HEX HALL

HEX HALL

RACHEL HAWKINS

Disney • HYPERION BOOKS
NEW YORK

First Edition
1 3 5 7 9 10 8 6 4 2
V567-9638-5-09349
Printed in the United States of America

Library of Congress Cataloging-in-Publication Data on file.
ISBN 978-1-4231-2130-5

Reinforced binding

Visit www.hyperionteens.com

SUSTAINABLE FORESTRY INITIATIVE
Certified Fiber Sourcing
www.sfiprogram.org

THIS LABEL APPLIES TO TEXT STOCK

For Mama and Daddy,
For John and Will,
For everything . . .

My mother says I must not pass
Too near the glass;
She is afraid that I will see
A little witch that looks like me;
With a red, red mouth to whisper low,
The very thing I should not know!

—Sarah Morgan Bryan Piatt

PROLOGUE

Felicia Miller was crying in the bathroom. Again.

I knew it was her because in the three months I'd been going to Green Mountain High, I'd already seen Felicia crying in the bathroom twice. She had a really distinctive sob, high and breathy like a little kid's, even though Felicia was eighteen, two years older than me.

I'd left her alone before, figuring that it was every girl's right to cry in a public bathroom from time to time.

But tonight was prom night, and there was something really sad about sobbing in formal wear. Besides, I'd developed a soft spot for Felicia. There was a girl just like her at every school I'd ever been to (nineteen and counting). And while I may have been a weirdo, people weren't mean to me; they mostly just ignored me. Felicia, on the other hand, was the class punching bag. For her,

1

school had been nothing but a constant parade of stolen lunch money and nasty remarks.

I peeked under the stall door and saw a pair of feet in strappy yellow sandals. "Felicia?" I called, rapping softly on the door. "What's wrong?"

She opened the door and looked up at me with angry, bloodshot eyes. "What's wrong? Well, let's see, Sophie, it's prom night of my senior year and do you see a date anywhere near me?"

"Um . . . no. But you *are* in the ladies' room, so I thought—"

"What?" she asked as she stood up and wiped her nose with a huge wad of toilet paper. "That my date's out there waiting for me?" She snorted. "Please. I lied to my parents and said I had a date. So they bought me this dress"—she slapped at the yellow taffeta like it was a bug she was trying to kill—"and I told them my date was meeting me here, so they dropped me off. I just . . . I couldn't tell them I didn't get invited to my senior prom. It would have broken their hearts." She rolled her eyes. "How pathetic is that?"

"It's not that pathetic," I said. "Lots of girls come to prom alone."

She glared at me. "Do you have a date?"

I did have a date. Sure, it was Ryan Hellerman, who might have been the only person at Green Mountain High

2

less popular than I was, but it was still a date. And my mom had been so excited that someone had asked me. She saw it as my finally making an attempt at Fitting In.

Fitting In was really important to my mom.

I watched Felicia standing there in her yellow dress, wiping at her nose, and before I could stop myself, I said something totally stupid: "I can help."

Felicia looked up at me through puffy eyes. "How?"

I looped my arm through hers, pulling her to her feet. "We have to go outside."

We made our way out of the bathroom and through the crowded gym. Felicia seemed wary as I led her through the big double doors and out into the parking lot.

"If this is some sort of prank, I have pepper spray in my purse," she said, holding her little yellow clutch close to her chest.

"Relax." I looked around to make sure the parking lot was deserted.

Even though it was late April, there was still a chill in the air, and both of us shivered in our dresses. "Okay," I said, turning back to her. "If you could have anyone as your prom date, who would it be?"

"Are you trying to torture me?" she asked.

"Just answer the question."

Staring at her yellow shoes, she mumbled, "Kevin Bridges?"

I wasn't surprised. SGA president, football captain, all-around hottie . . . Kevin Bridges was the guy almost any girl would pick to be her prom date.

"Okay, then. Kevin it is," I muttered, cracking my knuckles. Lifting my hands to the sky, I closed my eyes and pictured Felicia in Kevin's arms, her in her bright yellow dress, him in a tux. After just a few seconds of focusing on that image, I started to feel a slight tremor under my feet and a feeling like water rushing all the way up to my outspread hands. My hair started to float from my shoulders, and then I heard Felicia gasp.

When I opened my eyes, I saw exactly what I'd hoped. Overhead, a huge dark cloud was swirling, sparks of purplish light flashing inside of it. I kept concentrating, and as I did, the cloud swirled faster until it was a perfect circle with a hole in the center.

The Magic Doughnut, as I'd dubbed it the first time I'd created one on my twelfth birthday.

Felicia cowered between two cars, her arms raised over her head. But it was too late to stop.

The hole in the center of the cloud filled with bright green light. Focusing on that light and the image of Kevin and Felicia, I flexed my fingers and watched as a bolt of green lightning shot out of the cloud and raced across the sky. It disappeared behind some trees.

The cloud vanished, and Felicia stood up on shaky

legs. "W-what was that?" She turned to me, wide-eyed. "Are you like a witch or something?"

I shrugged, still feeling pleasantly buzzed by the power I'd just unleashed. *Magic drunk*, Mom always calls it. "It was nothing," I said. "Now let's go inside."

Ryan was hanging out by the punch table when I came back inside.

"What was that about?" he asked, nodding toward Felicia. She looked dazed as she stood on tiptoes, scanning the dance floor.

"Oh, she just needed some air," I said, picking up a glass of punch. My heart was still racing, and my hands were shaking.

"Cool," Ryan said, bouncing his head in time with the music. "Wanna dance?"

Before I could answer, Felicia ran up and grabbed my arm. "He's not even here," she said. "Didn't that . . . that thing you did make him my prom date?"

"Shhh! Yes it did, but you'll have to be patient. As soon as Kevin gets here, he'll find you, trust me."

We didn't have to wait long.

Ryan and I were only halfway through our first dance when a huge crash echoed through the gym.

There was a rapid succession of loud pops, almost like gunshots, that sent kids screaming and diving under the refreshment table. I watched the punch bowl plummet to the floor, splashing red liquid everywhere.

But it wasn't a gun that had made the popping sounds; it was balloons. Hundreds of them. Whatever had happened had sent the huge balloon arch swooping to the ground. I watched as one white balloon escaped the carnage and rose into the rafters of the gym.

I looked over and saw several of the teachers running for the doors.

Which weren't there anymore.

That was because a silver Land Rover had crashed through them.

Kevin Bridges staggered out of the driver's seat. He'd cut both his forehead and his hand, and was bleeding on the shiny hardwood as he bellowed, "Felicia! FELICIA!"

"Holy crap," Ryan murmured.

Kevin's date, Caroline Reed, scrambled out of the passenger side. She was sobbing. "He's crazy!" she shrieked. "He was fine, and then there was this light and . . . and . . ." She broke off into more hysterics, and I felt sick to my stomach.

"FELICIA!" Kevin continued to scream, wildly searching the gym. I looked around and saw Felicia hiding under one of the tables, her eyes huge.

I was careful this time, I thought. I'm better at this now!

Kevin found Felicia and yanked her out from under the table. "Felicia!" He smiled broadly, his whole face lit up, which, what with the blood and all, was terrifying. I didn't blame Felicia for screaming her head off.

One of the chaperones, Coach Henry, sprinted over to help, grabbing Kevin's arm.

But Kevin just turned, one hand still clutching Felicia, and backhanded Coach Henry across the face. The coach, who was six foot two and easily over two hundred pounds, went flying backward.

And then all hell broke loose.

People were stampeding for the doors, more teachers were swarming Kevin, and Felicia's screams had taken on a desperate, keening edge. Only Ryan seemed unfazed.

"Awesome!" he enthused as two girls scrambled over the Land Rover and out of the gym. "*Carrie* prom!"

Kevin was still holding one of Felicia's hands, and by now he was on one knee. I couldn't be sure, thanks to all the screaming, but I think he was singing to her.

Felicia wasn't screeching anymore, but she was fishing in her handbag for something.

"Oh no," I groaned. I started running toward them, but I slipped and fell in the punch.

Felicia whipped out a small red can and sprayed the contents in Kevin's face.

His song broke off in a garbled cry of pain. He

dropped her hand to claw at his eyes, and Felicia ran.

"It's okay, baby!" he shouted after her. "I don't need eyes to see you! I see you with the eyes of my heart, Felicia! My HEART!"

Great. Not only was my spell too strong, it was also *lame*.

I sat in the pool of punch while the chaos I'd created raged around me. A lone white balloon bobbed by my elbow, and Mrs. Davison, my algebra teacher, stumbled past, shouting into her cell phone, "I *said* Green Mountain High! Um . . . I don't know, an ambulance? A SWAT team? Just send *somebody!*"

Then I heard a shriek. "It was her! Sophie Mercer!"

Felicia was pointing at me, her whole body shaking.

Even over all the noise, Felicia's words echoed in the cavernous gym. "She's . . . she's a witch!"

I sighed. "Not *again*."

CHAPTER 1

"Well?"

I stepped out of the car and into the hot thick heat of August in Georgia.

"Awesome," I murmured, sliding my sunglasses on top of my head. Thanks to the humidity, my hair felt like it had tripled in size. I could feel it trying to devour my sunglasses like some sort of carnivorous jungle plant. "I always wondered what it would be like to live in somebody's mouth."

In front of me loomed Hecate Hall, which, according to the brochure clutched in my sweaty hand, was "the premier reformatory institution for Prodigium adolescents."

Prodigium. Just a fancy Latin word for monsters. And that's what everyone at Hecate was.

That's what I was.

I'd already read the brochure four times on the plane from Vermont to Georgia, twice on the ferry ride to Graymalkin Island, just off the coast of Georgia (where, I learned, Hecate had been built in 1854), and once as our rental car had rattled over the shell and gravel driveway that led from the shore to the school's parking lot. So I should have had it memorized, but I kept holding on to it and compulsively reading it, like it was my wubby or something:

The purpose of Hecate Hall is to protect and instruct shape-shifter, witch, and fae children who have risked exposure of their abilities, and therefore imperiled Prodigium society as a whole.

"I still don't see how helping one girl find a date *imperiled* other witches," I said, squinting at my mom as we reached into the trunk for my stuff. The thought had been bugging me since the first time I'd read the brochure, but I hadn't had a chance to bring it up. Mom had spent most of the flight pretending to be asleep, probably to avoid looking at my sullen expression.

"It wasn't just that one girl, Soph, and you know it. It was that boy with the broken arm in Delaware, and that teacher you tried to make forget about a test in Arizona. . . ."

"He got his memory back eventually," I said. "Well, most of it."

Mom just sighed and pulled out the beat-up trunk

we'd bought at The Salvation Army. "Your father and I both warned you that there were consequences for using your powers. I don't like this any more than you do, but at least here you'll be with . . . with other kids like you."

"You mean total screwups." I pulled my tote bag onto my shoulder.

Mom pushed her own sunglasses up and looked at me. She seemed tired and there were heavy lines around her mouth, lines I'd never seen before. My mom was almost forty, but she could usually pass for ten years younger.

"You're not a screwup, Sophie." We hefted the trunk between us. "You've just made some mistakes."

Had I ever. Being a witch had definitely not been as awesome as I'd hoped it would be. For one thing, I didn't get to fly around on a broomstick. (I asked my mom about that when I first came into my powers, and she said no, I had to keep riding the bus like everyone else.) I don't have spell books or a talking cat (I'm allergic), and I wouldn't even know where to get a hold of something like eye of newt.

But I can perform magic. I've been able to ever since I was twelve, which, according to sweaty brochure, is the age all Prodigium come into their powers. Something to do with puberty, I guess.

"Besides, this is a good school," Mom said as we approached the building.

But it didn't look like a school. It looked like a cross between something out of an old horror movie and Disney World's Haunted Mansion. For starters, it was obviously almost two hundred years old. It was three stories tall, and the third story perched like the top tier of a wedding cake. The house may have been white once, but now it was just sort of a faded gray, almost the same color as the shell and gravel drive, which made it look less like a house and more like some sort of natural outcrop of the island.

"Huh," Mom said. We dropped the trunk, and she walked around the side of the building. "Would you look at that?"

I followed her and immediately saw what she meant. The brochure said Hecate had made "extensive additions to the original structure" over the years. Turns out, that meant they'd lopped off the back of the house and stuck another one onto it. The grayish wood ended after sixty feet or so and gave way to pink stucco that extended all the way to the woods.

For something that had clearly been done with magic—there were no seams where the two houses met, no line of mortar—you would've thought it would have turned out a little more elegantly. Instead it looked like two houses that had been glued together by a crazy person.

A crazy person with really bad taste.

Huge oak trees in the front yard dripped with Spanish moss, shading the house. In fact, there seemed to be plants everywhere. Two ferns in dusty pots bracketed the front door, looking like big green spiders, and some sort of vine with purple flowers had taken over an entire wall. It was almost like the house was being slowly absorbed by the forest just beyond it.

I tugged at the hem of my brand-new Hecate Hall–issue blue plaid skirt (kilt? Some sort of bizarre skirt/kilt hybrid? A skilt?) and wondered why a school in the middle of the Deep South would have wool uniforms. Still, as I stared at the school, I fought off a shiver. I wondered how anyone could ever look at this place and *not* suspect its students were a bunch of freaks.

"It's pretty," Mom said in her best "Let's be perky and look on the bright side" voice.

I, however, was not feeling so perky.

"Yeah, it's beautiful. For a prison."

My mom shook her head. "Drop the insolent-teenager thing, Soph. It's hardly a prison."

But that's what it felt like.

"This really is the best place for you," she said as we picked up the trunk.

"I guess," I mumbled.

It's for your own good seemed to be the mantra as far as me and Hecate were concerned. Two days after prom we'd gotten an e-mail from my dad that basically said I'd blown all my chances, and that the Council was sentencing me to Hecate until my eighteenth birthday.

The Council was this group of old people who made all the rules for Prodigium.

I know, a council that calls themselves "the Council." So original.

Anyway, Dad worked for them, so they let him break the bad news. "Hopefully," he had said in his e-mail, "this will teach you to use your powers with considerably more discretion."

E-mail and the occasional phone call were pretty much the only contact I had with my dad. He and Mom split up before I was born. Turns out he hadn't told my mom about him being a warlock (that's the preferred term for boy witches) until they'd been together for nearly a year. Mom hadn't taken the news well. She wrote him off as a nut job and ran back to her family. But then she found out she was pregnant with me, and she got a copy of *The Encyclopedia of Witchcraft* to go along with all her baby books, just in case. By the time I was born, she was practically an expert on things that go bump in the night. It wasn't until I'd come into my powers on my twelfth birthday that she'd reluctantly opened the lines of communication with Dad. But she was still pretty frosty toward him.

In the month since my dad had told me that I was going to Hecate, I'd tried to come to terms with it. Seriously. I told myself that I'd finally be around people that were like me, people I didn't have to hide my true self from. And I might learn some pretty sweet spells. Those were all big pros.

But as soon as Mom and I had boarded the ferry to take us out to this isolated island, I'd started to feel sick to my stomach. And trust me, it wasn't seasickness.

According to the brochure, Graymalkin Island had been selected to house Hecate because of its remote location, the better to keep it a secret. The locals just thought it was a super-exclusive boarding school.

By the time the ferry had approached the heavily forested spit of land that would be my home for the next two years, the second thoughts had majorly set in.

It seemed like most of the student body was milling around on the lawn, but only a handful of them looked new, like me. They were all unloading trunks, toting suitcases. Some of them had beat-up luggage like mine, but I saw a couple of Louis Vuitton bags, too. One girl, dark-haired with a slightly crooked nose, seemed about my age, while all the other new kids looked younger.

I couldn't really tell what most of them were, whether they were witches and warlocks or shapeshifters. Since we all look like regular people, there was no way to tell.

The faeries, on the other hand, were very easy to spot. They were all taller than average and very dignified looking, and every one of them had straight shiny hair, in all sorts of different colors, from pale gold to bright violet.

And they had wings.

According to Mom, faeries usually used glamours to blend in with humans. It was a pretty complex spell since it involved altering the mind of everyone they met, but it meant that humans could only see the faeries as normal people instead of bright, colorful, winged . . . creatures. I wondered if the faeries that got sentenced to Hecate were kind of relieved. It had to be hard, doing that big of a spell all the time.

I paused to readjust my tote bag on my shoulder.

"At least this place is safe," Mom said. "That's something, right? I won't have to be constantly worrying about you for once."

I knew Mom was anxious about my being so far from home, but she was also happy to have me in a place where I wasn't risking getting found out. You spend all your time reading books about the various ways people have killed witches over the years, it's bound to make you a little paranoid.

As we made our way toward the school, I could feel sweat pooling up in weird places where I was pretty sure I had never sweat before. How can your *ears* sweat? Mom, as usual, appeared unaffected by the humidity. It's like a natural law that my mother can never look anything less than obscenely beautiful. Even though she was wearing jeans and a T-shirt, heads turned in her direction.

Or maybe they were staring at me as I tried to discreetly wipe sweat from between my breasts without appearing to get to second base with myself. Hard to say.

All around me were things I'd only read about in books. To my left, a blue-haired faerie with indigo wings was sobbing as she clung to her winged parents, whose feet hovered an inch or two above the ground. As I watched, crystalline tears fell not from the girl's eyes, but from her wings, leaving her toes dangling over a puddle of royal blue.

We walked into the shade of the huge old trees— meaning the heat diminished by maybe half a degree. Just as we neared the front steps, an unearthly howl echoed in the thick air.

Mom and I whirled around to see this . . . *thing* growling at two rather frustrated-looking adults. They didn't look scared; just vaguely annoyed.

A werewolf.

No matter how many times you read about werewolves, seeing one right in front of you is a whole new experience.

For one thing, it didn't really look much like a wolf. Or a person. It was more like a really big wild dog standing on hind legs. Its fur was short and light brown, and even from a distance I could see the yellow of its eyes. It was also a lot smaller than I'd thought one would be. In fact, it wasn't nearly as tall as the man it was growling at.

"Stop it, Justin," the man spat. The woman, whose hair, I noticed, was the same light brown as the werewolf's, put a hand on his arm.

"Sweetie," she said in a soft voice with a hint of a Southern accent, "listen to your father. This is just silly."

For a second the werewolf, er, Justin, paused, his head cocked to the side, making him look less like a throat-ripping-out beastie and more like a cocker spaniel.

The thought made me giggle.

And suddenly those yellow eyes were on me.

It gave another howl, and before I even had time to think, it charged.

CHAPTER 2

I heard the man and woman cry out a warning as I frantically racked my brain for some sort of throat-repairing spell, which I was clearly about to need. Of course the only words I actually managed to yell at the werewolf as he ran at me were, "BAD DOG!"

Then, out of the corner of my eye, I caught a flash of blue light on my left. Suddenly, the werewolf seemed to smack into an invisible wall just inches in front of me. Giving a pitiful bark, he slumped to the ground. His fur and skin began to ripple and flow until he was a normal boy in khakis and a blue blazer, whimpering pitifully. His parents got to him just as Mom ran to me, dragging my trunk behind her.

"Oh my God!" she breathed. "Sweetie, are you okay?"

"Fine," I said, brushing grass off my skilt.

"You know," someone said off to my left, "I usually find a blocking spell to be a lot more effective than yelling 'Bad dog,' but maybe that's just me."

I turned. Leaning against a tree, his collar unbuttoned and tie loose, was a smirking guy. His Hecate blazer was hanging limply in the crook of his elbow.

"You *are* a witch, aren't you?" he continued. He pushed himself off the tree and ran a hand through his black curly hair. As he walked closer, I noticed that he was slender almost to the point of skinny, and that he was several inches taller than me. "Maybe in the future," he said, "you could endeavor not to suck so badly at it."

And with that, he sauntered off.

Between nearly being attacked by Justin the Dog-face Boy, and having some strange guy who was not *that* hot tell me I sucked at witchcraft, I was now thoroughly pissed.

I checked to see if Mom was watching, but she was asking Justin's parents something that sounded like, "Was he going to bite her?!"

"So I'm a bad witch, huh?" I said under my breath as I focused on the boy's retreating back.

I raised my hands and thought up the nastiest spell I possibly could—one involving pus and bad breath and severe genital dysfunctions.

And nothing happened.

There was no sensation of water rushing up to my fingers, no quickening heartbeat, no hair standing on end.

I was just standing there like an idiot, pointing all of my fingers at him.

The heck? I'd never had trouble doing a spell before.

And then I heard a voice that sounded like a magnolia dragged through molasses say, "That's enough, my dear."

I turned toward the front porch, where an older woman in a navy suit stood between the scary ferns. She was smiling, but it was one of those creepy doll smiles. She pointed one long finger at me.

"We do not use our powers against other Prodigium here, no matter how provoked we may be," she said, her voice soft, smoky, musical. In fact, if the house could have talked, I'd have expected it to sound exactly like this woman.

"May I add, Archer," the woman continued, turning to the dark-haired boy, "that while this young lady is new to Hecate, you know better than to attack another student."

He snorted. "So I should have let him eat her?"

"Magic is not the solution for everything," she replied.

"Archer?" I asked, raising my eyebrows. Hey, you might be able to take away my magical powers, but the power of sarcasm was still at my disposal. "Is your last name Newport or Vanderbilt? Maybe followed by some numbers? Ooh!" I said, widening my eyes, "or maybe even Esquire!"

I'd hoped to hurt his feelings or, at the very least, make him angry, but he just kept smiling at me. "Actually, it's Archer *Cross*, and I'm the first one. Now what about you?" He squinted. "Let's see . . . brown hair, freckles, whole girl-next-door vibe going on . . . Allie? Lacie? Definitely something cutesy ending in *ie*."

You know those times when your mouth moves but no sound actually comes out? Yeah, that's pretty much what happened. And then, of course, my mom took that opportunity to end her conversation with Justin's parents and call out, "Sophie! Wait up."

"I knew it." Archer laughed. "See you, Soph*ie*," he called over his shoulder as he disappeared into the house.

I turned my attention back to the woman. She was around fifty, with dark blond hair that had been twisted, teased, and probably threatened into a complicated updo. From her practically regal bearing and her suit in Hecate Hall's signature royal blue, I assumed she was the school's headmistress, Mrs. Anastasia Casnoff. I didn't have to look at the brochure to remember that. A name like *Anastasia Casnoff* tends to stick with you.

The blond woman was in fact the awesomely named leader of Hecate Hall. My mom shook her hand. "Grace Mercer. And this is Sophia."

"*Soh-fee-yuh*," Mrs. Casnoff said in her Southern lilt, turning my relatively simple name into something that sounded like an exotic appetizer at a Chinese restaurant.

"I go by Sophie," I said quickly, hoping to avoid being known forever as Sohfeeyuh.

"Now, y'all are not originally from this area, am I correct?" Mrs. Casnoff continued as we walked toward the school.

"No," Mom answered, switching my duffel bag to her other shoulder, the trunk still between us. "My mother is from Tennessee, but Georgia is one of the few states we haven't lived in. We've moved around quite a bit."

Quite a bit is something of an understatement.

Nineteen states over the course of my sixteen years. The longest we've ever stayed anywhere was Indiana, when I was eight. That was four years. The shortest we ever lived anywhere was Montana three years ago. That was two weeks.

"I see," Mrs. Casnoff said. "And what do you do, Mrs. Mercer?"

"*Ms.*" Mom said automatically, and just a little too loudly. She bit her lower lip and tucked an imaginary piece of hair behind her ear. "I'm a teacher. Religious studies. Mostly mythology and folklore."

I trailed behind them as we ascended the imposing front steps and entered Hecate Hall.

It was blessedly cool, meaning that they apparently had some sort of air-conditioning spell going on. It also smelled like all old houses, that weird scent that's a combination of furniture polish, old wood, and the musty smell of aged paper, like in a library.

I'd wondered if the smushed-together houses would be as obvious on the inside as they had been on the outside, but all the walls were covered in the same fugly burgundy wallpaper, making it impossible to see where the wood ended and the stucco began.

Just inside the front door, the massive foyer was dominated by a mahogany spiral staircase that twisted up three stories, seemingly supported by nothing. Behind the staircase was a stained-glass window that started at the second-floor landing and soared all the way up to the ceiling. The late-afternoon sun shone through it, filling the foyer with geometric patterns of brightly colored light.

"Impressive, isn't it?" Mrs. Casnoff said with a smile. "It depicts the origin of Prodigium."

The window showed an angry-faced angel standing just inside golden gates. In one hand the angel held a black sword. The other hand was pointing, clearly indicating that the three figures in front of the gates should get the heck out. Only, you know, angelically.

The three figures were also angels. They all looked

pretty bummed. The angel on the right, a woman with long red hair, even had her face buried in her hands. Around her neck was a heavy golden chain that I realized was actually a series of small figures holding hands. The angel on the left was wearing a crown of leaves and looking over his shoulder. And in the middle, the tallest angel looked out straight in front of him, his head high and shoulders back.

"It's . . . something," I said at last.

"Do you know the story, Sophie?" Mrs. Casnoff asked.

When I shook my head, she smiled and gestured to the fearsome angel behind the gates. "After the Great War between God and Lucifer, those angels who refused to take sides were cast out of heaven. One group"—she pointed to the tall angel in the middle—"chose to hide itself away under hills and deep in forests. They became faeries. Another group chose to live among animals and became shapeshifters. And the last chose to intermingle with humans and became witches."

"Wow," I heard Mom say, and I turned to her with a smile.

"Good luck explaining to God that you used to spank one of his heavenly beings."

Mom gave a startled laugh. "Sophie!"

"What? You did. I hope you like hot weather, Mom, that's all I'm saying."

Mom laughed again, even though I could tell she was trying not to.

Mrs. Casnoff frowned before clearing her throat and continuing her tour. "Students at Hecate range in age from twelve to seventeen. Once a student has been sentenced to Hecate, he or she is not released until his or her eighteenth birthday."

"So some kids could be here for, like, six months, and others could be here for six years?" I asked.

"Precisely. The majority of our students are sent here soon after they come into their powers. But there are always exceptions, such as yourself."

"Go me," I muttered.

"What are the classes here like?" Mom asked, shooting me a look.

"The classes at Hecate are modeled after those found at Prentiss, Mayfair, and Gervaudan."

Mom and I both nodded at her like we knew what those words meant. I guess we didn't fool her, because Mrs. Casnoff said, "The premier boarding schools for witches, faeries, and shapeshifters, respectively. Classes are assigned based on both the student's age and the particular struggles that student was having blending into the human world."

She gave a brittle smile. "The curriculum can be challenging, but I have no doubt that Sophie will do very well."

Never had encouragement sounded so much like a threat.

"The girls' dormitories are located on the third floor," Mrs. Casnoff said, gesturing up the stairs. "Boys are on the second. Classes are held here on the first floor as well as in the surrounding outbuildings." She pointed to the left and right of the staircase where long narrow hallways branched off from the foyer. What with the pointing and the blue suit, she brought to mind a flight attendant. I expected her to tell me that in the event of an emergency, my brand-new Hecate blazer could be used as a flotation device.

"Now, are the students separated by . . . um . . ." Mom waved her hand.

Mrs. Casnoff smiled, but I couldn't help but notice that the smile was as tight as her bun.

"By their abilities? No, of course not. One of the founding principles of Hecate is teaching the students how to coexist with every race of Prodigium."

Mrs. Casnoff turned to lead us to the other end of the foyer. Here, three huge windows soared up to the third-floor landing. Beyond them was the courtyard, where kids were already beginning to gather on stone benches under live oak trees. I say kids. I guess they were all *things,* like me, but you couldn't tell. They just looked like any normal bunch of students. Well, except for the faeries.

I watched one girl laugh as she offered a tube of lip gloss to another, and something in my chest tightened a little bit.

I felt something cold brush my arm, and I jumped back, startled, as a pale woman in blue swept past me.

"Ah, yes," Mrs. Casnoff said with a small smile. "Isabelle Fortenay, one of our resident spirits. As I'm sure you read, Hecate is home to a number of spirits, all of them the ghosts of Prodigium. They're quite harmless— completely noncorporeal. That means they're unable to touch you or anything else. They may give you a fright now and then, but that's all they can do."

"Great," I said as I watched Isabelle fade into a paneled wall.

As she did, I caught a movement out of the corner of my eye and turned to see another spirit standing at the foot of the stairs. She was a girl about my age, wearing a bright green cardigan over a short flowered dress. Unlike Isabelle, who hadn't seemed to notice me, this girl was staring straight at me. I opened my mouth to ask Mrs. Casnoff who she was, but the headmistress had already turned her attention to someone across the foyer.

"Miss Talbot!" she called. I was amazed at the way her voice crossed the huge room without sounding even remotely like yelling.

A tiny girl, barely five feet tall, appeared at Mrs.

Casnoff's elbow. Her skin was nearly snow white, as was her hair, with the exception of a hot-pink stripe running through her bangs. She had on thick, black-rimmed glasses, and even though she was smiling, I could tell it was just for Mrs. Casnoff's benefit. Her eyes looked totally bored.

"This is Jennifer Talbot. I believe you'll be rooming with her this semester, Miss Mercer. Jennifer, this is Soh-fee-yuh."

"Sophie is fine," I corrected, just as Jennifer said, "Jenna."

Mrs. Casnoff's smile tightened, like there were screws on either side of her mouth. "Gracious. I don't know what it is with children these days, Ms. Mercer. Given perfectly lovely names, and determined to mangle and change them at the first opportunity. In any case, Miss Mercer, Miss Talbot is, like you, a relative newcomer. She only joined us last year."

Mom beamed and shook Jenna's hand. "Nice to meet you. Are you, um, are you a witch like Sophie?"

"Mom," I whispered, but Jenna shook her head and said, "No, ma'am. Vamp."

I could feel Mom stiffen beside me, and I knew Jenna did too. Even though I was embarrassed for her, I shared Mom's freak-out. Witches, shapeshifters, and fae were one thing. Vampires were monsters, plain and simple. That whole sensitive Children of the Night thing was total b.s.

"Oh, okay," Mom said, struggling to recover. "I . . . uh, I didn't know vampires attended Hecate."

"It's a new program we have here," Mrs. Casnoff said, reaching out to run a hand over Jenna's hair. Jenna had a polite, if kind of blank look on her face, but I saw her tense up slightly. "Every year," Mrs. Casnoff continued, "Hecate takes a young vampire and offers him or her a chance to study alongside Prodigium in the hopes that we can eventually reform these unfortunates."

I glanced over at Jenna, because . . . *unfortunates?* Ouch.

"Sadly, Miss Talbot is the only vampire student we currently have, although one of our instructors is a vampire as well," Mrs. Casnoff said. Jenna just smiled that weird nonsmile again, and we all stood around in awkward silence until Mom said, "Sweetie, why don't you let . . ." She looked up helplessly at my new room-mate.

"Jenna."

"Right, right. Why don't you let Jenna show you your room? I've got a few things I want to go over with Mrs. Casnoff, then I'll be up to say bye, okay?"

I looked toward Jenna, who was still smiling, but her eyes seemed to be already looking past us.

I shifted my tote again and went to grab my trunk from Mom, but Jenna beat me to it.

"You really don't have to help—" I started, but she waved her free hand.

"No problem. The one bonus to being a blood-sucking freak is upper-body strength."

I didn't know what to say to that, so I just lamely replied, "Oh." She carried one side, and I grabbed the other.

"No chance of an elevator, I guess?" I was only half joking.

Jenna snorted. "Nah, that would be too convenient."

"Why don't they just have, like, a luggage-moving spell or something?"

"Mrs. Casnoff's a real stickler for not using magic as an excuse to be lazy. Apparently, carrying heavy suitcases up stairs is character-building."

"Right," I said as we struggled past the second-story landing.

"So what do you think of her?" Jenna asked.

"Mrs. Casnoff?"

"Yeah."

"Her bun is very impressive." Jenna's smirk confirmed that I had said the right thing.

"I know, right? I swear to God, that hairdo is like, epic."

There was only a trace of Southern lilt in her voice. It was pretty.

"Speaking of hairdos," I ventured, "how do you get away with that stripe?"

Jenna smoothed the pink streak with her free hand. "Oh, they don't really care about the poor vamp scholarship student that much. I guess as long as I'm not munching on my peers, I'm free to have any hair color I want."

When we reached the third-floor landing, she studied me. "I could do yours if you want. Not pink, though. That's my thing. Maybe purple?"

"Um . . . maybe."

We had stopped in front of room 312. Jenna set down her end of the trunk and pulled out her keys. Her key chain was bright yellow and had her name spelled out in sparkly pink letters.

"Here we are!"

She unlocked the door and pushed it open. "Welcome to The Twilight Zone!"

CHAPTER 3

The "Holy-crap-that's-a-lot-of-pink" Zone would have been a more accurate description.

I don't know what I was expecting a vampire's room to look like. Maybe lots of black, a bunch of books by Camus . . . oh, and a sensitive portrait of the only human the vamp had ever loved, who had no doubt died of something beautiful and tragic, thus dooming the vamp to an eternity of moping and sighing romantically.

What can I say? I read a lot of books.

But this room looked like it had been decorated by the unholy lovechild of Barbie and Strawberry Shortcake. It was bigger than I expected, but still small. There was enough room for two twin beds, two desks, two dressers, and one battered futon. The curtains were beige canvas, but Jenna had twined a hot-pink scarf over the drapery rod. Between the two desks was one of those old Chinese screens, but even this bore Jenna's stamp, as the wood had been painted—you guessed it: pink. The top of the screen was draped with pink Christmas lights. Jenna's bed was covered in what appeared to be deep pink Muppet fur.

Jenna caught me staring at it. "Awesome, right?"

"I . . . I didn't know pink existed in that particular shade."

Kicking off her loafers, Jenna threw herself down on her bed, upsetting two sequined pillows and a ratty stuffed lion. "It's called 'Electric Raspberry.'"

"That's the perfect name for it." I smiled as I pulled my trunk over to my bed, which looked as plain as . . . well, as plain as me next to Jenna.

"So, did your old roommate like pink too?"

Jenna's face froze for a split second. Then the strange look was gone, and she was leaning off the bed to scoop up her pillows and lion. "Nah, Holly just stuck with the blue stuff they give you if you don't bring your own. You brought your own, right?"

I opened my trunk and pulled out the corner of my mint green bedspread. Jenna looked a little disappointed, but sighed, "Well, it's better than regulation blue. So"— she flopped back onto the bed and began fishing around in her bedside table—"what brings you to Hex Hall, Sophie Mercer?"

"Hex Hall?" I repeated.

"Hecate is kind of a mouthful," Jenna explained. "Most people just say Hex. Besides, it feels kind of appropriate."

"Oh."

"So what was it?" she asked again. "Did you make it rain frogs, or turn some guy into a newt?"

I leaned back on my bed, trying to imitate Jenna's air of nonchalance, but it turns out that's really hard to do on a bare mattress, so I sat up and started pulling things out of my trunk. "I did a love spell for this girl in my class. It went badly."

"Didn't work?"

"Worked too well." I gave her the short version of the Kevin/Felicia episode.

"*Day*-um," she said, shaking her head. "That's hard core."

"Apparently," I said. "So you're . . . uh, you're a vampire. How exactly did that happen?"

Her eyes didn't meet mine, but her tone was casual. "Same way it happens to everyone else: met a vamp, got bitten. Not really that interesting."

I couldn't blame her for not wanting to share the whole story with someone she'd only known for fifteen minutes.

"So your mom is normal, huh?" she asked.

Hmm. Not exactly something *I* wanted to get into on the first day, but hey, this was what Fitting In was all about, right? Sharing makeup, clothes, and dark secrets with your roommate.

I cleared my throat. "Yeah, my dad is a warlock, but they're not together or anything anymore."

"Oh," Jenna said knowingly. "Say no more. A lot of the kids here come from divorced families. Even magic doesn't ensure a happy marriage, apparently."

"Are your parents divorced?"

She finally found the nail polish she'd been searching for. "No, they're still disgustingly happy. Or, I mean . . . I guess they are. I haven't seen them since I, uh, changed, or whatever."

"Oh wow," I replied. "That sucks."

"No pun intended?" she asked.

"Right." I finished putting the sheets on my bed. "So if you're a vamp, do I have to be really careful about not opening the drapes in the morning?"

"Nope. See this?" She tugged on a silver chain around her neck and held up a small pendant. It was about the size and shape of a jelly bean, and dark red. Anyone else might mistake it for a ruby, but I'd seen pictures of something like it in one of Mom's books.

"A bloodstone?" Bloodstones were clear, hollow stones that could be filled with the blood of a powerful witch or warlock. The stone acted as a protection against lots of different things. I guess in Jenna's case it negated all her vampire issues, which was a relief. At least now I knew I could eat garlic in front of her.

Jenna started painting her left hand. "So what about blood?" I asked.

She let out a huge sigh. "It's completely embarrassing. I have to go to the infirmary. They have a minifridge in there with a bunch of bags of blood, like it's the Red Cross or something."

I suppressed a shudder at the image. Blood is so very gross to me. If I give myself a paper cut, I nearly hyperventilate. I was really glad to hear Jenna wouldn't be snacking in our room. I could never date a vampire. Just the thought of blood breath . . . ugh.

Then I noticed that Jenna was staring at me. Crap. Had my disgust been written all over my face? Just in case, I faked a smile and said, "Awesome. Like a bloody Capri Sun."

Jenna laughed. "Nice one."

We sat in companionable silence for a moment before Jenna asked, "So your parents' breakup was ugly?"

"Apparently," I answered. "It happened before I was born."

She looked up from her nails. "Whoa."

I walked to my desk. Someone, Mrs. Casnoff, I guess,

had left my class schedule there. It looked like a normal enough schedule, but said things like "M-F, 9:15-10:00, *Magical Evolution*, Yellow Sitting Room."

"Yeah. Mom doesn't talk about it much, but whatever happened, it was bad enough that she won't let him meet me."

"So you've never seen your own *dad*?"

"I have a picture. And I've talked to him on the phone, and e-mail."

"Damn. I wonder what he did. Did he, like, hit her or something?"

"I don't know!" It came out more sharply than I had intended.

"Sorry," she murmured.

I turned to my bed and began smoothing my comforter. After I'd fixed about five imaginary wrinkles (and Jenna had painted one nail three times), I turned back and said, "I didn't mean to snap—"

"No, it's cool. That was none of my business anyway."

That cozy feeling of companionship was completely gone now.

"It's just . . . for like, my whole life, I've lived with only my mom, and I'm just not used to this whole telling-your-life-story thing yet. I guess we've always been pretty private."

Jenna nodded, but she still wasn't looking at me.

"I guess you and your old roommate told each other everything, huh?"

That dark look came over her face again. She abruptly capped her bottle of nail polish. "No," she said softly. "Not everything."

She tossed the bottle into her drawer and hopped off her bed. "See you at dinner."

As she left, she nearly smacked into Mom, mumbling an apology as she ran off.

"Soph," Mom said, dropping down onto my bed. "Don't tell me you already had a fight with your roommate."

She was annoyingly good at reading my moods. "I dunno. I think I'm just really bad at this girl stuff, you know? I mean, the last friend I had was in sixth grade. It's not like you can find a best friend when the longest you ever stay anywhere is six months, so I gue—Oh, Mom, I didn't mean to make you feel bad."

She shook her head and wiped away the stray tears. "No, no, sweetie, it's fine. I just . . . I just wish I could have given you a more normal childhood."

I sat down and wrapped my arm around her. "Don't say that. I've had an awesome childhood. I mean, how many people get to live in nineteen states? Think of all I've seen!"

It was the wrong thing to say. If anything, Mom just looked sadder.

"And this place is awesome! I mean, I have this cool, extremely pink room, and Jenna and I seem to have bonded enough to fight, which is a pretty important part of the girl-friendship thing, right?"

Mission accomplished. Mom was smiling. "Are you sure, sweetie? If you don't like it, you don't have to stay. I'm sure there's something we could do to get you out of here."

For a second I thought about saying, "Yes, please, let's catch the next ferry out of this freak show."

Instead, what I said was: "Look, it's not forever, right? Just two years, and I'll have Christmas and summers off. Just like regular school. I'll be fine. Now go before you make me cry and I look like a huge dork."

Mom's eyes teared up again, but she pulled me into a tight hug. "I love you, Soph."

"Love you too," I said, my throat tight.

Then, after making me swear to call at least three times a week, Mom was gone.

And I lay down on my not-pink bed and cried like a huge dork.

CHAPTER 4

Once I'd gotten that out of my system, I still had an hour until dinner. I decided to do some exploring. I'd opened the two small doors in our room, vainly hoping for private bathrooms, but no. Just closets.

The only bathroom on the whole floor was at the opposite end of the hall, and it, like the rest of the house, was spooky. The only light in it came from a few low-wattage bulbs surrounding a big mirror over the bank of sinks. That meant that the shower stalls in the back of the room were shrouded in darkness. Giving the showers a closer look, it occurred to me that I'd never had a true reason to use the word "dank" before now.

I knew I should have packed flip-flops.

In addition to the mildew-rific showers, there were also a bunch of claw-foot tubs against one wall, separated by waist-high partitions. I wondered who would ever want to take a bath in front of a bunch of other people?

Risking all manner of communicable diseases, I went to one of the sinks and splashed water on my face. Looking at myself in the mirror, I saw that the water hadn't really helped. My face was still bright red from crying, which had the charming effect of making my freckles stand out even more.

I shook my head, as if that would suddenly improve what I was seeing. It didn't. So with a sigh I set out to investigate the rest of Hecate Hall.

There wasn't much happening on my floor; just the usual chaos that occurs when you throw roughly fifty girls together. There were four hallways on the third floor, two to the left of the staircase, two to the right. The landing was huge, so it had been converted into a lounge. There were two couches and several chairs, but none of the furniture matched, and it all looked a little worse for wear. Since all the seats were taken, I hovered near the staircase.

The faerie I'd seen earlier, the one with the blue tears, had apparently recovered. She was draped over a chartreuse fainting couch, laughing with another faerie. This one had light green wings that beat softly against the back of the sofa. I'd always though faeries' wings would be like butterflies', but they were thinner and more translucent. You could see veins running through them.

They were the only faeries in the room. The other couch was taken up by a group of girls who looked about twelve. They were whispering nervously to each other, and I wondered if they were witches or shifters.

The dark-haired girl I'd seen on the lawn sat in an ivory wingback chair, idly flipping channels on the tiny television sitting on top of a small bookcase.

"Could you please turn that down?" the green-winged faerie said, turning to glare at the girl in the chair. "Some of us are trying to have conversations, Dog Girl."

None of the twelve-year-olds reacted to that, so I figured they were all witches. Surely a shifter would've looked more offended.

The blue faerie laughed as the dark-haired girl stood and turned off the TV. "My name is Taylor," she said, tossing the remote at the green faerie. "*Taylor*. And I turn into a mountain lion, not a dog. If we're going to live together for the next few years, you might want to remember that, Nausicaa."

Nausicaa rolled her eyes, her green wings beating softly. "Oh, we will not be living together for long, I assure you. My uncle is king of the Seelie Court, and as soon as I tell him I am sharing a room with a shifter . . . well, let's just say I expect my living arrangements to change."

"Yeah, well, it doesn't look like your uncle could keep you out of this place," Taylor fired back. Nausicaa's face was still blank, but her wings beat faster.

"I will not live with a shifter," she said to Taylor. "I certainly don't want to deal with your litter box."

The blue faerie laughed again, and Taylor turned bright red. Even from several feet away I saw her brown eyes turn gold. She was breathing hard as she said, "Shut up! Why don't you go and hug a tree or something, you faerie freak?"

Her words sounded garbled, like she was mumbling around a mouthful of marbles. Then I realized that she was mumbling around a mouthful of *fangs*.

Nausicaa had the good sense to look a little scared. She turned to the blue faerie and said, "Come on, Siobhan. Let's let this animal get control of herself."

The two of them rose. They glided past me and down the stairs.

I looked back at Taylor, who was still panting, her eyes squeezed shut. After a moment, she shuddered, and when she opened her eyes, they were brown again. Then she looked up and saw me standing there.

"Faeries," she said with a nervous laugh.

"Right," I said. Like I'd ever seen a faerie before today.

"This your first day too?" she asked.

When I nodded, she said, "I'm Taylor. Shifter, obviously."

"Sophie. Witch."

"Cool." She knelt on the couch the faeries had

vacated, folding her arms on the back and looking at me with those dark eyes.

"So what did you do to get in here?"

I glanced around. No one was paying attention to us.

Still, I kept my voice kind of quiet. "Love spell gone wrong."

Taylor nodded. "There's a bunch of witches in here for stuff like that."

"You?" I ventured.

She pushed her hair out of her eyes and said, "Pretty much what you just saw. Lost my temper with some girls at marching band practice, lioned out. But that's nothing compared to the crap some of the kids here have pulled." She leaned forward and her voice dropped to a near whisper. "This one werewolf, Beth? I hear she actually *ate* some girl. Still," she sighed, looking past me toward the stairs, "I'd rather have somebody like that for a roommate than a snotty faerie."

She looked back at me. "What are you rooming with?"

I didn't like the way she said "What," so my tone was a little sharp when I said, "Jenna Talbot."

Her eyes widened. "Dude. The vamp?" She chuckled. "Forget it. I'll take a bitchy faerie over that any day."

"She's not so bad," I said automatically.

Taylor shrugged and picked up the remote she'd

thrown at Nausicaa. "If you say so," she murmured, turning the TV back on.

Apparently our conversation was over, so I headed to the second floor. That was Boy World, so I couldn't really do any exploring. The layout was identical to the third floor, but their lounge area looked even more beat up than ours. Stuffing was leaking out of one of the couches, and a card table leaned crookedly in the corner. There was no one in there, but I did glance down one of the halls. I saw Justin trying to maneuver a huge trunk into what I guessed was his room. He paused, and his shoulders sagged with defeat. I felt a little sorry for him. Watching him try to push around a trunk that was nearly as tall as he was reminded me that, vicious werewolf or not, he was just a little kid. Then he turned, saw me, and, I boy you not, snarled.

I hurried down the stairs and onto the first floor. It was quiet down there. I only saw a couple of people hanging around, including a tall jock-looking guy all in denim and flannel. I wondered if he was someone's older brother, since he looked too old to be at Hecate, and he was wearing jeans instead of khakis.

My footsteps were muffled by a thick oriental rug in swirling shades of red and gold as I turned down one of the hallways off the main foyer.

I peeked into the first room I came to. It looked like

it had once been a dining room, or maybe a large parlor. Directly across from the door, one wall was nothing but windows, finally allowing me a good look at the grounds. This room overlooked a small pond with a pier and a pretty, ramshackle cabin. But what really struck me was all the green. The grass, the trees, the thin coat of algae on the pond, where I really, *really* hoped we wouldn't be canoeing or anything . . . all of it was this bright, hurt-your-eyes green that was like nothing I'd ever seen before. Even the heavy clouds that were beginning to swell with the threat of an afternoon thunderstorm seemed lime-tinted.

The carpet in this room was also green, and it felt soft, almost mushy underfoot, making me think of moss or fungus. Pictures covered the other three walls. Every one showed the same thing: a group of Prodigium gathered on the front porch. I didn't know if they were witches or shifters, but there were no faeries. A tiny gold plaque at the base of every frame told the year, starting in 1903 and ending with last year's picture, just to the right of the door.

There were only six adults in the oldest picture, and all of them looked really serious, like they'd probably kicked kittens for fun. Younger Prodigium didn't start showing up until 1967. I wondered if that was the first year Hecate Hall had become a school. And if so, what was it before then?

Last year, there were nearly a hundred kids, and everybody looked a lot more relaxed. I spotted Jenna in the front, standing next to a taller girl. They had their arms slung over each other's shoulders, and I wondered if this was the mysterious Holly.

To be honest, I felt a little jealous. I couldn't imagine ever being close enough to someone to casually put my arm around them in a picture. In all my old school pictures I was always the one standing alone in the back with my hair in my face.

Was that why Jenna had seemed so weird when I'd mentioned her old roommate? Had they been best buddies, and now I was the interloper trying to take Holly's place? Great.

"Sophia?"

Startled, I turned around.

The three most beautiful girls I'd ever seen in my life were standing behind me.

Then I blinked.

No, they weren't all drop-dead gorgeous. It was just the one in the middle. She had auburn hair that fell in soft bouncy curls nearly to her waist. She probably didn't even have to use a diffuser. I bet she woke up with her hair looking like something out of a Pantene commercial while little bluebirds circled around her head, and raccoons brought her breakfast or something.

I also couldn't help but notice that she didn't have any freckles, which was enough to make me hate her instantly.

The girl to her right was a blonde, and even though she had that whole California girl thing going— stick-straight hair, tan skin, deep blue eyes—her eyes were too close together, and when she smiled at me, I noticed she had a pretty bad overbite.

Rounding out the trio was an African American girl who was even shorter than I was. She was prettier than the blonde, but nowhere near as lovely the redheaded goddess in the middle. Still, looking at the plainer of the three, it was like my brain *wanted* them to be beautiful. My eyes wanted to skip over all of their imperfections.

A glamour. That was the only explanation, but I'd never heard of a witch using one. That was some serious magic.

I must have been looking at them like I was mentally damaged or something, because the blonde snickered and said, "Sophia Mercer, right?"

It was about then that I realized my mouth was literally hanging open. I closed it so quickly, it made a clacking sound that was really loud in the quiet room.

"Yeah, I'm Sophie."

"Great!" said the short girl. "We've been looking for you. I'm Anna Gilroy. This is Chaston Burnett"—she gestured to the blonde. "And this is Elodie Parris."

"Oh," I said, smiling at the redhead. "That's pretty. Like 'Melody' without the 'M.'"

She smirked. "No, like Elodie."

"Be nice," Anna admonished before turning back to me. "Chaston, Elodie, and I are sort of like the welcoming committee for new witches. So . . . welcome!"

She stuck her hand out, and I briefly wondered if I was supposed to kiss it, before I came to my senses and shook it.

"You three are witches?"

"That's what we just said," Elodie retorted, earning another sharp look from Anna.

"I'm sorry," I said. "It's just that I've never met any other witches before."

"Really?" Chaston asked. "Like, never met any witches at all, or just never met any other *dark* witches before?"

"Excuse me?"

"Dark witches," Elodie repeated, giving Nausicaa a run for her money in the Snottiest Tone Ever competition.

"I . . . um . . . I didn't know there were types of witches."

Now all three of them were looking at me as if I'd just spoken in a foreign language. "Yes, but you *are* a dark witch?" Anna asked, pulling a piece of paper from her blazer. It was some sort of list, and she scanned it intently.

"Let's see, Lassiter, Mendelson . . . here, Mercer, Sophia. Dark Witch. That's you."

She handed me the list, which was titled "New Students." There were about thirty names, all with classifications in parentheses. "Shapeshifter," "Faerie," and "White Witch." Mine was the only one that said "Dark Witch."

"Dark and white? What, are we like chicken meat?" Elodie glared at me.

"You really don't know?" Anna asked gently.

"Really don't," I said casually, but inside I was kind of annoyed. I mean, hello, what is the point of having a mom who's supposed to be some sort of witch expert if she doesn't know the really important stuff?

I get that it's not really her fault, and that most modern witchcraft information is highly secretive since they're so freaked out about being discovered . . . but damn, this was getting embarrassing.

"White witches—" Anna began, but Elodie cut her off.

"White witches do weenie spells. Love spells, fortune reading, locator spells, and . . . I don't know, making bunnies and kittens and rainbows appear out of thin air or whatever," she said, waving her hand dismissively.

"Oh," I said, thinking of Felicia and Kevin. "Yeah. Weenie spells."

"Dark witches do the bigger things," Chaston offered. "And our powers are a hell of a lot stronger. We can make barrier spells, and if we're really good, control the weather. We're also necromancers if—"

"Whoa!" I held up my hand. "Necromancers? Like, power over dead things?"

All three girls nodded eagerly, like I'd just suggested going to the mall instead of raising zombies.

"Ew!" I exclaimed without thinking.

Mistake. Simultaneously, their smiles disappeared, and a distinct chill came over the room.

"*Ew?*" Elodie sneered. "God, how old are you? Power over the dead is the most coveted power there is, and you're grossed out by it? I swear," she said, turning back to the other two, "are you serious about wanting her for the coven?"

I'd heard of covens, but Mom always said they'd fallen out of favor in the last fifty years or so. These days, it was more like every witch for herself.

"Hold up," I started, but Anna cut in like I hadn't even spoken.

"She's the only other dark witch here, and you know we need four."

"And I have the power of invisibility, apparently," I muttered, but they all ignored me.

"She's worse than Holly," Elodie said. "And Holly

was the most pathetic excuse for a dark witch ever."

"Elodie!" Chaston hissed.

"Holly?" I asked. "Like, Holly who used to room with Jenna Talbot?"

Anna, Chaston, and Elodie managed a three-way glance, which is no easy feat.

"Yes," Anna said guardedly. "How do you know about Holly?"

"I'm rooming with Jenna, and she mentioned her. So she's a dark witch too? Did she graduate or something, or just move out?"

Now all three of them looked genuinely freaked out. Even Elodie's perma-sneer was replaced by a look of shock.

"You're rooming with Jenna Talbot?" she asked.

"That's what I just said," I snapped, but Elodie seemed totally unfazed by my attempt at bitchiness.

"Listen," she said, taking my arm. "Holly didn't graduate or leave. She died."

Anna moved in on the other side of me, her eyes wide and frightened. "And Jenna Talbot killed her."

CHAPTER 5

When someone tells you somebody's been murdered, laughing is probably not the best response. You know, for future reference.

But laughing is exactly what I did.

"Jenna? Jenna Talbot killed her? What did she do, smother her with pink glitter or something?"

"You think this is funny?" Anna asked with a slight scowl.

Chaston and Elodie were glaring at me, and I figured my temporary membership into their club was about to be revoked.

"Well, yeah, kind of. I mean," I amended quickly, afraid smoke might actually start pouring out of Elodie's ears, "not that someone died. That's awful, 'cause . . . you know, death—"

"Yeah, we know. 'Ew,'" Elodie said, rolling her eyes.

"But the idea that Jenna could kill anyone is just . . . funny," I finished lamely.

Again with the three-way glance. Seriously, did they practice in front of a mirror?

"She's a vampire," Chaston insisted. "Can you think of any other way Holly ended up with two holes in her neck?"

All three of them had gathered around me now, like we were in a huddle. Outside, the late afternoon sun had finally disappeared behind heavy clouds, making the room feel even gloomier and more claustrophobic. Thunder had started rumbling, and I could smell that faint metallic scent that always comes before a storm.

"When Holly started two years ago, we formed a coven," Anna began. "The four of us were the only dark witches here, and you need four people for a really strong coven, so it seemed natural that we would become friends. But then Jenna Talbot showed up at the beginning of last year, and she and Holly became roommates."

"Next thing we know," Chaston interjected, "Holly won't hang out with us anymore. She starts spending all her time with Jenna, totally blowing us off. When we asked her why, all she would say was that Jenna was fun. Like, more fun than us."

She gave me a look that clearly said anyone being

55

more fun than the three of them was impossible.

"Wow," I said faintly.

"Then one day in March, I find Holly in the library crying," Elodie said. "All she would tell me was that it was about Jenna, but she wouldn't tell me what."

"Two days later, Holly was dead," Chaston said, her voice dark and somber. I waited for another crack of thunder, thinking one surely had to follow a statement like that. But the only sound was the soft shushing of the rain.

"They found her in the upstairs bathroom." Elodie's voice was almost a whisper. "She was in a tub, with two holes in her neck, and almost no blood left in her body."

By now my stomach was somewhere south of my knees, and I could actually feel my heart pounding in my ears. No wonder Jenna had freaked when I'd mentioned her roommate. "That's horrible."

"Yeah. It was." Chaston nodded.

"But—"

"But what?" Elodie's eyes narrowed.

"If everyone's so sure it was Jenna, why is she still here? Wouldn't the Council have staked her or something?"

"They did send someone," Chaston said, tucking her hair behind her ear. "But the guy said Holly's wounds couldn't have been made by fangs. They were too . . . neat."

I swallowed. "Neat?"

"Vampires are messy eaters," Anna replied.

I tried really hard to keep my face blank as I said, "Well, if the Council said it wasn't Jenna, then it wasn't her. Pretty sure those guys wouldn't let a rabid vampire go to school with Prodigium kids."

Elodie was the only one of the three who would meet my eyes. "The Council was wrong," she said flatly. "Holly was living with a vampire and she was killed by someone draining her blood *through her neck*. What else could have happened?"

Chaston and Anna still weren't looking at me. Something was definitely off here. I wasn't sure why these girl were so determined make me believe Jenna was a killer, but I wasn't buying it. Besides, the last thing I wanted to do on my first day was get wrapped up in some sort of witch/vamp gang war.

"Look, I still have some unpacking to do—" I started to say, but Anna decided to change tactics.

"Forget about the vamp for just a second, Sophie. Hear us out." Her voice slid into a whine. "We really need a fourth for our coven."

"Yeah," Chaston added. "And we could teach you so much about being a dark witch. No offense, but you seem like you could use the help."

"I'll, uh, think about it, okay?"

I turned to leave, but the door slammed shut inches from my face. Suddenly a wind seemed to blow through the room and the pictures on the walls rattled. When I turned back to the girls, all three of them were smiling at me, their hair rippling around their faces like they were underwater.

The one lamp in the room flickered and went out. I could just make out silvery traces of light passing under the girls' skin, like mercury. Even their eyes were glowing. They began to levitate, the tips of their Hecate-issue loafers barely brushing the mossy carpet. Now they weren't homecoming queens or supermodels—they were witches, and very dangerous ones at that.

Even as I fought the urge to fall to my knees and throw my hands over my head, I was wondering, was this what I was capable of? If I hadn't been busy doing "weenie spells" like Felicia's, would I have looked like this, my skin lit up with silver and my eyes on fire? The power I sensed surging up through them made me feel like I was in the room with a tornado, like I was about to be blown out of that wall of windows and into that scummy pond. As it was, the energy was enough to send the glass splintering out of three of the framed photographs. One thin sliver sliced my forearm, but I hardly felt it.

Then, as quickly as it had started, the wind died down and the pictures stilled. The three girls in front of me no longer looked like primeval goddesses. They were just normal, if stunning, teenagers again.

"See?" Anna said eagerly. "That's what we can do with only three. Imagine what we could accomplish with four."

I stared at them. Had that been their sales pitch? *Look! We're really scary! Come be scary too!*

"Wow," I finally said. "That was . . . yeah. Really something."

"So are you in?" Chaston asked.

She and Anna were still smiling at me, but Elodie was looking off to the side, bored.

"Can I get back to you?" I asked.

Chaston's and Anna's smiles vanished. "Told you so," Elodie said.

And then, like I suddenly ceased to exist, they walked out.

I collapsed into one of the wingback chairs, my knees drawn up under my chin, watching as the rain died down.

That's where Jenna found me nearly an hour later, just after the dinner bell rang.

"Sophie?" she asked, poking her head in.

"Hey." I attempted a smile.

Which must have been pretty pathetic, because Jenna immediately furrowed her brow. "What's up?" But before I could explain about the Witches of Clinique, Jenna rushed on, her words coming so fast that I could practically see them tumbling out of her mouth. "Look, I'm sorry about earlier. None of that was any of my business."

"No, no," I said, rising to my feet. "Jenna, it's not you. Really. We're cool."

Relief washed over her face. Then she glanced down. It happened so quickly that I couldn't be sure, but I thought I saw her eyes darken for a split second. I looked at my arm and saw the cut where the flying glass had hit me.

Right. I'd forgotten about that. It was deeper than I'd expected. Now, as I looked down, I could see splotches of my own blood staining the carpet.

I looked up at Jenna, who was obviously trying not to stare at my arm.

An uncomfortable prickling sensation crawled over the back of my neck.

"Oh, that," I said, covering the wound. "Yeah, I was looking at the pictures and a couple of them fell. The glass broke and I cut myself. I'm really clumsy."

But Jenna had already turned to the wall to see that none of the pictures had fallen; that just three of them had shattered. "Let me guess," she said softly. "You had a run-in with the Trinity."

"Who?" I said, lamely forcing a laugh. "I don't even know—"

"Elodie, Anna, and Chaston. And the fact that you didn't want to tell me about it means they must have told you about Holly."

Great. Was my only chance at friendship here destined to be thwarted at every turn?

"Jenna," I started, but now it was her turn to cut me off.

"Did they tell you I killed Holly?"

When I didn't answer, she made this sound that I think was supposed to be a sarcastic laugh, but she was clearly holding back tears.

"Right, 'cause I'm a monster who can't control herself and would eat her . . . her best friend." The corners of her mouth had started to tremble a little. "They're the ones who are into the really dark stuff, but I'm the monster," she continued.

"What do you mean?"

She looked back at me for a second before turning away again. "I don't know," she mumbled. "Just some stuff Holly said. Some sort of spell they were trying to do to get more power or something."

I thought of them hovering over the carpet, skin on fire. Whatever "stuff" they'd tried, it had clearly worked.

Jenna started sniffling. I felt sorry for her, but I couldn't stop thinking about that look I'd seen on her face before.

It was hunger.

I pushed the thought away and stepped closer to her. "Screw them."

Except I didn't say "screw." There are certain times when only really bad words will work, and this was one of them. Jenna's eyes got huge, and relief visibly flowed through her. "Damn straight." She agreed with such a strong nod that we both burst into giggles.

As we made our way to the dining hall, I looked over at Jenna, who was now babbling about how awesome the pecan pie was. I thought about those three girls, how wrong they'd been; there was no way Jenna could hurt anyone.

But even as I laughed at her rapturous descriptions of pie, I felt a small shiver at the base of my spine, thinking about her eyes as she'd watched my blood drip to the carpet.

CHAPTER 6

The dining hall was completely bizarre. After hearing that it was a converted ballroom, I'd expected something fancy: crystal chandeliers, shiny dark wood floors, a wall of mirrors . . . the full-on fairy-tale ballroom.

Instead, it had the same decayed feeling as the rest of the house. Oh sure, there were chandeliers, but they were covered with what looked to be big trash bags. And there was a wall of mirrors, but it was covered from floor to ceiling in big sheets of canvas.

The dining hall was a jumble of tables of all sizes and shapes shoved into the massive room. There was a huge oval oak table right next to a Formica and steel table that looked like it had been stolen from a diner. I even thought I spotted a picnic bench. Wasn't this school run by witches? Was there not, like, a furniture-creating spell or something?

But then I caught sight of the long low table that held all the food: big heaping silver bowls of shrimp, steaming pans full of roasted chicken, vats of gooey macaroni and cheese.

I gaped at the towering chocolate cake, easily three feet tall, covered in dark creamy frosting and dotted with thick red strawberries.

"This is a first-night spread only," Jenna warned.

Once I had piled my plate high, Jenna and I looked around for a place to sit. I saw Elodie, Chaston, and Anna sitting at a glass-top table near the end of the room, so I immediately started to look for a table far away from them. There were a couple of empty spots available at nearly every table, and I could hear my mom saying, "Now, Sophie, please make an effort to meet new people."

But Mom wasn't here, and I could see that Jenna wasn't really in the mood to socialize either. Then I spotted a small white table near the doors, and pointed it out to Jenna.

It looked like it had once been used for some little girl's tea party, but it was the only table for two, so, you know, beggars, choosers, and all that.

I sat in one of the little white chairs. My knees thwacked into the edge of the table, causing Jenna to snort with laughter.

While I devoured the delicious food on my plate, I

asked Jenna questions about various people in the dining hall. I started with the huge ebony table that sat on a raised platform at one end of the room. It was clearly the teachers' table, since not only was it the nicest, it was also the biggest. Besides Mrs. Casnoff picking at her salad at the head of the table, there were five other adults—two men and three women. The faerie teacher was easy to spot, what with the wings, and Jenna told me that the big man next to her was Mr. Ferguson, a shifter.

On his right was a young woman with bright, nearly purple hair and thick-framed glasses like Jenna's. She was so fair-skinned I guessed she was the vampire Mrs. Casnoff had mentioned earlier, but Jenna said she was actually Ms. East, a white witch.

"The guy next to her, he's the vamp," Jenna said through a mouthful of pie. She pointed to a really good-looking guy in his thirties with black curly hair. "Lord Byron."

I snorted. "Oh God, how angsty can you be, naming yourself after a dead poet?"

But Jenna just looked at me. "No, he's the real Lord Byron."

Now it was my turn to stare. "No freaking way! Like, 'She Walks in Beauty' and all that? He's a vampire?"

"Yup," Jenna confirmed. "One of them turned him while he was dying in Greece. The Council actually held him prisoner for a really long time since he's kind of conspicuous. Kept wanting to go back to England and turn everybody into vampires. When they opened this place, they sentenced him to be a teacher here."

"Wow," I breathed softly, watching the guy I'd written a paper about last year boldly scowl at all of us. "How bad would that suck to be immortal and have to spend eternity *here*?"

Then I remembered who I was talking to. "Sorry," I said, looking at my food.

"Don't be," Jenna said, shoving a forkful of pie into her mouth. "I don't plan on spending the rest of my very long life at Hecate, trust me."

I wanted to ask Jenna some more questions about what it was like to know you'd live forever. I mean, vamps are the only Prodigium that get to do that. Even faeries will blink out eventually, and witches and shifters don't live any longer than regular people.

Instead I gestured to the tall woman with curly brown hair who was sitting across the table from Mrs. Casnoff.

"Who's that?"

Jenna rolled her eyes and groaned. "Ugh. Ms. Vanderlyden. Or the Vandy as we all call her. Not to her face," she quickly added. "Do that and you'll never get out of detention. She's a dark witch, or at least she was.

The Council stripped her of her powers years ago. Now she's kind of like our dorm mother or something, and she teaches P.E. or what passes for it at Hex. She's in charge of making sure we follow the rules and stuff. She's also totally evil."

"She's wearing a scrunchie," I said. I had rocked some scrunchies in my day, but that had been when I was, like, seven. The thought of wearing one as a grown woman was just tragic.

"I know." Jenna shook her head. "We have this theory that it's her Portable Portal to hell. You know, she just stretches it out and steps through whenever she needs to recharge her evilness."

I laughed, even as I wondered if Jenna was actually being serious.

"There's also a groundskeeper," Jenna added. "Callahan, but we all call him Cal. I don't see him tonight."

We moved on to the students. I noticed that Archer was sitting at a table with a bunch of other guys. They were laughing at something Archer was saying. I really hoped it wasn't the "Bad Dog" story. "What about that guy?" I asked with forced casualness.

"Archer Cross, resident bad boy and total heartthrob. Warlock. Every girl here is at least, like, half in love with him. Crushing on Archer Cross might as well be a class."

"What about you?" I asked. "You have a crush on him?"

Jenna studied me for a moment before saying, "He's not really my type."

"What, you don't do tall, dark, and handsome?"

"No," she said lightly. "I don't do guys."

"Oh," was all I could say to that. I'd never had a gay friend. Then again, I'd never really had a lot of friends.

Still looking at Archer, I said, "Yeah, well, I attempted to kill him earlier."

After Jenna recovered from the sweet tea that nearly shot out of her nose, I filled her in on the actual story.

"Mrs. Casnoff didn't seem very impressed with him," I said.

"She wouldn't be. Archer was always in trouble last year. Then he left in the middle of the school year for almost a month, and there were all these rumors about him. People thought he went to London."

"Why? So he could ride one of those double-decker buses?"

Jenna gave me a funny look. "No, London is where Council headquarters is. Everybody thought he'd gone through the Removal."

I'd read something about that in one of Mom's books. It was this really intense ritual that took away magical powers. But something like one in a hundred Prodigium survive it. I'd never heard of anyone going through it voluntarily.

"Why would he do that?" I asked.

She pushed her food around on her plate. "He and Holly were . . . really close, and he was in a bad place after she died. A couple of people said they heard him telling Casnoff that he hated what he was, wanted to be normal, stuff like that."

"Huh," I said. "So he and Holly were a couple?"

"You could say that."

I clearly wasn't going to get any more out of Jenna about *that*, so I said, "Well, apparently he didn't go through the Removal. He's still got powers."

"Yeah, powers over your pants," Jenna said with a giggle.

I threw a roll at her, but before she could retaliate, Mrs. Casnoff rose from her seat. She raised her hands over her head and the room fell quiet so quickly, you would have thought she'd just cast a silencing spell.

"Students," she drawled. "Dinner is now concluded. If this is not your first night at Hecate, please exit the dining hall. The rest of you are to remain seated."

Jenna gave me a sympathetic look and cleared our empty plates. "Sorry in advance for what you're about to see."

"What?" I asked as the dining hall began to empty. "What's going to happen?"

Jenna shook her head. "Let's just say you may regret that second piece of cake."

Oh my God. Regret cake? Whatever was about to happen must be truly evil.

Everyone was filing out when Mrs. Casnoff's voice rang out. "Mr. Cross? Where are you going?"

Archer was only a few feet from me and about to head out the door. I also noticed that he was holding hands with Elodie. Interesting. Of course it made total sense that the two people who already seemed to dislike me the most would be dating.

Archer stared down the length of the ballroom at Mrs. Casnoff. "This isn't my first year," he said. The line out the door had frozen, everyone's curious faces turned toward Archer. Elodie placed her other hand—the one that wasn't clutching Archer's like he was a prize she'd won at a carnival—on his shoulder.

"I've seen all this crap before," he insisted.

The shifter teacher, Mr. Ferguson, rose to his feet. "Language!" he bellowed.

But Archer's eyes were on Mrs. Casnoff, who looked calm and cool.

"And yet I don't believe it has sunk in," she told Archer. She gestured to the Jenna's now-empty chair. "Kindly have a seat."

I'm pretty sure he muttered an even worse string

of words as he grabbed the chair across from me. "Hey there, Soph*ie*."

I gritted my teeth. "Hi. So what is this?"

Archer settled into his seat, a grim look on his face. "Oh, you'll see."

And then everything went black.

CHAPTER 7

As soon as the lights went out, I expected that usual thing that happens when a teacher turns off the lights: laughter, *oooohs*, and the rustling of clothing and squeaking of chairs that tells you people are scooting closer together, probably to make out. Instead the room was silent. Of course, there were only about twenty of us in there.

Next to me, I heard Archer sigh. It always feels weird to sit next to a guy in the dark, even if it was a guy I didn't like. Because I couldn't see him, I was very aware of him breathing, shifting in his chair, even the way he smelled (which, admittedly, was clean and soapy).

I was about to ask him again just what I was in for when a tiny square of light appeared at the front of the room next to Mrs. Casnoff. The square grew larger and larger until it was roughly the size of a movie screen. It hovered there, blank and glowing, until, very slowly, an image began to appear, like a photo developing. It was a black-and-white painting of a group of stern-faced men wearing the black suits and big hats of Puritans.

"In 1692, two witches in Salem, Massachusetts, came into their powers and created a panic that left eighteen innocent humans dead," Mrs. Casnoff began. "A group of warlocks from nearby Boston wrote to the warlocks and witches in London and created the Council. It was hoped that with structure and resources, the Council could better control magical activity and prevent other tragedies like this from occurring."

The picture faded and morphed into a portrait of a redheaded woman in a green satin dress with a huge hoop skirt.

"This is Jessica Prentiss," Mrs. Casnoff continued, her voice filling the huge room. "She was an enormously powerful white witch from New Orleans. In 1876, after her younger sister, Margaret, perished while having her powers stripped by the Council, Miss Prentiss proposed the idea of a safe house of sorts, a place where witches whose powers were potentially harmful could live in peace."

The portrait faded and the old photograph that I'd seen earlier, the one of the school in 1903, appeared.

"It took almost thirty years, but her dream was realized in 1903," Mrs. Casnoff continued. "In 1923, the Council granted shapeshifters and fae the right to come to Hecate as well."

No mention of vamps, of course.

"This isn't so bad," I whispered to Archer. "Just a history lecture."

He shook his head slightly. "Just wait."

"In 1967, the Council realized that it needed a place to train and mold young Prodigium who were using their powers without the proper level of discretion. A school where they would learn more about the history of Prodigium, and of the dreadful consequences of exposing their abilities to humans. And so Hecate Hall was born."

"Juvie for monsters," I muttered under my breath, earning me a low laugh from Archer.

"Miss Mercer," Mrs. Casnoff said, making me jump. I was afraid she was going to bust me for talking, but instead she asked, "Can you tell us who Hecate is?"

"Um, yeah. She's the Greek goddess of witchcraft."

Mrs. Casnoff nodded. "Indeed. But she is also the goddess of the crossroads. And that is where all of you children now find yourselves. And now"—Mrs. Casnoff's voice rang out—"a demonstration."

"Here we go," Archer murmured.

Once again, a small speck of light sparkled in the front

of the room, but this time, no screen appeared. Instead, the light took the form of an old man, maybe around seventy. He would have looked completely real if it hadn't been for the slight shimmer that clung to him, making him glow in the dark room. He was dressed in overalls and a plaid shirt, and a brown hat was pulled low over his eyes. A scythe dangled from his right hand. For a moment he was totally motionless, but then he turned and began swinging the scythe near the ground, like he was cutting grass that wasn't there. It was . . . eerie. It was like we were watching a movie, but the action was happening live.

"This is Charles Walton," Mrs. Casnoff announced. "He was a white warlock from a village in England called Lower Quinton. He kept to himself and earned one pitiful shilling an hour as a hedge cutter for a local farmer. In addition to that, he performed simple spells for the people of Lower Quinton: potions for gout, the occasional love spell . . . simple harmless things. But then, in 1945, the village had a bad harvest." As she spoke, more figures began to materialize behind the man. There were four of them in all: normal-looking people in cardigans and sensible shoes. Two of them had their backs to me, but I could see a short, squat woman with a rosy face and steel gray hair, and a skinny guy wearing a deep burgundy hat with earflaps. They looked like they should be on a box of shortbread. Both also wore stark, scary expressions on their faces, and the skinny guy was holding a pitchfork.

"The people of Lower Quinton decided that Charles must have been to blame for their crops failing, and . . . well, you can see the rest."

The man with the pitchfork darted forward and grabbed the old man by the elbow, whirling him around. The old man looked terrified, and even though I knew what was coming, I couldn't turn away. Instead I watched as three people, people who looked like they should be baking pies or sipping tea, forced the old man to the ground, and the skinny man drove the pitchfork through his neck.

I thought for sure someone would scream; that someone in the room would cry out or even faint. But it seemed like everyone was as frozen as I was. Even Archer had stopped slouching in his seat. Now he was leaning forward, his elbows on his thighs, hands clenched.

The sweet grandmotherly woman knelt down next to the body and picked up the scythe, and just as I was thinking that I really did regret that cake, the scene in front of us shimmered and vanished.

Mrs. Casnoff filled us in on what we hadn't seen. "After stabbing him, the villagers went on to carve symbols on Mr. Walton's body, which they hoped would ward off his 'evil' magic. After five decades of trying to help his fellow villagers, this is how Charles Walton was repaid by humans."

And suddenly the room was full of images and sounds. Just behind Mrs. Casnoff, a family of vampires were staked by a group of men in black suits. I could actually hear the horrible wet sound, almost like a loud kiss, as the wooden stakes pierced their chests.

From the left I heard the sharp rattle of gunfire, and I instinctively ducked as a werewolf collapsed, riddled with silver bullets fired by an old woman in, of all things, a pink housecoat.

It was like being thrust into a horror movie, and it was *everywhere*. In the center of the room, I now saw two faeries, both with translucent gray wings, forced to their knees by three men in brown robes. As the faeries screamed, their wrists were shackled in iron that immediately seared their flesh, filling the room with a smell that was disturbingly like barbecue.

My mouth went so dry I could feel my lips sticking to my teeth. That's why I couldn't even gasp when a gallows full of hanged witches sprung up right next to me.

Instead of fading in as the other pictures had done, this one shot straight up from the ground like a jack-in-the-box. Their bodies actually jolted and started spinning on their nooses, their faces purple, tongues protruding from swollen lips. I could hear faint screaming, but I wasn't sure if it was from my fellow students or the images themselves. I wanted to cover my face, but my hands felt heavy and clammy, my heart stuck in my throat.

Something warm settled on the back of my hand. I tore my eyes away from those dangling bodies and saw that Archer had covered my hand with his. He was staring straight at the witches, and I realized they weren't just women. There were warlocks hanging too. Without really thinking, I curled my fingers around his.

And then, just when I was sure I was going to be sick, the images vanished and the dining hall lights came on.

Mrs. Casnoff stood at the front of the room, smiling serenely, but when she spoke, her voice was cold and hard. "This is why all of you are here. This is what you all risked when you recklessly used your powers in the presence of humans. And for what?" She looked around the room. "To gain acceptance? To show off?" Her eyes fell on me for a second before she continued. "We've been persecuted unto death by humans who will happily use our powers if it suits them. And what you just saw"—she swept her hand around, and I could almost see those hanged witches again, their eyes cloudy, their lips blue—"is just what *normal* humans have done. This is nothing compared to what is done by those who've made it their life's work to eliminate our kind."

My heart was still pounding, but my stomach was

no longer threatening mutiny. Next to me, Archer had resumed slouching, so I guess he was feeling better too.

Mrs. Casnoff waved her hand again, and like before, images sprang up behind her, only this time they were still pictures instead of movies from hell. "There's a group that calls themselves the Alliance," she said, sounding almost bored as she gestured to a group of bland-looking men and women in suits. I thought her tone was awfully dismissive for a lady who worked for a council called "the Council," but I had to agree that "the Alliance" was pretty lame.

"The Alliance is made up of agents from several different government agencies from several different governments. Luckily, they stay so bogged down with paperwork that they're rarely an actual threat."

That picture faded as a trio of women with the brightest red hair I'd ever seen appeared. "And, of course, the Brannicks, an ancient family from Ireland who have been fighting 'monsters,' as they call us, since the time of Saint Patrick. These are the current keepers of the flame, Aislinn Brannick, and her two daughters, Finley and Isolde. They tend to be a little more dangerous, as their ancestor was Maeve Brannick, an incredibly powerful white witch who renounced her race to join with the church. They're therefore imbued with more power than your regular human."

She waved her hand again, and the women disappeared.

"And then there is our most forceful enemy," Mrs. Casnoff continued. As she spoke, a black image formed over her head. It took me a minute to figure out that it was an eye. But not an actual eye—more like a really stylized tattoo sketched all in black, except for the iris, which was deep gold.

"*L'Occhio di Dio*. The Eye of God," she said. I heard the room draw in a collective breath.

"What's that?" I whispered to Archer.

He turned. That sarcastic smile was hovering around his lips again, so I figured our earlier camaraderie was pretty much over. He confirmed it, saying, "You can't do a blocking spell, *and* you've never heard of L'Occhio? Man, what kind of witch are you?"

I had an incredibly nasty retort ready that involved his mother and the U.S. Navy, but before I could get it out, Mrs. Casnoff said, "L'Occhio di Dio is the greatest threat to any Prodigium. They are a group based in Rome, and their express purpose is wiping our kind off the face of the earth. They see themselves as holy knights, while we are the evil that must be purged. Last year this group alone was responsible for the deaths of more than one thousand Prodigium."

I stared up at The Eye and felt the hair on the back

of my neck stand up. Now I remembered why it looked so familiar. I'd seen it once in one of Mom's books. I'd been about thirteen, just idly flipping through the pages, admiring the glossy pictures of famous witches. And then I'd turned to a painting of a witch's execution in Scotland, maybe around 1600 or so. The picture was so gruesome that I hadn't been able to stop staring at it. I could still see the witch lying on her back, strapped to a wooden plank. Her blond hair streamed to the ground, a look of sheer terror on her face. Standing over her was a dark-haired man holding a silver knife. He wasn't wearing a shirt, and just above his heart was a tattoo—a black eye with a golden iris.

"In the past we've more than held our own against these three groups, but that's when they were separate and at odds. Now we've received word that they may be forging a sort of peace. If this happens . . ." She sighed. "Well, let's just say we can't let that happen."

The Eye faded, and Mrs. Casnoff clapped her hands together. "Now. Enough of that. You all have a very big morning tomorrow, so you are dismissed. Lights out in half an hour."

She sounded so bright and businesslike that I wondered if I had hallucinated the part where she basically told us we were all going to die. But one look around the room and I knew that my classmates were just as shell-shocked and confused as I was.

"Well," Archer said, slapping his hands on his thighs. "That was new."

Before I could ask what he meant, he was out of his seat and disappearing among the crowd of students.

CHAPTER 8

Thanks to his long-legged stride, I nearly had to jog to catch up with Archer.

By the time I reached him, he was halfway up the stairs.

"Cross!" I called. I just couldn't bring myself to say "Archer" out loud. I'd have felt like I was in an episode of *Masterpiece Theatre*: "Archer! Let us fetch a spot of tea, old boy!"

He paused on the stairs and turned to face me. Shockingly, he wasn't smirking.

"Mercer," he replied, making me roll my eyes.

"Look, what did you mean by 'that was new'? I thought you'd seen all that before."

He came down a couple of steps. "I have," he answered when he was only two steps above me. "Three years ago, when I was fourteen. My first year here. But it was different then."

"Different how?"

He shrugged out of his blazer, rolling his shoulders as if the jacket had been heavy. "They still did the Charles Walton thing; that seems to be a favorite. And there was a werewolf getting shot, and maybe one or two faeries on fire. But there weren't as many images. And they weren't all at once like that."

He looked down at me like he was sizing me up. "No hanged witches and warlocks either. I have to say, I'm a little impressed."

I crossed my arms over my chest and scowled. I didn't like the way he was looking at me. "Impressed by what?"

"When I saw that show three years ago, I had to run into that little bathroom over there"—he pointed to a small door across the foyer—"and puke my guts out. What we saw tonight was a lot worse, and you don't even look pale. You're tougher than I thought."

I fought the urge to laugh. My face may have looked calm, but my belly still felt like a mosh pit. Briefly amused by the image of my organs wearing eyeliner and ripped jeans, I gave Archer what I hoped was a look of cool nonchalance. "I just don't believe all that."

He raised an eyebrow, which made me totally jealous. I've never been able to do that. I always just end up raising both of them and looking surprised or scared instead of sardonic.

"Don't believe all what?"

"All that about humans wanting to kill us in lots of nasty ways."

"I think history pretty well supports that hypothesis, Mercer. Hell, humans have wiped out thousands of their own kind trying to get to us."

"Yeah, but that was in the past," I argued. "Back when they also thought drilling a hole in your head, or draining your blood would cure you of a disease. Humans are a lot more enlightened now."

"That a fact?" He was smirking again. I wondered if his face hurt if he took too long a break from it.

"Look," I said. "My mom is human, okay? And she loves Prodigium. She'd never do a thing to hurt one. She even got a—"

"Her daughter's one."

"What?"

He heaved a sigh and tossed his jacket over one shoulder, holding it with the tip of his index finger. I thought only male models in GQ did that. "Your mom may be an awesome person, but do you honestly believe she'd feel all warm and fuzzy about witches if she weren't raising one?"

I wanted to answer yes. I really did. But he had a point. Mom may have become a monster expert for my sake, but hadn't she run from my dad the minute he'd told her what he really was?

"You're right," Archer said, his tone softening a little. "Humans aren't what they used to be. But all those images were real, Mercer. Humans are always going to be scared of us. They're always going to be envious of our powers, and suspicious of our motives."

"Not all of them," I said, but my voice sounded weak, and I was thinking of Felicia, hysterical and screaming, "It was her! She's a witch!"

Archer shrugged again. "Maybe not. But you've been living with one foot in each world, and you can't do that anymore. You're at Hecate now."

His words hit hard. It had never occurred to me that I was different, that most Prodigium grew up in households with two parents just like them. And some of the kids here had had hardly any interactions with humans once they'd come into their powers. Despite the doubt that was crawling over my skin like bugs, I said, "Yeah, but—"

"Arch!"

Elodie was standing on the landing above us, one hand on her basically nonexistent hip. Normally when this kind of thing happens in movies, the girlfriend is glaring down at the other girl with bright green jealousy, but since Elodie was a goddess, and I was, well, not, she didn't look even the littlest bit threatened. More bored, actually.

"Be right there, El," Archer called up to her. She executed that combination eye-roll/hair-flip/hand-wave thing that only beautiful girls irritated with their boyfriends can pull off, and walked up to the third floor. I think she put a little too much swing in her hips as she went, but, hey, matter of opinion.

"'Arch'?" I asked once she was gone, attempting the raised-eyebrow thing. As usual, it didn't work, so I probably just looked startled.

"See ya, Mercer," was all he replied. But as he turned to go, I couldn't help blurting out, "Do you think they might have a reason sometimes?"

He turned back to me. "Who?"

I glanced around, but the hall was empty.

"Those people. The Alliance and those Irish girls. The Eye," I answered. "I mean, what we saw was *awful*, but aren't there dangerous Prodigium too?"

For a moment we held each other's gaze. At first I thought he was pissed at me, but then I realized the look in his eyes wasn't anger. It was more like he was . . . I don't know . . . studying me or something.

I felt a weird sort of heat travel from my stomach to my cheeks. I don't know if he noticed it, but he smiled at me, a real smile this time, and I actually felt my breath hitch in my chest. It was the same feeling I'd had in the fourth grade when Suzie Strelzyck dared me to touch the bottom of the pool at the YMCA. I'd done it, but kicking back up to the surface, my chest had felt like it was caught in a trash compactor, and I was light-headed by the time I'd broken through the water.

That's how I felt now, staring up into Archer Cross's eyes.

He walked down the two steps between us until he was on the same stair as me. I still had to look up at him, but at least it didn't make my neck hurt. He leaned in close, and I caught that clean soapy smell.

"I wouldn't say that kind of thing around here if I were you, Mercer," he whispered. I could feel his breath warm against my cheek, and although I wouldn't swear to it, I think my eyes may have fluttered.

But just a little.

As I watched him lope up the stairs, I gritted my teeth and repeated a mantra in my head:

I will not have a crush on Archer Cross, I will not have a crush on Archer Cross, I will not . . .

When I got back to my room, Jenna was sitting cross-legged on her bed, reading a book.

I heaved a sigh and leaned against the door, pushing it shut with a loud click.

"What's wrong? The Moving Picture Show get to you?" Jenna asked without looking up.

"No. I mean, yeah, of course. That stuff was messed up."

"Mm-hmm," Jenna agreed. "Anything else?"

"I have a crush on Archer Cross."

Jenna laughed. "How original of you."

I flopped down on my bed. "Why?" I moaned into my pillow. I rolled over and stared at the ceiling. "Okay, so he's cute. Big deal. Lots of guys are cute."

Clearly my whining about a boy I liked was interfering with Jenna's reading, because she uncrossed her legs and came to perch on the edge of her desk. "Archer's not cute," she amended. "Puppies are cute. Babies are cute. *I'm* cute. Archer Cross is smokin' hot. And I'm not even into guys."

Okay, so Jenna was not going to be much assistance in squashing the crush. "He's a jerk," I pointed out. "Remember the whole werewolf thing this morning?"

"Yeah," Jenna said drily. "Saving you from a werewolf. What a tool."

I groaned. "You're not helping."

"Sorry."

We sat in silence for a moment, me looking at a suspicious mildew stain on the ceiling, Jenna leaning back on her elbows, drumming her feet against the desk drawers. Outside, I could hear howling. It was a full moon, so the shifters got free run of the grounds. I wondered if Taylor was out there.

"Ooh!" Jenna said suddenly, sitting up so fast she

knocked over her cup of pens. "He has a total bitch for a girlfriend!"

"Yes!" I said, sitting up and pointing at her. "Thank you! Evil girlfriend who already hates me, no less. And any guy who willingly spends time with Elodie is not a guy worth liking."

"Too true," Jenna said with an emphatic nod.

Feeling better, I rolled onto my stomach to grab a book from beside the bed. "It's weird, though," Jenna said.

"What is?"

"Archer and Elodie. She was after him all last year, but he never wanted anything to do with her. Like, ever. Then he came back from wherever he was, and bam! Suddenly they're a couple. It's weird."

"Not that weird," I countered. "I mean, she's incredibly beautiful. Maybe hormones finally got the best of him."

"Maybe," Jenna said, resting her chin in her hand. "But still. Archer is smart and funny in addition to being hot. Elodie is stupid and dull."

"And hot," I added. "And even smart boys are dumb when it comes to hot girls."

"True," Jenna agreed.

I was about to bring up the subject of Holly again when Casnoff's voice drifted through the room, almost like she was on a PA system. I guessed it was some sort of voice amplification spell.

"Ladies and gentlemen, in light of tomorrow's busy schedule, you are expected to retire early tonight. Lights out in ten minutes."

I glanced at my watch. "It's eight o'clock," I said incredulously. "She wants us to go to bed at eight o'clock?"

Sighing, Jenna went to her closet and pulled out her pajamas. "Welcome to life at Hecate, Sophie."

There was a mad rush for the bathroom to brush teeth, but it was all shifters and witches. I guess faeries have naturally clean teeth. Once I made it back from that, I only had three minutes left to put on my pajamas and dive into bed. At 8:10 exactly, the lights blinked out.

My mind was whirling, and I didn't know how I was ever going to get to sleep. "Is it weird for you," I asked Jenna, "going to bed at night? I mean, aren't vampires supposed to sleep during the day?"

"Yeah," she replied. "But as long as I'm here, I have to follow Hecate's schedule. It's gonna be a bitch once I get to leave."

I didn't ask Jenna *when* she would get to leave. Everybody else was released from Hecate at eighteen, but the rest of us aged like humans. Jenna would always be fifteen.

I settled into my bed and tried to think sleepy thoughts. It seemed like I had just closed my eyes when I heard the door creak open.

Panicked, I sat up, heart pounding. The clock by my bed said it was a few minutes after midnight.

A dark figure slid into the room.

I gasped. "Relax," Jenna muttered from her bed. "It's probably just one of the ghosts. They do that sometimes."

Then there was the soft snick of a match being lit, and a small pool of light illuminated the figure.

Elodie.

She was wearing purple silk pajamas, a black candle cradled in her hands. Two other candles blazed to life, and I saw Chaston and Anna, also pajama-clad, standing behind Elodie.

"Sophia Mercer," Elodie intoned, "we have come to induct you into our sisterhood. Say the five words to begin the ritual."

I blinked at her. "Are you freaking kidding me?"

Anna gave an exasperated sigh. "No, the five words are 'I accept your offer, sisters.'"

I brushed my hair out of my face and said, "I told you earlier, I'm not sure if I want to join your coven. I'm not saying any words to begin any ritual."

"Saying the five words doesn't mean you automatically join," Chaston said, stepping forward. "It just means that the ritual of acceptance can start. You can back out any time."

"Oh, just go with them," Jenna said. I could see her in the candlelight, sitting up in her bed, her dark eyes wary. "They're not going to leave you alone until you hear them out."

Elodie's mouth tightened, but she didn't say anything.

"Fine," I said, pushing off my covers and standing up. "I . . . I accept your offer, sisters."

CHAPTER 9

The three of them led me to Elodie and Anna's room.

"How did you two get to room together?" I whispered. "I thought the big thing at Hecate was learning to live with other Prodigium."

Elodie was searching her desk for something and gave no sign of hearing me, so Chaston said, "Witches sometimes have to pair up since there are always way more of us than faeries or shifters."

"Why is that?" I asked.

Anna answered me as she lit some more candles, bathing the room in a soft glow. "Faeries and shifters don't attempt to travel in the human world as much as witches do. Less chance of them getting sent to this place."

Elodie had found a piece of chalk in her desk and was busy drawing a large pentagram on the hardwood floor. Once she was done, she drew a circle around it.

"Normally we'd do this ritual outside, preferably in a ring of trees," she said, sitting at the head of the pentagram. Chaston and Anna sat on either side of her, so I took my place at the other end. "But we're not allowed in the woods. Mrs. Casnoff is, like, insanely strict about that."

The four of us sat around the pentagram holding hands. I wondered if we were about to sing "Kumbaya."

"Sophie, what was the first magic you put out into the universe?" Elodie asked.

"What?"

"The first spell you ever cast," Chaston said, leaning forward, her blond hair spilling over her shoulders. "It's a sacred thing for a witch, that first spell. When I was twelve, I created a storm that lasted *three days*. And Anna froze time for . . . how long?"

"Ten hours," Anna answered.

I looked across the circle at Elodie. The light from the candles flickered in her eyes.

"What about you?" I asked her.

"I turned day to night."

"Oh."

"What was yours, Sophie?" Chaston asked eagerly.

I thought about lying. I could say I turned someone to stone, or something. But then again, maybe if they knew what a crappy witch I was, they'd back off from this coven business.

"I turned my hair purple."

I was met with three identical stares.

"Purple?" Anna asked.

"It wasn't on purpose or anything," I said. "I was trying to permanently straighten it, but I guess I did something wrong because instead it turned purple. Only for three weeks, though. So . . . yeah, that was the first magic I ever did."

They were silent. Anna and Chaston exchanged looks across the circle.

"Maybe I should go," I said.

"No!" Chaston said, squeezing my hand.

"Yeah, don't go," Anna added. "So your first magic was . . . well, kind of stupid. You've done bigger spells than that since then, right?" She nodded at me encouragingly.

"What spell got you in here?" Elodie asked. She was sitting perfectly still, her eyes glittering. "Surely that was something."

I met her gaze across the circle. "I did a love spell."

Anna and Chaston heaved identical sighs and dropped my hands.

"A love spell?" Elodie sneered.

"What about you?" I looked around the circle at

the three of them. "What did you do to get sent to Hecate?"

Anna spoke first. "I turned a boy in my English class into a rat."

Chaston shrugged. "I told you. I made it storm for three days."

Elodie glanced down at the floor for a second. I wasn't sure, but I thought she took a deep breath. When she raised her head, she looked calm. Relaxed, even. "I made a girl vanish."

I swallowed. "For how long?"

"Forever."

Now *I* took a deep breath. "So all three of you did spells that hurt people."

"No," Anna replied. "We did powerful spells befitting our kind. Humans just . . . got in the way."

That was all I had to hear. I stood up. "All right, well, thanks for the offer, but . . . yeah. I don't think this is gonna work out."

Chaston reached up and grabbed my hand again. "No, don't go," she said. Her eyes were huge and shining in the candlelight.

"Oh, let her," Elodie said in a disgusted voice. "She clearly thinks she's better than us anyway."

"Okay, that's not what I said—"

"But we need a fourth," Chaston broke in.

"Not if that fourth is dead weight," Elodie retorted.

"She's the only other dark witch here. We *need* her," Anna said in a low voice. "Without four, we won't be strong enough to hold it."

"Hold what?" I asked, but at the same time, Elodie hissed, "*Shut up, Anna.*"

"It didn't work anyway," Chaston said glumly.

"Seriously, are you guys talking in code or something?" I asked.

"No," Elodie said, rising to her feet. "They're talking about things related to the coven. Things that don't concern you."

I don't think anyone has ever looked at me with that much anger. I was kind of baffled by it. I mean, sure I'd turned down the invitation to join their coven, but it wasn't like I'd spit in their faces or anything.

"I'm sorry if I hurt your feelings," I said, "but . . . um, it's not you, it's me?"

Oh, that *was original, Sophie.*

Anna and Chaston were both standing by now. Anna was scowling at me, but Chaston still looked worried.

"You need us too, Sophie," Chaston said. "It won't be easy for you without your sisters to protect you."

"Protect me from what?"

"Do you honestly think people here are going to welcome you with open arms?" Elodie asked. "Between that leech you room with and your father, you're looking at total pariahdom without us."

My stomach dropped. "What about my dad?"

The three of them glanced at each other.

"She doesn't know," Elodie murmured.

"Know *what?*"

Chaston opened her mouth to reply, but Elodie stopped her. "Let her figure it out on her own." She opened the door. "Good luck surviving Hecate, Sophie. You'll need it."

If that wasn't a dismissal, I didn't know what was.

I was so distracted thinking about my dad that I walked right into the middle of the circle, kicking over the candle as I did. I hissed as hot wax spilled over my bare foot. I could've sworn I heard Anna giggle.

I limped to the door. Before I left, I turned to Elodie. She was watching me stonily.

"I'm sorry," I said again. "I didn't realize turning down a coven was such a big deal."

For a second I thought she wasn't going to reply. Then she dropped her voice and said, "I spent years in the human world being looked at like I was a monster. No one gets to look at me like that anymore." Her hard, green eyes narrowed. "Certainly not a loser witch like you."

Then she slammed the door in my face.

I stood there in the hall, very aware of the sound of my own breathing. Had I looked at her like she was a monster? I thought of how I'd felt when she said she'd made some poor girl disappear.

Yeah, I'd probably looked at her like that.

"Okay, that is IT!" someone shouted.

A door flew open across the hall, and Taylor stomped out of her room. She was wearing an oversize nightshirt, and her hair was tangled around her face. Once again her mouth was full of fangs.

"Get OUT!" she cried, pointing down the hall. Through the open door I could see Nausicaa and Siobhan, along with a couple of other faeries, sitting cross-legged on the floor. A green light glowed from the center of the circle, but I couldn't tell what it was.

The group stood. "You cannot keep me from performing the rituals of my people," Nausicaa said.

Taylor pushed her hair away from her face. "No, but I *can* tell Casnoff that you four were trying to communicate with the Seelie Court with that mirror thingie."

Nausicca frowned and bent down to pick up the glowing circle of green glass. "It is not a 'mirror thingie.' It is a pool of dew collected from night-blooming flowers found on the highest hill in—"

"WHAT. EVER," Taylor shouted. "I have to be in Classifications of Shapeshifters at eight, and I can't sleep with your stupid *mirror thingie* shining in my face."

Siobhan leaned over, her blue hair obscuring her face, and whispered something in Nausicaa's ear.

Nodding, Nausicaa gestured to the other faeries. "Come. We may continue this somewhere less . . . primitive."

Taylor rolled her eyes.

The faeries glided past me. Siobhan shot me a disdainful glance, and then they transformed into circles of light, roughly the size of tennis balls, and drifted down the hall.

"Good freaking riddance," Taylor said under her breath before turning to me with a bright smile. Her fangs were nearly gone now, but her eyes were still golden. "Hi again."

"Hi," I said weakly, giving a wave.

"So what are you doing up and about?"

I nodded my head toward Elodie's door. "Just, you know, socializing. Shouldn't you be outside, running in the woods or . . . whatever?"

Taylor looked confused. "No, that's only the weres."

"There's a difference?"

The friendliness vanished from her face. "Yes," she snapped. "I'm a shifter. That means I become an actual animal. Weres are somewhere between animal and person." She shuddered. "Freaks."

"Don't listen to her," a voice growled from behind me.

The werewolf was bigger than Justin had been, and her fur was reddish instead of gold. She was standing at the opposite end of the hallway, near the stairs.

"Shifters are just jealous because we're so much more powerful than they are," she continued, leaning against the wall. It was a very human posture, and it made her look that much scarier.

I gulped and shrank back against Elodie's door. Taylor didn't look scared, just annoyed. "Keep telling yourself that, Beth." To me she said, "See you tomorrow, Sophie."

"See you."

The werewolf stayed put at the end of the hall, her tongue lolling out and her eyes bright. I would have to pass her to get to my room.

I struggled to keep my face impassive as I strolled toward her. My foot still stung from the wax, but I wasn't limping anymore.

When I reached the werewolf, she startled me by thrusting out one large hand, tipped in deadly-looking claws. For a second I thought she was trying to disembowel me. But then she said, "I'm Beth," and I realized I was supposed to shake her paw.

I did, gingerly. "Sophie."

She smiled. It was terrifying, but that wasn't her fault. "Nice to meet you," she said, her voice thick.

Okay, this wasn't so bad. I could handle this. So she had eaten someone. She didn't seem to want to—

She plunged her snout into my hair and took a deep shuddering breath.

A warm string of drool dripped from her open maw onto my bare shoulder.

I forced myself to stay very calm, and after a moment, she released me.

Giving a bashful shrug, she said, "Sorry. Werewolf thing."

"Hey, no problem," I said, even though all I could think was, *Slobber! Werewolf slobber! On my skin!*

"See you around!" she called after me as I hurried past her.

"Yeah, sure thing!" I said over my shoulder.

When I reached my room, I dashed over to my desk and pulled out a handful of tissues. "Ugh, ugh, ugh!" I moaned, scrubbing at my shoulder. Once I was de-drooled, I flipped on my lamp to search for some hand sanitizer.

I remembered Jenna, and turned to look at her bed. "Oh, sor—"

Jenna was sitting up in bed, a bag of blood pressed against her mouth. Her eyes were bright red.

"Sorry," I finished weakly. "About the lamp."

Jenna lowered the bag, a smear of blood on her chin. "Midnight snack. I . . . I figured you wouldn't be back for a while," she said softly. The red slowly faded from her eyes.

"It's fine," I said, sagging into my desk chair. My stomach was turning over, but I wasn't about to let Jenna know it. I remembered Archer's words:

You're at Hecate now.

And man, had tonight proved that.

"Believe it or not, it's not the weirdest thing I've seen this evening."

She wiped her chin with the back of her hand, still not meeting my eyes.

"So did you join their coven?"

"Oh, heck no," I said.

She did look at me then, obviously surprised. "Why not?"

I rubbed my eyes. I was suddenly really tired. "It's just not my thing."

"Probably because you're not an evil bimbo."

"Yeah, I think my lack of evil bimbo-ness was the death knell. Then I watched a shifter fight with some faeries—Oh, by the way, what the heck is a Seelie?"

"The Seelie Court? It's a group of good faeries who use white magic."

"I would hate to see the bad guys, then," I muttered.

Jenna nodded toward the tissues in my hand
up with that?"

"Huh? Oh, right. After the faerie fight, a
smelled my hair and drooled all over me. It's b
a night."

"And then you came back to your room t(
vampire chowing down," Jenna said. Her tone
but she was twisting her Electric Raspberry cor
her hands.

"Don't worry about it," I said. "Hey, w(
gotta drool, vampires gotta eat. . . ."

She laughed before picking up the blood
shyly asking, "Do you mind if I . . ."

My stomach clenched again, but I made m)
and said, "Knock yourself out."

I flopped back on my bed. "They were pre
off at me."

Jenna stopped slurping. "Who?"

"The coven. They said I needed their p
against social ruin because of, uh . . ."

"Because I'm your roommate?"

I sat up. "Yeah, that was part of it. But the)
something about my dad."

"Huh," Jenna said thoughtfully. "Who's yo

I lay back down, pushing my pillow under
"Just a regular warlock, as far as I know. James A

"Never heard of him," Jenna said. "But then I'm always out of the loop. So you think Elodie and those girls are mad at you?"

I remembered Elodie's hard eyes. "Oh yeah," I said softly.

Suddenly Jenna burst out laughing.

"What?"

She shook her head, her pink stripe falling in front of one eye. "Just thinking. Man, Sophie, it's only your first day and you've already befriended the school outcast, pissed off the most popular girls at Hecate, and developed a full-blown thing for the hottest guy. If you can manage to get detention tomorrow, you'll be like, *legendary*."

CHAPTER 10

By Jenna's definition, it took me a week and a half to become legendary. The first week went smoothly, all things considered. For one thing, the classes were ridiculously simple. They mostly seemed to be excuses for our teachers to talk us to death. Even Lord Byron, whose class I'd been really excited about, turned out to be a major snoozefest. When he wasn't waxing poetic on his own awesomeness, he was sulking behind his desk and telling us all to shut up—although there were a few days when he let us take long walks around the pond to "be one with nature." That was kind of fun.

I'd hoped for classes on how to do spells, but according to Jenna, those classes were only taught at the "real" Prodigium schools, the fancy places where powerful Prodigium sent their kids. Since Hecate was technically a reformatory school, we were stuck learning about witch hunts in the sixteenth century and things like that. Lame.

The one bright spot was that Jenna was in almost all of my classes. "They don't have any special vampire classes," she'd explained. "So last year they just gave me the same schedule as Holly. Guess they decided to do the same thing this year."

The only class Jenna didn't have with me was P.E., or as they called it at Hecate, "Defense." It was on my schedule every other week, so I was halfway into my second week at Hecate before I went.

"Why is it only every other week?" I asked Jenna that morning. "All our other classes meet every day."

I was pulling on my truly heinous Hecate-blue P.E. uniform, which consisted of bright blue cotton pants and a slightly-too-tight-for-comfort blue T-shirt with "HH" printed in swirly white script just above my left boob.

"Because," Jenna answered, "if you had Defense every day, or even every week, you'd be in the hospital."

So I wasn't feeling exactly confident as I headed down to the converted greenhouse they used as a gym.

It was maybe a quarter of a mile from the main house, but by the time I'd walked thirty feet, I was soaked in sweat. I wasn't stupid: I'd known that Georgia was hot, and I'd lived in hot places before. But those places, like

Arizona and Texas, didn't have this kind of heat, the kind that seemed to suck all the will to live from me. This was a wet kind of heat that made you feel like mildew must be growing on your skin.

"Sophie!"

I turned and saw Chaston, Anna, and Elodie walking toward me. They looked amazing in the fugly gym uniforms. Shocker.

However, when they got closer, I saw that they too were sweating, which made me feel better. The three of them were in several of my classes, but they hadn't spoken to me since the first night. I wondered what was up with them now.

"Hey," I said casually, as they caught up with me. "What now? Coming to warn me of my impending death at the hands of fluffy bunnies? Or shoot lightning bolts at me?"

Chaston laughed, and to my utter surprise, looped her arm through mine. "Look, Sophie, we were talking, and we feel really bad about the other night. So you don't want to join our coven. No biggie!"

"Yeah," Anna added, coming up on my other side. "We overreacted."

"You think?" I said.

"We're trying to apologize," Elodie added, walking backward in front of us. I really, really hoped she'd walk into a tree. "I was talking to Archer, and he said you were all right."

"Really?" I asked before I could stop myself.

Great, Sophie, I thought. Way to be cool.

"Yeah, and he told me you didn't know anything about Prodigium. Said it was kind of pathetic, actually."

I tried to smile, but there was something dark and sharp twisting in my stomach that was making it a little difficult. "Huh."

"Yeah," Chaston said. "And then we got to thinking that we probably freaked you out."

"You could say that." I could see the greenhouse now. It was a huge white wood-and-glass building, with windows that caught the early morning sun and sparkled so brightly it hurt my eyes. Unlike the rest of Hecate, it looked pretty cheery. There were a bunch of students milling around, looking like blueberries.

"And we're sorry," Anna added. I wondered if they had rehearsed this weird three-way-talking thing they had going on. I imagined them sitting in a circle in their dorm room, brushing their hair and saying, "Okay, so I'll say we feel bad, and then *you'll* say that your hot boyfriend thinks she's pathetic."

"So can we start over?" Chaston asked. "Friends?"

They were all smiling hopefully at me, even Elodie. I should have known right then and there that this could not end well, but I stupidly smiled back and said, "Yeah. Friends."

"Great!" Chaston and Anna squealed in unison. Elodie sort of muttered it a split second afterward.

"Okay," Chaston said as we approached the greenhouse. "So as your friends, we thought we should give you a heads up about Defense."

"The Vandy teaches it, and she's awful," Elodie said.

"Right, the scrunchie lady."

Simultaneous eye roll. Were these girls synchronized swimmers in their spare time?

"Yes," Anna sighed. "That stupid scrunchie."

"Jen . . . um, I heard someone call it her portable portal to hell."

All three of them laughed at that. "She wishes," Anna snorted.

"The Vandy was a pretty decent dark witch," Elodie explained, "but she got a little big for her britches, as they say down here. She worked for the Council. Tried to make a play for running Hecate, and . . . well, it's a long story. But it ended with her getting sent to the Council for the Removal."

"And," Anna added in a conspiratorial whisper, "part of her punishment was that she had to come to Hecate but not as a headmistress. Just a regular teacher. She's supposed to be an example to others. That's why she's such a bitch."

"She'll definitely pick on you because you're new," Chaston said.

"But," Elodie cut in, "she's super vain. So if you get in trouble, compliment her on her tattoos."

"Tattoos?" I asked. Up close, the greenhouse was even bigger than I'd thought. What the hell had they grown in it? Redwoods?

"She has these really pretty purple tattoos all over her arms. They're magical symbols of some kind, like runes or something," Elodie continued. "She's really proud of them. Say you like them, and you're in for life with the Vandy."

We walked through the front door of the greenhouse, Chaston's arm still in mine. The room was huge, and felt especially big because only about fifty people were in there. Defense wasn't split up by age for some reason, so I noticed a couple of *very* freaked-out-looking twelve-year-olds. It was bright, obviously, but not hot. There was cool air flowing all around me, so I figured this building had the same spell going on as the main house.

In a lot of ways it was like a normal high school gym: wooden floors, blue exercise mats, weights. But I couldn't help noticing that some things were most definitely not normal.

Like several iron manacles bolted to the wall. And a full-size gallows erected at the back of the room.

Elodie immediately ran off to find Archer, who, it turns out, was not as skinny as I'd thought. The boys' uniforms were basically the same as the girls', and his blue T-shirt clung to a chest that was a lot more defined than I would have guessed. I tried not to look, and I definitely tried to stamp down the little icy spark of jealousy that shot through me when he lowered his lips to Elodie's for a quick kiss.

A tall redhead waved at me. "Hi, Sophie!"

I waved back, wondering who the heck . . . Oh, right. Red hair. Beth the werewolf. I liked her lots better when she wasn't drooling on me. She gestured for me to come stand by her, but before I could, a loud nasal voice broke through the chatter.

"All right, people!"

The Vandy moved through the crowd, wearing the same uniform we were. I immediately noticed the tattoos. They were a deep vibrant purple that looked even brighter against her pale flabby skin.

The ever-present scrunchie held back her brown hair. She had small piggish dark eyes that scanned the crowd, and even from a distance, I could see this weird eager look on her face. Like she was hoping someone would defy her so that she could squash them like a bug.

Put simply, she freaked me the hell out.

"Listen up!" she barked in a thin voice. Like Mrs.

Casnoff, she had a Southern accent, but hers sounded harsh instead of smooth and melodic. "I'm sure your other teachers will tell you that your classes in *Magical History* or *Classifications of Vampires*, or, what, *Personal Grooming of Werewolves*"—I noticed a few boys, including Justin, bristle, but the Vandy continued—"are more important than this one. But tell me this: how much are those classes going to help you when you're under attack from a human? Or a Brannick? Or, worst of all, an Eye? You think books are going to save you when L'Occhio di Dio comes calling?"

I guess we didn't look sufficiently impressed, because she seemed to puff up with anger. Her finger practically pierced the clipboard in front of her as she pointed to something.

"Mercer! Sophia!" she shouted.

I hissed a very bad word under my breath, but I raised my hand. "Um . . . here. Me."

"Come forward!"

I did. She yanked me by my arm until I was standing next to her. "Now, Miss Mercer, it says here on the chart that this is your first year at Hecate, correct?"

"Yes."

"Yes, what?"

"Uh . . . yes, ma'am."

"So apparently you did a love spell that got you sent

to Hecate. Was it for you, or were you just trying to make some human your friend, Miss Mercer?"

I heard snickers from the crowd, and I knew my face was flaming red. Stupid pale skin.

Apparently, it was a rhetorical question, because the Vandy didn't wait for an answer. She turned and knelt down beside a large canvas bag. When she straightened up, she was holding a wooden stake.

"How would you defend yourself against this, Miss Mercer?"

"I'm a witch," I said automatically, and again I heard the crowd murmur and giggle. I wondered if Archer was laughing, but then decided I really didn't want to know.

"You're a witch?" the Vandy repeated. "So, what? A large pointy piece of wood slamming into your heart won't kill you?"

Stupid, stupid, stupid. "I, uh, I guess it would, yeah."

The Vandy smiled, and it was one of the most disturbing smiles I've ever seen. Clearly I was the bug for today.

Turning away from me, she looked though the crowd until she saw someone who made her eyes narrow. "Mr. Cross!"

Oh God, I thought weakly. Oh please, please, no . . .

Archer made his way to the front and stood on the other side of the Vandy, crossing his arms over his chest. The sunlight coming in through the windows glinted off his hair, which wasn't black after all, but the same deep dark brown as his eyes.

Then the Vandy turned to me and put the stake in my hand.

I don't know what kind of stakes vampire killers normally use, but this one was pretty crappy. It was made of some cheap yellow wood that felt prickly against my palm. It also felt totally wrong in my grip, and I let it just sort of dangle at my side. But the Vandy grabbed my elbow and positioned my arm so that I was holding it up as if I were ready to jam it through Archer's chest.

I looked up at him, and saw that he was struggling not to laugh. His eyes were nearly watering, and his lips were twitching.

My hand tightened on the stake. Maybe shoving it into his heart wasn't such a bad idea.

"Mr. Cross," the Vandy said, still smiling sweetly, "kindly disarm Miss Mercer using Skill Nine."

Instantly, all levity vanished from his face. "You've got to be kidding."

"Either you demonstrate it or I will."

CHAPTER 11

For a second I thought he was still going to refuse, but then he looked back at me and muttered, "Fine."

"Excellent!" the Vandy trilled. "Now, Miss Mercer, attack Mr. Cross."

I stared at her. I had never so much as wielded a flyswatter in my life, and this woman expected me to just lunge at a guy with a pointy wooden stick?

The Vandy's smile hardened. "Any day now."

I wish I could say that I suddenly discovered my inner warrior princess and expertly leaped at Archer, weapon hoisted high, teeth bared. That would have been cool.

Instead I raised the stake to about shoulder height and took two, maybe three shuffling steps forward.

Then viselike fingers clenched my throat, the stake was wrenched from my hand, and a sharp stabbing pain shot up my right thigh as I landed on the ground with a thump that knocked the breath out of me.

And as if that wasn't bad enough, once I landed, something hard and heavy—his knee, I thought—hit me right in the sternum. You know, just in case there was one last breath left in my lungs. The point of the stake scraped the sensitive skin just under my chin. I looked up, wheezing, into Archer's face.

He was off of me in a heartbeat, but all I could do was roll onto my side, draw my knees up to my chest, and wait for oxygen to reenter my body.

"Very good!" I heard the Vandy say from somewhere far off. I was literally seeing stars, and every ragged breath I took felt like I was trying to breathe through broken glass.

On the upside, my crush on Archer was totally gone. Over. Once a boy has slammed his kneecap into your rib cage, I think any romantic feelings should naturally go the way of the ghost.

Then I felt hands under my arms, lifting me to my feet. "I'm sorry," Archer murmured, but I just glared at him. My throat still felt thick and swollen, and I didn't want to try to push any words through it.

Much less all the words I wanted to say to him.

"Now," the Vandy was saying brightly, "Mr. Cross showed excellent technique there, although I would have definitely stayed on the opponent's chest longer."

Archer nodded very slightly at me when she said that, and I wondered if he was trying to say that's why he'd done it; I would have been worse off if it had been the Vandy. I really didn't care. I was still pissed.

"And now, Mr. Cross, Skill Four," the Vandy chirped.

But this time Archer shook his head. "No."

"Mr. Cross," the Vandy said sharply, but Archer just tossed the stake at her feet. I waited for the disemboweling or the caning or, at the very least, the writing up, but once again, the Vandy just smiled her tight smile. She picked up the stake and handed it to me.

I was certain I was going to throw up. Wasn't there some other newbie she could torture? I glanced around and caught a few sympathetic looks, but everyone else just seemed relieved it wasn't them about to get squashed.

"Very well. Watch and learn, people. Skill Four. Come at me, Miss Mercer."

I just stood there staring at her.

She pursed her lips in irritation, and then, without warning, her hand shot out to grab me. But I was ready this time, and angry and hurt. Without thinking, I pulled my leg up and thrust it out.

Hard.

I saw my sneaker-clad foot slam into her chest as if that foot belonged to someone else. It couldn't possibly have been mine. I'd never kicked anyone in my life; I certainly wouldn't kick a teacher.

But I had. I had kicked the Vandy in the chest, and she went sprawling onto the blue mat, not far from the very spot where I had sprawled earlier.

I heard the other students draw in a collective breath. I mean, really. All fifty of them seemed to gasp at the same time.

It was right about then that the enormity of what I'd done hit me.

I knelt down and offered her my hand. "Oh my God! I . . . I didn't mean . . ."

She threw off my hand and got to her feet, nostrils flaring. I was so very, very screwed.

"Miss Mercer," she said, breathing heavily, making me think of a bull, "is there any reason you can think of that I shouldn't give you detention for the next month?"

My mouth moved, but nothing came out.

Then, like a godsend, I remembered Elodie's advice. "I like your tattoos!" I blurted out.

I only thought the class had gasped before. Now the sound they made was like the air escaping from a balloon.

The Vandy tilted her head at me and narrowed her tiny eyes. "You what?"

"I . . . I like your tattoos. Your ink. Your, um, tats. They're really cool."

I'd never seen anyone have an aneurysm before, but I was afraid that was exactly what the Vandy was about to do. Frantic, I looked out at the crowd of students until I met Elodie's eyes. She was grinning, and I realized that I had just made a truly horrible mistake.

"I hope you weren't planning on having any free time here at Hecate, Miss Mercer," the Vandy sneered. "Detention. Cellar duty. Rest of the semester."

The semester? I shook my head. Who had ever heard of detention that lasted eighteen weeks? That was insane! And cellar duty? What was that?

"Oh, come on," I heard someone say, and I looked up to see Archer glaring at the Vandy. "She didn't know, okay? She wasn't raised like us."

The Vandy shoved a lock of hair off her forehead. "Really, Mr. Cross? So you think Miss Mercer's punishment is unfair?"

He didn't answer, but she nodded as though he had. "Fine. Share it, then."

Elodie squawked, and I took some satisfaction in that.

"Now, both of you get out of my gym and report to Mrs. Casnoff," the Vandy said, rubbing her chest.

Archer was out the door almost before the words left the Vandy's mouth, but I was still feeling a little stunned, not to mention hurt. I limped toward the exit, ignoring Elodie and Chaston's glares.

★ ★ ★

Archer was already way ahead of me and walking so fast that I could hardly catch up.

"You like her 'ink'?" he all but snarled when I was finally next to him. "Like she doesn't have enough reasons to hate you."

"I'm sorry, but are you pissed at me? Me? I'm the one who had your knee practically crushing my spine, buddy, so let's check the attitude."

He stopped so suddenly that I actually walked three steps past him and had to turn around.

"If the Vandy had pulled that maneuver, you'd be at the infirmary right now. Sorry for trying to save your ass. Again."

"I don't need anyone saving my ass," I shot back, my face hot.

"Right," he drawled before walking toward the house. But then something he'd said struck me.

"What do you mean she has enough reasons to hate me?"

He clearly wasn't going to stop walking, so I had to jog to catch up.

"Your dad's the one who gave her those 'tats.'"

I grabbed his elbow, my fingers slipping on his sweaty skin. "Wait. What?"

"Those marks mean she's gone through the Removal.

122

They're a symbol of her screwup, not a point of pride with her. Why would you . . ."

He trailed off, probably because I was glaring at him. "Elodie," he muttered.

"Yeah," I fired back. "Your girlfriend and her friends were really helpful in filling me in on the Vandy this morning."

He sighed and rubbed the nape of his neck, which had the effect of pulling his T-shirt even tighter across his chest. Not that I cared. "Look, Elodie . . . she's—"

"*So* do not care," I said, holding up my hand. "Now, what did you mean when you said my dad gave her those tattoos?"

Archer looked at me incredulously. "Whoa."

"What?"

"You seriously don't know?"

I'd never been able to actually feel my blood pressure rising before, but it certainly was now. It felt kind of the way magic used to feel, only with more homicidal rage thrown in.

"Don't. Know. *What?*" I managed to say.

"Your dad is the head of the Council. As in, the guy who sent us all here."

CHAPTER 12

After that little tidbit of information, I did something I have never done in my entire life.

I had a full-on drama queen meltdown.

By which I mean I burst into tears. And not tragically beautiful, elegant tears either. No, I had the big messy ones involving a red face and snot.

I usually make it a point not to cry in front of people, especially hot boys that I'd been totally crushing on before they'd tried to choke me.

But for some reason, hearing that there was yet another thing I didn't know just sent me right on over the edge.

Archer, to his credit, didn't look exactly horrified by my sobbing, and he even reached out like he might grab hold of my shoulders. Or possibly smack me.

But before he could either comfort me or commit further acts of violence upon my person, I spun away from him and made my drama queen moment complete by running away.

It wasn't pretty.

But by that point I was beyond caring. I just ran, my chest burning, my throat aching from a combination of Archer's chokehold and tears.

My feet pounded against the thick grass with dull thumps, and all I could think was what an idiot I was.

Don't know about blocking spells.

Don't know about tattoos.

Don't know about big, stupid, evil Italian Eyes.

Don't know about Dad.

Don't know anything about being a witch.

Don't know, don't know, don't know.

I wasn't sure exactly how far I'd run, but by the time I got to the pond at the back of the school, my legs were shaking and my side ached. I had to sit down. Luckily, there was a little stone bench right next to the edge of the water. I was so out of breath between the running and the crying that I totally overlooked the moss creeping over the seat and flopped down. It was hot from the sun, and I winced a little.

I sat there, my elbows on my knees and my head in my hands, listening to my breath saw in and out of my lungs.

Sweat dripped from my forehead to my thighs, and I started to feel a little dizzy.

I was just so . . . *pissed.* Okay, so Mom had been freaked out by Dad being a warlock. Fair enough. But why couldn't she at least have let me talk to the guy? It would have been nice to get a little heads up about the Vandy. You know, just a friendly "Oh, and by the way, your gym teacher hates me a lot, and so, by extension, hates you! Best o' luck!"

I groaned and lay across the bench, only to come shooting back into a sitting position when the hot stone touched my bare arm.

Without really thinking, I laid my hand on the bench and thought, *Comfy.*

A tiny silver spark flew from my index finger, and immediately the bench under me began to stretch and undulate until it morphed itself into a pretty, lush, velvet chaise lounge covered in hot-pink zebra stripes. Clearly, Jenna was rubbing off on me.

I settled back onto my newly comfy resting spot, a pleasant buzz humming through me. I hadn't done magic since coming to Hecate, and I'd forgotten how good even the littlest spells could make me feel. I couldn't create something out of nothing—very few witches could, and that was some seriously dark magic anyway—but I could change things into different versions of themselves.

So I put a hand on my chest and smiled as my gym uniform rippled and receded until I was wearing a white tank top and khaki shorts. Then I pointed a finger at the water's edge and watched as a stream spiraled upward from the surface of the lake, spinning into a cylinder until I had a glass of iced tea hovering in the air in front of me.

I was feeling pretty satisfied with myself, and more than a little magic drunk, as I leaned back against the chaise lounge and took a sip of tea. I may be a loser, but hey, at least I'm a loser who can do magic, right?

I sat there with my sweaty arm over my eyes for several minutes, listening to the birds, the gentle lap of the water against the shore, and for those few moments I was able to forget that I was in some serious trouble when I got back to the school.

Lowering my arm, I turned my head to look at the pond.

There, just across the water, was a girl standing on the opposite shore. The pond was pretty narrow, so I could see her clearly: it was the ghost in green I'd seen my first day at Hecate. And just like on that first day, she was staring right at me.

It was beyond creepy, to say the least. Not sure what to do, I raised my hand and lamely waved hello.

The girl raised her hand in reply. And then she

vanished. There was no gradual fading away like I'd seen with Isabelle's ghost. Just one minute she was there, then she was gone.

"Curiouser and curiouser," I said, my voice just a little too loud in the quiet, and creeping me out even more.

My good mood had started to fade as the spell buzz wore off, and I looked down to see that my cute and much cooler outfit had dissolved back into my gym uniform. That was weird. My spells usually lasted a lot longer than that. The lounge beneath me was starting to feel a little harder too, and I figured it was only about five more minutes before I was sitting on hot mossy stone again.

My thoughts turned back to my parents and their apparent penchant for being big ol' liars. But even as I tried to work up righteous anger at them for getting me into this mess, I knew that wasn't what had my ugly gym shorts in a twist.

It was that my worst fear seemed to be coming true. It's one thing to be different around people who you're really, well, *different* from. It's a whole other problem to be an outcast in a group of outcasts.

I sighed and lay down on the lounge, which now had moss creeping up one side. I closed my eyes.

"Sophia Alice Mercer, a freak among freaks," I mumbled.

"Pardon?"

I opened my eyes to see a figure hovering above me. The sun was directly behind her, turning her into a black shadow, but the shape of her hair made Mrs. Casnoff easily identifiable.

"Am I in trouble?" I asked without getting up.

It was probably a hallucination brought on by the heat, but I was pretty sure I saw her smile as she leaned down to place a hand under my shoulder and maneuver me into a sitting position.

"According to Mr. Cross, you have cellar duty for the rest of the semester, so yes, I would say you are in a great deal of trouble. But that is Ms. Vanderlyden's concern, not mine."

She looked down at my hot-pink lounge, and her mouth twisted into a little pucker of disgust. She placed her hand on the back of the chair and my spell fell away in a shower of pink sparkles until my lounge became a perfectly respectable light blue love seat covered in big pink cabbage roses.

"Better," she said crisply, sitting down beside me.

"Now, Sophia, would you care to tell me why you're here by the pond instead of reporting to your next class?"

"I'm experiencing some teenage angst, Mrs. Casnoff," I answered. "I need to, like, write in my journal or something."

She snorted delicately. "Sarcasm is an unattractive quality in young ladies, Sophia. Now, I'm not here to indulge whatever pity party you have decided to hold for yourself, so I would prefer it if you told me the truth."

I looked over at her, perfectly turned out in her ivory wool suit (again with the wool in the heat! What was wrong with these people?), and sighed. My own mom, who was super cool, barely got me. What help could this fading steel magnolia with her shellacked hair be?

But then I just shrugged and spilled it. "I don't know anything about being a witch. Everyone else here grew up in this world, and I didn't, and that sucks."

Her mouth did that puckering thing, and I thought she was about to bust me for saying "sucks," but instead she said, "Mr. Cross told me that you didn't know your father is the current head of the Council."

"Yeah."

She picked a small piece of lint off her suit and said, "I'm hardly privy to your father's reasons for doing things, but I'm sure he had a reason for keeping his position from you. And besides, your presence here is very . . . sensitive, Sophia."

"What's that supposed to mean?"

She didn't answer for a long time; instead she stared out at the lake. Finally she turned to me and covered my hand with hers. Despite the heat, her skin felt cool and

dry, slightly papery, and as I looked into her face, I realized that she was older than I'd originally thought, with
tons of fine lines radiating from her eyes.

"Follow me to my office, Sophia. There are some
things we need to discuss."

CHAPTER 13

Her office was on the first floor, off the sitting room with the spindly chairs. I noticed as we walked through this time that the spindly chairs had been replaced with prettier, much sturdier-looking wingback chairs, and the vaguely moldy-looking couches had been reupholstered in a cheery white-and-yellow-stripe fabric.

"When did you get new furniture?" I asked.

She glanced over her shoulder. "We didn't. It's a perception spell."

"Excuse me?"

"One of Jessica Prentiss's ideas. The furnishings of the house reflect the beholder's mind. That way we can gauge your comfort level with the school by what you see."

"So I imagined the gross furniture?"

"In a way, yes."

"What about the outside of the house? No offense, or anything, but it still looks pretty rank."

Mrs. Casnoff gave a low laugh. "No, the spell is only used in the public rooms of the house: the lounge areas, the classrooms, and so forth. Hecate must maintain *some* of its brooding air, don't you think?"

I turned in the doorway of Mrs. Casnoff's office and looked again at the sitting room. Now I could see the way the couches, chairs, even the curtains shimmered and wavered slightly, like heat rising off a road.

Weird.

I'd thought Mrs. Casnoff would have the biggest, grandest room in the house. You know, something filled with ancient books, with heavy oak furniture and floor-to-ceiling windows.

Instead she led me into a small windowless room. It smelled strongly of her lavender perfume, and another stronger, bitter smell. After a moment I realized it was tea. A small electric kettle was bubbling away on the edge of the desk, which wasn't the wooden monstrosity I'd imagined, but simply a small table.

There were books, but they were stacked in vertical rows around three of the four walls. I tried to make out the titles on the spines, but those that weren't too faded to read were in languages I didn't know.

The only thing in Mrs. Casnoff's office that was even

remotely like I'd expected was her chair. It was less of a chair, really, and more like a throne: a tall, heavy chair covered in purple velvet.

The chair on the other side of the desk was lower by a good five inches, and as I sat in it, I immediately felt about six years old.

Which, I guessed, was the point.

"Tea?" she asked after primly arranging herself on her purple throne.

"Sure."

A few more moments passed in silence as she poured me a cup of thick red tea. Without asking, she added milk and sugar.

I took a sip. It tasted exactly like the tea my mom made for me on rainy winter days: days we'd spent curled up on the couch, reading or talking. The familiar taste was comforting, and I felt myself relax slightly.

Which, again, had probably been the point.

I looked up at her. "How did you—"

Mrs. Casnoff just waved her hand. "I'm a witch, Sophia."

I scowled. Being manipulated has always been one of my least favorite things. Right up there with snakes. And Britney Spears.

"So you know a spell that makes tea taste like . . . tea?"

Mrs. Casnoff took a sip from her cup, and I got the

impression she was trying to hold back a laugh. "Actually, it's a little more than that." She gestured to the kettle. "Open it."

I leaned forward and did just that.

It was empty.

"Your favorite drink is your mother's Irish breakfast tea. Had it been lemonade, you would have found that in your cup. Had it been hot chocolate, you would have had that. It's a basic comfort spell that's very useful for putting people at ease. As you were before your naturally suspicious nature kicked in."

Wow. She was good. I had never even attempted an all-purpose spell before.

But not like I was going to let her know I was impressed.

"What if my favorite drink had been beer? Would you have given me a frosty mug of that?"

She lifted her shoulders in something that was far too elegant to be called a shrug. "There, I may have been somewhat stymied."

Pulling a leather portfolio out of a stack of folders on her desk, she settled back into her throne.

"Tell me, Sophia," Mrs. Casnoff said, "what exactly do you know about your family?"

She was leaning back in her chair, one ankle crossed over the other, looking as casual as was possible for her.

"Not much," I said warily. "My mom's from Tennessee, and both her parents died in a car accident when she was twenty—"

"That is not the side of your family I was referring to," Mrs. Casnoff said. "What do you know of your father's people?"

Now she wasn't even trying to disguise her eagerness. I suddenly felt like something very important depended on my next answer.

"All I know is that my father is a warlock named James Atherton. Mom met him in England, and he said he grew up there, but she wasn't sure if that was true."

With a sigh, Mrs. Casnoff put down her cup and began rummaging through the leather portfolio. She slid her glasses down from their usual spot on top of her head as she muttered, "Let's see, I just saw . . . Ah yes, here it is."

She reached into the portfolio, then suddenly stopped and looked up at me.

"Sophia, it is imperative that what we discuss in this room remains in this room. Your father asked me to share this with you when I thought the time was appropriate, and I feel that time has come."

I just nodded. I mean, what can you say to a speech like that?

Apparently that worked for her, and she handed me a black-and-white picture. A young woman stared back at me. She looked maybe a few years older than me, and from the style of her clothes, I could guess that the picture had been taken some time in the 1960s. Her dress was dark, and it fluttered around her calves as though a gentle breeze had just caught it. Her hair was light, probably blond or red.

Just behind her, I could make out the front porch of Hecate Hall. The shutters had been white back then.

She was smiling, but the smile looked tight, forced.

Her eyes. Large, widely spaced, and very light.

And very familiar.

The only other eyes I'd even seen like that had been my father's, in the only picture I had of him.

"Who—" My voice broke a little. "Who is this?"

I looked up at Mrs. Casnoff to find her watching me closely. "That," she said, pouring herself another cup of tea, "is your grandmother, Lucy Barrow Atherton."

My grandmother. For the longest moment I felt like I couldn't breathe. I just stared at the face, trying desperately to find myself in it.

I couldn't find anything. Her cheekbones were sharp and high, and my face is slightly rounded. Her nose was too long to resemble mine, and her lips too thin.

I looked into her face, which despite the smile, looked so sad.

"She was here?" I asked.

Mrs. Casnoff placed her glasses on top of her head and nodded. "Lucy actually grew up here at Hecate, back before it *was* Hecate, of course. I believe that picture was taken shortly after your father was born."

"Did you , , , did you know her?"

Mrs. Casnoff shook her head. "I'm afraid that was before my time. But most Prodigium know of her, of course. Her story was a very unique one."

For sixteen years I had wondered who I really was, where I came from. And here was the answer right in front of me. "Why?"

"I told you the story of the origins of Prodigium your first day here. Do you remember?"

It was like two weeks ago, I thought. Of course I remember. But I decided to store the sarcasm, and said, "Right. Angels. War with God."

"Yes. However, in your case, your family did not gain its powers until 1939, when your great-grandmother Alice was sixteen."

"I thought you had to be born a witch. Mom said that only vampires start out as human."

Mrs. Casnoff nodded. "Usually that is the case. However, there is always the odd human who attempts to change their fate. They find a spell book or a special incantation, some way to imbue themselves with the divine, the mystical. Very few survive the process. Your great-grandmother was one of the few."

Not knowing what to say, I took a long drink of my tea. It was cold, and the sugar had settled at the bottom, making it syrupy.

"How?" I finally asked.

Mrs. Casnoff sighed. "There, I am sadly at a loss. If Alice ever spoke in depth to anyone about her experiences, it was never recorded. I only know what I've picked up here and there. Apparently, she had gotten mixed up with a particularly nasty witch who was attempting to enhance her own powers through the aid of black magic, magic that has been outlawed by the Council since the seventeenth century. No one is exactly sure how Alice was involved with this woman—a Mrs. Thorne, I believe her name was—or even if she knew what the woman was. Somehow the spell that was meant for Mrs. Thorne transformed Alice instead."

"Wait, but you said Mrs. Thorne was using black magic for this spell, right?"

Mrs. Casnoff nodded. "Yes. Truly terrible stuff, too. Alice was very lucky she wasn't killed during the transformation. Mrs. Thorne was not as fortunate."

I suddenly felt like I'd swallowed a tray of ice cubes, but even as my stomach froze, beads of sweat broke out on my forehead.

"So my . . . my great-grandmother was made into a

witch by black magic? As in, the worst, most dangerous kind of magic ever?"

Again, Mrs. Casnoff nodded. She was still looking at me very closely.

"Your great-grandmother was an aberration, Sophia. I'm sorry. I know that's a very ugly word, but there's no way around it."

"How"—my voice came out as a croak, and I cleared my throat—"what happened to her?"

Mrs. Casnoff sighed. "She was eventually found by a member of the Council in London. She'd been committed to an asylum, ranting and raving about witches and demons. The Council member brought her and your grandmother Lucy to Hecate."

"My grandmother?" I looked down at the photo in my hands.

"Yes. Alice was pregnant when she was found. They waited until your grandmother was born to bring them both here."

She poured herself another cup of tea. I got the feeling that she didn't really want to say anything else, but I had to ask. "So what happened then?"

Mrs. Casnoff stirred her tea with the sort of concentration usually reserved for brain surgery. "Alice did not adjust well to her transformation," she answered without looking at me. "After three months here at Hecate, she somehow contrived to escape. Again, no one is sure how, but Alice had some very powerful magic at her disposal. And then . . ." Mrs. Casnoff paused to take a sip of tea.

"And then?" I repeated.

Finally she lifted her eyes to mine. "She was murdered. L'Occhio di Dio."

"How did we know it was—"

"They're very distinctive in their disposal of us," she replied briskly. "In any case, Lucy, who had been left behind, stayed here at Hecate so the Council could observe her."

"What, like a science experiment?" I didn't mean to sound so angry, but I was beyond freaked out.

"Alice's power had been off the charts. She was literally the strongest Prodigium that had ever been recorded. It was vital that the Council know if that level of magic had been passed down to her daughter, who was, after all, half human."

"Had it?"

"Yes. And that power was also passed to your father." Her eyes met mine. "And to you."

CHAPTER 14

After our little meeting, Mrs. Casnoff gave me the rest of the afternoon off to, as she put it, "reflect on what you've learned." However, I didn't feel like doing much reflecting. I marched straight to the third floor. In the small alcove off my hallway, there was a bank of bright red telephones that students could use. They were dusty with non-use since most of the Prodigium at Hecate didn't need telephones to communicate with their families. Vampires could use telepathy, but it wasn't like Jenna was calling home. The shapeshifters had some sort of pack mentality thing going on, and the faeries used the wind or a flying insect to deliver messages. I'd seen Nausicca murmuring to a dragonfly just that morning.

As for witches and warlocks, there were supposedly a bunch of different spells you could use to talk to people—

everything from making your words appear in writing on a wall, to making a cat channel your voice. But I didn't know any of those spells, and even if I had, they were only useful for communicating to other witches. Since Mom was human, human communication it was.

I picked up the phone, grimacing at the gritty feel of it in my sweaty hand.

A few seconds later, Mom picked up.

"My dad is the head of the Council," I said before she could even finish her hello.

I heard her sigh. "Oh, Sophie, I wanted to tell you."

"But you didn't," I said, and I was surprised to feel my throat constricting.

"Soph . . ."

"You didn't tell me anything." My eyes stung and my voice sounded thick. "You didn't tell me who my dad was, you didn't tell me that I'm apparently the most powerful witch, you know, *ever*. You didn't tell me that Dad is the one who . . . who sentenced me to go here."

"He didn't have a choice," Mom said, her voice tired. "If his daughter were exempt from punishment, how would that have made him look to other Prodigium?"

I wiped my cheek with the heel of my hand. "Well, I certainly wouldn't want him to *look bad*," I said.

"Honey, let me call your dad, and we can get this—"

"Why didn't you tell me that people want to kill me?"

Mom gasped a little. "Who told you that?" she demanded, and now she sounded even angrier than I was.

"Mrs. Casnoff," I answered. Right after she'd dropped the bomb about my powers, Mrs. Casnoff had told me one of the reasons that my dad had sent me to Hecate—to keep me safe.

"You can't blame him," she had said. "L'Occhio di Dio killed Lucy as well, in 1974, and your father has had numerous attempts made on his life. For the first fifteen years of your life, your father was able to keep your existence a secret. But now . . . It was only a matter of time before L'Occhio di Dio discovered your existence, and you would have been defenseless in the regular world."

"What . . . what about those Irish people?" I'd croaked.

Mrs. Casnoff's eyes had slid away from mine. "The Brannicks are not a concern at this time," was all she had said. I knew she was lying, but I'd been too shell-shocked to call her on it.

"Is it true?" I asked Mom now. "Did Dad put me here because I'm in danger?"

"I want you to put Mrs. Casnoff on the phone right now," Mom said, not answering my question. There was a lot of anger in her voice, but there was fear too.

"Is it true?" I repeated.

When she didn't answer, I shouted, *"Is it true?"*

A door somewhere in the hall opened, and I glanced over my shoulder to see Taylor sticking her head out of her room. When she saw me, she just shook her head slightly and closed her door.

"Soph," Mom was saying, "look, we'll . . . we'll talk about this when you're home for winter break, okay? This is not something I want to get into over the phone."

"So it *is* true," I said, crying.

There was such a long silence on the other end that I wondered if she'd hung up. Then she gave a long sigh and said, "We can talk about this later."

I slammed down the receiver. The phone made a jangly sound of protest.

I slid down the wall to the floor and drew my knees in so I could rest my head on them.

For a long time I stayed that way, breathing slowly in and out, trying to stop the steady flow of tears. There was a little part of me that felt weirdly guilty, like I should be super pumped about being a kick-ass witch or something. But I wasn't. I felt more than happy to leave the glowing skin and floating hair and smiting to Elodie and those girls. I could just run a little tea shop or something, where I could sell books about astrology and chakras. That would be fun. I could maybe wear a floaty purple muu—

I lifted my head and cut off my mental rant. That weird goose-bump feeling was back.

I looked up and saw the girl from the lake standing at the end of the hall. Up close I could see that she was about my age. She was frowning at me, and I noticed that her green dress was flapping around her calves as though a wind were blowing.

Before I could open my mouth to ask her who she was, she turned abruptly on her heels and walked off. I listened for her shoes on the wooden steps, but there was no sound.

Now the goose bumps weren't just on my neck, but everywhere. It probably seems weird to go to a school populated by monsters and still be afraid of ghosts, but this whole thing was getting ridiculous. This was the third time that I'd seen this girl, and every time she seemed to be studying me. But why?

I slowly stood up and walked down the hall.

I paused before rounding the corner, afraid she might be standing there, waiting for me.

What's she going to do, Sophie? I thought. Yell "Boo"? Walk through you? She's a ghost, for God's sake.

But I was still holding my breath as I hurried around the corner.

And ran into something very solid.

I tried to scream, but it came out more of a breathy "Urrrgh!"

Hands reached out to steady me. "Whoa," Jenna said with a little laugh.

"Oh. Hi," I said, out of breath from the collision, and overcome with relief.

"Are you okay?" She studied my face with a look of concern.

"It's been a long day."

She smiled a little. "I'm sure. I heard about what happened with the Vandy."

I groaned. What with the family secrets and assassins and ghosts, I'd forgotten all about my more imminent danger.

"It's my own fault. I never should have listened to Elodie."

"No, you shouldn't have," Jenna said, twirling her pink streak. "Is it true you have cellar duty for the rest of the semester?"

"Yeah. What is that, by the way?"

"It's awful," she replied flatly. "The Council stores all its reject magical artifacts here, and they're all just jumbled up in the cellar. People who get cellar duty have to try to catalogue all that junk."

"Try?"

"Well, it's all crap, but it's magic crap, so it moves

around. Cataloguing it is pointless because it doesn't stay in the same place."

"Great," I muttered.

"Careful, Sophie. The Leech is looking kind of hungry."

I looked over Jenna's shoulder and saw Chaston standing at the end of the hall. I'd never seen her without Elodie and Anna, and the effect was a little jarring.

Chaston sneered at us, but it looked more like an impression of Elodie than a genuine expression.

"Shut up, Chaston," I said irritably.

"Witch: It's what's for dinner," she said with a nasty laugh before disappearing into her room.

Next to me, Jenna looked even paler than normal. It could have been a trick of the light, but for just a second I thought her eyes flashed red.

"The Leech," she murmured. "That's new."

"Hey," I said, giving her a little shake. "Don't let them get to you. Especially not *that* one. She's not worth it."

Jenna nodded. "You're right," she said, but she was still looking at Chaston's door. "So, you coming to Classifications of Shapeshifters?"

I shook my head. "Casnoff gave me the day off," I said.

Thankfully, Jenna didn't ask why. "Cool. See you at dinner, then."

After Jenna left, I thought about going to my room to read or lie down, but instead I went downstairs and into the library. Like the rest of the house, the room now looked a lot less shabby to me. The chairs looked less like fungi ready to swallow me, and much comfier.

I only had to scan the shelves for a little while before I found what I was looking for.

The book was black, with a cracked spine. There was no title, but a large golden eye was stamped on the front.

I sat down in one of the chairs and pulled my legs underneath me, opening to the middle of the book. There were several glossy pages of pictures, most of them reproductions of paintings, although there were a few grainy photographs of a crumbling castle in Italy that was supposed to be the headquarters of L'Occhio di Dio. I flipped through the pages, stopping when I came to the same picture I'd seen in Mom's book. It was as horrible as I remembered: the witch on her back, her eyes wild with fright, and the dark-haired man crouched over her holding a silver knife. The Eye tattooed over his heart.

I turned away from the pictures to skim the text.

Formed in 1129, the society began in France as an offshoot of the Knights Templar. Originally a group of holy knights charged with ridding the world of demons, the group soon relocated to Italy, where they took on the official title, L'Occhio di Dio—The Eye of God. The group soon became well known for their brutal acts against all manner of Prodigium, but they were also known to attack any human who aided Prodigium. Over time they morphed from holy warriors into something more akin to a terrorist organization. Highly secretive, L'Occhio di Dio is an elite group of assassins with only one goal—the total destruction of all Prodigium.

"Well, that's nice," I murmured to myself.

I flipped through more pages. The rest of the book seemed to be a history of the group's leaders and their most notable Prodigium victims. I scanned the list of names, but I didn't see Alice Barrow on there. Maybe Mrs. Casnoff had been wrong and she wasn't that big a deal after all.

I was about to put the book back on the shelf when a black-and-white illustration caught my eye and sent chills through me. It showed a witch lying on a bed, her head lolling to the side, her eyes blank. There were two somber men in black standing behind her, looking down at the body. Their shirts were opened just enough so that I could see the tattoos over their hearts. One was holding a long thin stick with a pointed end, almost like an ice pick. The other man held a jar of suspicious-looking black liquid. I glanced down at the caption under the picture.

Although the removal of the heart is the most common means of execution employed by The Eye, the group has been known to drain the blood of Prodigium. Whether this is done to implicate vampires or some other reason is not known.

I shivered as I stared at that blank-eyed witch. There weren't any holes in her neck, like they'd found on Holly, but the men had clearly drained her blood somehow.

But that was impossible. We were on an island, and there were more protection spells around this place than I could count. Surely there was no way a member of The Eye could get in undetected.

I flipped back through the book, looking for any chapters about The Eye getting past protective spells, but everything I read said that The Eye didn't use magic, just brute force.

Later, after I'd snuck the book up to my room, I showed the picture to Jenna.

I thought she'd be interested, but instead she barely looked at it before turning away and climbing into her bed. "L'Occhio di Dio doesn't kill like that," she said as she turned out the lights. "They're never secretive, or anything. They want people to know it was them."

"How do you know that?" I asked.

She just lay there, and I thought she wasn't going to answer me.

Then, out of the darkness, she said, "Because I've seen them."

CHAPTER 15

Two days later I started cellar duty.

I should say upfront that I have never been in a cellar in my life. In fact, I can see no reason why anyone should ever go into a cellar unless there is wine involved.

This cellar seemed particularly unwelcoming. For one thing, the floor was just hard-packed dirt, which . . . ew. The air was cool despite the heat outside, and it smelled musty and damp. Add to that the high ceiling with its bare lightbulbs, the one tiny window that looked out on the compost pile behind the school, and the endless shelves of dusty junk, and I suddenly understood why a full semester of cellar duty sucked so bad. Not only that, but the Vandy had decided to be especially evil and give it to us three nights a week, right after dinner. So while everyone else was hanging out in their room, or working on one of Lord Byron's epic essays, Archer and I would be cataloguing a bunch of crap the Council thought was too important to throw away but not important enough to store at Council headquarters in London.

Jenna had tried to cheer me up that morning, saying, "At least you have it with a hot guy."

"Archer isn't hot anymore," I'd fired back. "He tried to kill me, and his girlfriend is Satan."

But I have to admit that as we stood beside each other on the cellar steps and listened to the Vandy ramble on about what we were supposed to do down there, I couldn't help but sneak sideways glances at him and notice that, homicidal tendencies and evil girlfriends aside, he was still hot. As usual, his tie was loose and his shirtsleeves were rolled up. He was watching the Vandy with this bored, vaguely amused look, arms crossed over his chest.

That pose did most excellent things for his chest and arms. How unfair was it that Elodie of all people got that as a boyfriend? I mean, where is the justice when—

"Miss Mercer!" the Vandy barked, and I jumped high enough to nearly lose my balance.

I clutched the banister next to me, and Archer caught my other elbow.

Then he winked, and I immediately turned my attention back to the Vandy like she was the most fascinating person I'd ever seen.

"Do you need me to repeat anything, Miss Mercer?" she sneered.

"N–no. I got it," I stammered.

She stared at me for a minute. I think she was trying to come up with a witty put-down. But the Vandy, like most mean people, was dumb, so in the end, she just sort of growled and pushed between me and Archer to stalk up the stairs.

"One hour!" she called over her shoulder.

The ancient door didn't so much creak as scream in pain as she pushed it closed.

To my horror, I heard a loud click.

"Did she just *lock us in*?" I asked Archer, my voice sounding way higher than I'd intended.

"Yep," he replied, jogging down the steps to pick up one of the clipboards the Vandy had left precariously perched on a row of jars.

"But that's . . . isn't that illegal?"

He smiled but didn't look up from his clipboard. "You've really gotta let go of charming human issues like legality, Mercer."

He looked up all of a sudden, his eyes wide. "Oh! Just remembered something."

He put the clipboard down and fished in his pocket for a second.

"Here," he said, walking over to me and pressing

something light into my open hand.

I looked down.

It was a wad of Kleenex.

"You're a jackass." I tossed the tissues at his feet and stomped past him. My face was flaming.

"No wonder Elodie's your girlfriend," I muttered as I picked up the clipboard. I made a big show of flipping through the pages. There were twenty in all, with about fifty items listed on each. My eyes skimmed over some of them, noting things like "Noose: Rebecca Nurse" and "Severed Hand: A. Voldari."

I ripped off the top ten pages and handed them to Archer, along with a pen.

"You take this half," I said, not meeting his eyes. Then I walked over to the shelf farthest from him, the one right under the little window.

He didn't move for a moment, and I could tell there was something he wanted to say, but in the end he just sighed and walked over to the opposite side of the room.

For about fifteen minutes we worked in total silence. Even though the Vandy had spent forever explaining the job to us, it was actually pretty easy, if ridiculously tedious, work. We had to look at the items on the shelves and then find them on the sheets of paper and write down which shelf they were on and what slot on that shelf they were in. The only thing that made it difficult was that none of the items were labeled, so it was sometimes hard to figure out what they were. Like, on Shelf G, Slot 5, there was a scrap of red cloth that could've been "Piece of Cover, Grimoire: C. Catellan" or "Fragment of Ceremonial Robe: S. Cristakos."

Or it could have been neither of those things and something on Archer's list. It would've gone faster if we'd worked together, but I was still pissed off about the Kleenex thing.

I squatted down and picked up a tattered leather drum. My eyes scanned the list, but I wasn't really seeing anything. I knew I shouldn't have cried in front of him, but I couldn't believe he'd be enough of a jerk to make fun of me for it. Not like we were best buddies or anything, but that first night I felt like we'd bonded a little.

Apparently not.

"It was a joke," he said suddenly. I whirled around to find him crouched behind me.

"Whatever." I turned back to the shelf.

"What did you mean about me and Elodie?" he asked.

I rolled my eyes as I stood up and walked to Shelf H. "Is it really that hard to figure out? I mean, she got quite a big laugh at my expense the other day, so it's only appropriate that you, as her boyfriend, would also enjoy mocking me. It's so sweet when couples can share hobbies."

"Hey," he snapped. "Elodie's little stunt got me in here too, remember? I tried to help you out."

"So did not ask you to," I replied, pretending to intently study what at first appeared to be a bunch of leaves floating in a jar of amber liquid.

Then I realized they weren't leaves but tiny faerie corpses.

Suppressing the urge to fling it away from me and make some sort of "NEEEEUUUUUNGGGHH!" sound, I rifled through my pages, looking for something that read "Small Dead Faeries."

"Well, don't worry," Archer snapped, flipping through his own pages. "It won't happen again."

We were quiet for a moment, both of us looking at our lists.

"Have you seen anything that could be part of an altar cloth?" he asked at last.

"Check Shelf G, Slot 5," I replied.

Then out of nowhere, he said, "She's not that bad, you know. Elodie. You just have to get to know her."

"Is that what happened with the two of you?"

"What?"

I swallowed, suddenly nervous. I really didn't want to hear Archer wax poetic about Elodie, but I was also genuinely curious.

"Jenna said that you used to be, like, a card-carrying

member of the We Hate Elodie club. What gives?"

He looked away and started picking up random things without really seeing them. "She changed," he said quietly. "After Holly died—you know about Holly?"

I nodded. "Jenna's roommate. Elodie, Chaston, and Anna filled me in."

He ran a hand through his dark hair. "Yeah. They're still really hung up on blaming Jenna. Anyway, Elodie and Holly had been really close when they started here, and Holly and I had been betrothed—"

"Hold up," I said, raising a hand. *"Betrothed?"*

He looked confused. "Yeah. All witches are betrothed to an available warlock on their thirteenth birthday. A year after they come into their powers."

He frowned. "Are you okay?" he asked. I'm sure I was making a pretty strange face. At thirteen I was thinking about allowing a boy's tongue into my mouth. Getting engaged would've been pretty far beyond me.

"Fine," I mumbled. "That's just weird to think about. It's so . . . Jane Austen."

"It's not that bad."

"Right. Arranged marriages for teenagers are a good thing."

He shook his head. "We don't get married as teen-agers, just betrothed. And the witch always has the right to refuse or accept the betrothal and change her mind later. But the match is usually a good one, based on complementary powers, personalities. Stuff like that."

"Whatever. I can't even imagine having a fiancé."

"You probably have one, you know."

I stared at him. "Excuse me?"

"Your dad is a really important guy. I'm sure he made a match for you when you were thirteen."

I didn't even want to get into that. The thought that there was some warlock out there who was planning on making me his missus one day was too much to handle. What if he was here at Hecate? What if I knew the guy? Oh God, what if it was that kid with bad breath who sat right behind me in Magical Evolution?

I made a mental note to ask my mom about all of this as soon as I decided to speak to her again.

"Okay," I said to Archer. "Just . . . go on with your story."

"I don't think anyone realized how much Holly's death got to Elodie. So we started talking over the summer, about Hecate and Holly, and one thing led to another . . ."

"And you can spare me the gory details," I said with a smile even as something painful twisted in my chest a little. So he really liked her. I'd been harboring this secret fantasy that he was only pretending to like her so that he could publicly dump her in the most embarrassing way possible, preferably on national television.

"Look," he said, "I'll get Elodie and her friends to lay off you, okay? And seriously, try to give her another chance. I swear she has hidden depths."

Without really thinking, I shot back, "I said spare me the gory details."

For a second I'm not sure I even realized what I'd just said. And then it sank in and I damned my sarcastic mouth straight to hell. Face on fire, I glanced over at Archer.

He was staring at me in shock.

And then he burst out laughing.

I started giggling too, and before long we were both sitting on the dirt floor wiping tears from our eyes. It had been a long time since I'd really laughed with someone, or made a dirty joke, for that matter, and I couldn't believe how good it felt. For a little bit I forgot that I was apparently made of evil, and that I was being stalked by a ghost.

It was nice.

"I knew I liked you, Mercer," he said when we'd finally stopped cackling, and I was glad I could blame my suddenly red cheeks on the laughter.

"But wait," I said, leaning on one of the shelves, trying to catch my breath. "If everybody gets betrothed at thirteen, isn't she already set to marry somebody else?"

He nodded. "But I told you, it's a voluntary thing. A betrothal can always be renegotiated. I mean, I'm considered something of a catch."

"And so modest too," I replied, tossing my pen at him.

He caught it with ease.

From above us, the door gave its death scream, and we both leaped to our feet guiltily, like we'd been making out or something.

Suddenly the image of me and Archer kissing against one of the shelves flooded my brain, and I felt the blush in my cheeks spread to the rest of my body. Without meaning to, I glanced at his lips. When I raised my eyes to his, he was looking at me with an expression that was totally inscrutable. But just like the look he'd given me on the stairs the first night, this one left me feeling breathless. I was actually glad when the Vandy shouted, "Mercer! Cross!"

Her harsh grating voice was the auditory equivalent of a cold shower, and the tension of the moment vanished. My lusty thoughts were pretty much gone by the time we were out of the cellar.

"Same time, same place, Wednesday," the Vandy said as we practically sprinted for the main staircase.

Naturally, Elodie was waiting for Archer in the

second-floor lounge. She was sitting on the grubby blue couch. A nearby lamp cast a soft golden glow on her flawless skin, and picked up the ruby highlights in her hair.

I turned to Archer, but he was staring at Elodie like . . . well, like I was staring at him.

I didn't even bother saying good night. I just jogged up the stairs to my room.

Jenna wasn't there, and after all that cellar grossness, I was in definite need of a shower. I grabbed a towel out of my trunk and a tank top and pajama bottoms out of my dresser.

Our floor was fairly deserted. Boys and girls didn't have to separate until nine, and it was just now seven, so I figured everybody was hanging out in the drawing rooms downstairs.

My mind still on Archer (and the general suckiness of having an unrequited crush on someone dating a goddess), I made my way to the bathroom and opened the door. The room was shrouded in heavy steam, and I could barely see in front of me. As I stepped forward, warm water sloshed around my feet. I could hear the sound of running bathwater.

"Hello?" I called.

There was no answer, so my first thought was that someone had left a faucet on as a joke. Mrs. Casnoff would *not* be amused. Hot water isn't great for two-hundred-year-old floors.

Then the steam began to part, flowing through the open door behind me.

And I saw why the faucet was still on.

It took a long time for my eyes to accept what they were seeing. At first I thought maybe Chaston was just asleep in the tub and that the water was tinted pink from bath salts or something. Then I realized her eyes weren't closed, but sort of half-mast, almost like she was drunk. And the water was pink from her blood.

CHAPTER 16

I noticed the tiny puncture wounds just below her jaw,
and longer, more vicious-looking slashes on both her
wrists, which were dripping blood onto the floor.

Without even thinking, I rushed to her side, mumbling a healing spell. It wasn't a very good one, I knew.
The most I'd ever been able to get it to do was heal
a skinned knee, but I thought it was worth a try. As I
watched, the small holes on her neck seemed to pucker
briefly, only to sag back open. I made a sound like a sob.
God, why was my magic so shitty?

Chaston's eyes fluttered for a moment, and she
opened her mouth like she was trying to say something.

I ran for the doorway. "Mrs. Casnoff! Anyone! Help!"

Several heads appeared in doorways.

"Oh God," I heard someone whimper. "Not again."

Mrs. Casnoff appeared at the top of the stairs in a robe, her hair in a long braid down her back. As soon as she saw where I was, her face paled. And for some reason, seeing her look so scared was what broke me. My knees started shaking and I felt my throat tighten with tears. "It's . . . it's Chaston," I managed to get out. "She . . . There's blood . . ."

Mrs. Casnoff grabbed me and looked into the bathroom. Her hands tightened on my shoulders. She leaned down and stared into my face. "Sophia, I need you to go get Cal as quickly as you can. Do you know where his quarters are?"

My brain felt like a scrambled egg, like in those old drug commercials. "The groundskeeper?" I asked stupidly. What could Mrs. Casnoff want with him? Was he like an EMT or something?

Mrs. Casnoff nodded, her grip still tight on my shoulders. "Yes. Cal," she repeated. "He lives next to the pond. Get him and tell him what's happened."

I turned and ran for the stairs. As I ran, I saw Jenna coming out of our room. I thought I heard her calling my name, but by then I was already out the front door and into the night.

Even though the day had been warm, now it was cold enough to make goose bumps stand up on my arms. The only light came from the school behind me, those huge windows making even bigger rectangles of light on the lawn. Knowing the lake was to my left, I turned that way and kept running, the cool air going in and out of my lungs like knives. I could just make out a dark lumpy shape that I really, really hoped was Cal's house, and not, like, a storage shack or something. Even though I was trying to push the panic away, all I could see was Chaston bleeding to death on those black-and-white tiles.

As I got closer, I saw that it was definitely a house. I could hear faint music coming from inside, and there was a little bit of light in the window.

By now I was breathing so hard I wasn't sure if I'd be able to get any words out.

I only had to bang on the door for about three seconds before it was flung open, and Cal stood before me.

I'd assumed he'd be old and burly with a side order of crotchety, so I was really shocked to find myself facing the jock guy I'd seen on the first day, the one I thought might have been someone's older brother. He couldn't have been more than nineteen, and his only concession to burliness was a flannel shirt and his vaguely annoyed expression.

"Students aren't allowed—" he started, but I cut him off.

"Mrs. Casnoff sent me to get you. It's Chaston. She's hurt."

As soon as I'd said "Mrs. Casnoff," he'd closed the door behind him. Then he was moving past me and running across the yard toward the house. Wiped out from my earlier sprint, I lagged behind.

By the time we got back to Chaston, she'd been pulled out of the tub and wrapped in a towel. Bandages covered the holes on her neck, and were wrapped tightly over both wrists. But she still looked really pale, and her eyes were closed.

Elodie and Anna were huddled against the sink in their pajamas, clutching each other and sniffling. Mrs. Casnoff was kneeling by Chaston's head, murmuring something. Whether it was comfort or magic, I didn't know.

She looked up when Cal came in, and her face seemed to sag in relief, making her look more like someone's concerned grandmother than a formidable headmistress. "Thanks be," she said softly. As she stood, I saw that her heavy silk robe was soaked at the knees and probably ruined. She didn't seem to notice.

"My office," she said to Cal as he knelt and scooped Chaston into his arms.

Mrs. Casnoff moved out into the hall, spreading her arms to part the crowd of students gathered outside the bathroom. "Back up, children, give us some room. I assure you, Miss Burnett will be fine. Just a small accident."

Everybody retreated, and the groundskeeper emerged,

with Chaston in his arms. Her cheek rested against his chest, and I saw that her lips were purplish.

As the three disappeared down the stairs, I heard someone behind me sigh, "Wow." I turned and noticed Siobhan lounging against the bathroom doorframe.

"What?" she said. "Don't tell me you wouldn't give up a little blood to get carried around by *that*."

Siobhan started when Elodie and Anna walked out of the bathroom looking shaky and pale. Then Elodie's eyes fixed on something behind me and narrowed. "It was *you*," she spat. I turned and saw Jenna standing outside our bedroom door.

"You did this," Elodie continued, slowly advancing on Jenna, who, proving herself either brave or completely insane, held her ground and continued to stare at Elodie.

The whole mood in the hallway changed. I think despite being worried about Chaston, we were all sort of anticipating an Elodie/Jenna smackdown, maybe to get our minds off the blood still pooled on the bathroom floor, maybe because teenage girls are horrible creatures who like to watch other girls fight. Who knows?

Jenna's cool faltered for just a second, and she glanced down at her feet. When she lifted her head, however, that same bored, languid look was in her eyes. "I don't know what you're talking about."

"Liar!" Elodie cried, and tears spilled down her cheeks. "You're killers, all of you vamps. You don't belong here."

"She's right," someone piped up, and I saw Nausicaa push her way through the crowd. Her wings were flapping angrily, stirring the air around her. Taylor was standing just behind her, dark eyes wide.

Jenna laughed, but it sounded forced. I looked around and realized the crowd had thinned around her, making her look very small and alone.

"And what?" she asked, her voice shaking a little. "None of your kind has ever killed? None of you witches or shapeshifters or fae? Vampires are the only ones who've ever taken a life?"

All eyes were on Elodie, and I think we expected her to lunge for Jenna's throat or something.

But she had the power and she knew it. Her green eyes were positively glittering as she sneered, "What do you know about anything? You're not even a real Prodigium."

The breath that everyone had been holding seemed to rush out all at once. She'd said it. The one thing they all thought but never acknowledged out loud.

"Our families' powers are ancient," Elodie continued, her face pale, except for two red spots on her cheeks. "We are the descendents of angels. And what are you?

A pathetic little human who was fed on by a parasite; a monster."

Jenna was shaking now. "So I'm the monster? What about you, Elodie? Holly told me what you and your little friends were trying to do."

I waited for Elodie to fire back with something, but instead she turned very pale. Anna had stopped crying and was clutching Elodie's shoulder. "Let's go," she implored in a high voice.

"I don't know what you're talking about," Elodie said, but she looked scared.

"The hell you don't. Your little coven was trying to raise a demon."

You'd think the crowd would have gasped. I think I gasped. But the rest of the hall was quiet.

Elodie just stared at Jenna, but I thought I heard Anna whimper.

In the face of that stare, Jenna started to babble. "She said you wanted more power, and that you wanted to do a summoning ritual, and you needed a sacrifice to do that. Y-you have to let the demon feed . . . feed on someone, so . . ."

Elodie had regained her composure. "A demon? You think we could raise a demon here and not have Mrs. Casnoff and the Vandy and the Council jump all over us? Please."

Someone in the crowd snickered, and the tension broke. One person laughing gives everyone permission to laugh, so that's what they did.

Jenna stood there listening to that mocking laughter a lot longer than I could have. Then she pushed past me and went down the hall and into our room. She slammed the door behind her.

Once she was gone, the murmuring began.

Nausicaa was talking to Siobhan. "Which one of us is next?"

Siobhan's blue wings shuddered as she replied, "All I did was fly to catch the bus! I don't deserve to be locked up here with killers."

"Jenna isn't a killer," I said, but I realized I didn't know that for sure. She was a vampire. Vampires feed off humans.

And maybe witches.

No. I shoved that thought away even as I remembered Jenna trying so hard not to look at my blood that first day.

To my surprise, it was Taylor who piped up next, saying, "Sophie's right. There's no proof Jenna killed anybody."

I have no idea if she said it because she actually believed it, or if she just wanted to irritate Nausicaa, but I was grateful anyway.

"Thanks," I said, but Beth stepped in between me and Taylor.

"I wouldn't listen to anything Sophie Mercer has to say, Taylor."

I stared at Beth. What happened to our whole hair-sniffing moment of bonding?

"I was talking to one of the other weres, and she said Sophie's dad is the head of the Council."

I heard a few murmurs at that, and some of the older girls glared at me. The younger ones just looked confused.

Crap.

"Her dad is the one who let vampires into Hex," Beth said. She looked back at me, and I saw the gleam of her fangs as they slid out of her gums. "Of course she's gonna say Jenna's innocent. Otherwise her daddy's job would be on the line."

I did not have time for this. "I've never even met my dad, and I'm certainly not here to further his political agenda or anything. I broke the rules and got sentenced to Hex. Just like everyone else."

Taylor narrowed her eyes. "Your dad is head of the Council?"

Before I could answer, Mrs. Casnoff appeared at the top of the stairs. She was still in her wet robe, and she looked majorly stressed, but she wasn't nearly as pale, so I took that as a good sign.

"Attention, ladies," she said in a voice that managed to be powerful without actually yelling. "Thanks to Cal's efforts, Miss Burnett has regained consciousness and appears to be on the mend."

The collective sigh of relief and following murmurs covered my leaning against Anna and whispering, "What does she mean about this Cal guy?"

I'd expected a snotty response about how stupid I was, but Anna was apparently too relieved about Chaston to be bitchy. "He's a white warlock," she replied. "A super-powerful one. He can heal wounds other witches and warlocks can't."

"Why didn't he heal Holly, then?" I asked, and that got me a snotty look. Good to know Anna was back to normal. "Holly was already dead when they found her, thanks to your little *friend*. Cal can only heal the living; he can't raise the dead. No one can."

"Oh," I said lamely, but she was already talking to Elodie.

"Her parents will come for her tomorrow," Mrs. Casnoff continued, "and I hope she will be able to rejoin us after winter break."

"Has she said anything?" Elodie asked. "Did she say who did it?"

Mrs. Casnoff frowned slightly. "Not at this time. And I encourage all of you to use your best judgment before you go around spreading rumors about this incident. We're obviously taking this very seriously, and the last thing we need is panic."

Elodie opened her mouth, but a look from Mrs. Casnoff stopped whatever nasty thing she was about to say.

"All right," Mrs. Casnoff said with a clap of her hands. "Everyone off to bed now. We can discuss this further in the morning."

CHAPTER 17

When I returned to my room, Jenna was inside, sitting on the dresser next to the window. Her forehead was resting on her knees.

"Jenna?"

She didn't look at me. "It's happening again," she said in a thick voice. "Just like Holly."

She took a deep shuddery breath and said, "When I saw them carrying Chaston out . . . it was exactly the same. The holes in her neck, the slashes on her wrists. The only difference is that Chaston was white. Holly w-was nearly . . . nearly *gray* when they p-pulled her out. . . ." Her voice broke.

I sat on my bed and laid a hand on her knee. "Hey," I said softly, "that wasn't your fault."

She looked up, her eyes red with anger. "Yeah, but

that's not what everyone else thinks, is it? They all think I'm what, a 'bloodsucking freak'?"

She hopped off the dresser. "Like I asked for this," she muttered in a low voice, pulling clothes out of her closet and tossing them on her bed. "Like I wanted to come to this damn school anyway."

"Jen," I started to say, but she whirled around on me.

"I *hate* it here!" she cried. "I . . . I hate taking stupid-ass classes like *A History of Nineteenth Century Witches*. God, I j-just wanna take algebra or something stupid like that. I wanna eat lunch—*real* lunch—in a cafeteria, and have an after-school job, and go to the prom."

With a sob, she sat down on her bed, like all the anger in her had evaporated. "I don't want to be a vampire," she whispered, and then she broke down crying, burying her face in the black T-shirt she was holding.

I looked around the room, and for the first time, all the pink didn't seem cheerful; it just seemed sad, like Jenna was trying to hold on to whatever life she'd had before. There are times when saying nothing is definitely the best course of action, and I felt like this was one of those times. So I just crossed the room and sat on her bed, stroking her hair like my mom did for me the night I'd found out I was going to Hecate.

And after a while, Jenna leaned back against her pillows and started talking.

"She was so nice to me," she said softly. "Amanda."

I didn't have to ask who Amanda was. I knew she was finally telling me the story of how she'd come to be a vampire.

"That was the biggest part. Not that she was cute, or smart, or funny. She was those things too, but it was the nice that got me. No one had ever paid so much attention to me before. When she told me what she was, that she wanted me to be with her forever, I didn't really believe it. I didn't believe it until I felt her teeth in my neck."

She paused, and there was no sound in the room except the soft rustling of the breeze in the oaks outside.

"When the Change happened, it was . . . amazing. I felt stronger and just *better*, you know? Like the rest of my life had been a dream. Those first two nights with her were the best nights of my whole life. And then they killed her."

"They?"

Her eyes met mine. My tiny reflection in her eyes looked very pale.

"The Eye," she replied, and an involuntary shiver ran through me.

"There were two of them. They broke into the motel where we were hiding, and they staked her while she was sleeping. But she woke up and she started . . . she started screaming, and it took both of them to hold her down.

So I got up ran out the door and I just kept running. For three days I hid in somebody's garden shed. I only left there because I was starving. So I stole some food from a convenience store.

"As soon as I put the first Twinkie in my mouth, I felt like was I going to die. I chewed it maybe twice before I had to spit it out. The—" She closed her eyes and took a deep breath. "The manager of the store came out and found me on my knees in the parking lot. He saw the wrapper and started yelling about calling the cops, and I—"

She broke off and wouldn't meet my eyes. I put my hand on her shoulder, trying to console her or let her know I didn't care that she'd drunk someone's blood, but I couldn't look at her face.

"After . . . after that, I felt better. I got a bus back into the city and found Amanda's parents. They were vamps too. Amanda's dad had been bitten years ago and had changed all of them. So they contacted the Council and I got sent here."

She looked at me again. "It wasn't supposed to be like this," she said plaintively. "I don't want to be like this without Amanda. I only wanted to be a vampire if we could be together forever. She *promised*." Tears were glistening in her eyes.

"Wow," I said. "Who knew girls sucked just as bad as boys?"

She sighed and tilted her head back against the head-board, eyes closed. "They're going to kick me out."

"Why?"

She looked incredulous. "Um . . . hello? They're totally going to pin Chaston on me. Holly was one thing, but two girls in a six-month period?" She shook her head. "Somebody's gonna go down for that, and you can bet it's gonna be me."

"Why?" I repeated. Jenna was the only person at Hecate I considered a friend. Well, maybe Archer and I were friends now, but there was still that whole possibly-being-in-love-with-him-maybe-a-little thing, and that pushed him out of the friend zone. If Jenna left, I'd be at the mercy of Elodie and Anna.

No way.

"You don't know that they're gonna kick you out. Chaston may remember what happened to her. Just wait and talk to Mrs. Casnoff, okay? Maybe by tomorrow everyone will have calmed down some."

Her derisive snort told me exactly how likely she found that scenario. After a moment she began putting her clothes back in the closet. I stood up and helped her.

"So how was cellar duty tonight?"

"Cellar-ific."

"And your stupendously futile crush on Archer Cross?"

"Still stupendous. Still futile."

She nodded as she hung up one of her many Hecate blazers. "Good to know."

We worked in companionable silence.

"What did you mean about Elodie and her coven trying to raise a demon?"

"That's what Holly told me they were working on," she said as she closed the closet. "Mrs. Casnoff was really pimping the whole *L'Occhio di Dio will kill us all* thing she's so big on, and their coven freaked out. Holly said they thought if they raised a demon, it would give them more power and they'd be safer should stuff go down."

"Did they do it?"

She shook her head. "I don't know."

The lights blinked out, plunging us into darkness. I heard a few startled shrieks from down the hall, but then Mrs. Casnoff's voice boomed, "Lights out is mandatory tonight. Go to bed, children."

Jenna sighed. "You gotta love Hex Hall."

Bumping into furniture and whispering bad words, we made our way to our respective beds.

I flopped down on mine with a low groan. I hadn't realized how exhausted I was until I felt my cool soft pillow under my head. So I was nearly asleep when I heard Jenna whisper, "Thank you."

"For what?" I mumbled.

"Being my friend."

"Wow," I replied. "That's like, the lamest thing anyone's ever said to me."

She gave a cry of mock outrage, and a second later one of her many pillows landed on my face.

"I was trying to be nice," she insisted, but I could hear the laughter in her voice.

"Well, don't," I retorted. "I like my friends mean and hateful."

"Will do," she replied, and a few minutes later we were both asleep.

I awoke to Jenna's screaming and the smell of smoke.

Confused, I sat up. Morning sunlight was streaming into the room and onto Jenna's bed. It took me a minute to realize that that's where the smoke was coming from.

Jenna's bed. Jenna.

She was frantically trying to stand up, but she was tangled in her sheets, and panic was making her clumsy.

My feet barely touched the floor as I leaped from my bed and tossed my comforter over her. As I did, I caught sight of her hand. The normally pale skin was bright red, and it was bubbling up in places.

Without thinking, I pushed her into her closet.

Once she was in, I grabbed one of her sheets and shoved it against the crack underneath the door. Jenna was crying, but she wasn't making that high-pitched sound of pain anymore.

"What happened?" I shouted through the wood.

"My bloodstone," she sobbed. "It's gone!"

I ran to her bed and crouched to peer under it.

Maybe it just fell off, I told myself. Maybe the clasp broke, or it got caught on her pillow.

I wanted it to be one of those things.

I pulled everything off the bed, even shoved the mattress off the box springs, but Jenna's bloodstone wasn't anywhere.

Rage surged inside of me.

"Wait here," I yelled to Jenna.

"Oh, like I'm going anywhere!" she replied when I was already halfway out the door.

There were a few girls in the hall. I recognized one, Laura Harris, from Magical Evolution. Her eyes went wide when she saw me.

I ran to Elodie's room and pounded on the door.

She opened it, and I pushed past her into the room.

"Where is it?"

"Where's what?" she asked. There were dark circles under her eyes.

"Jenna's bloodstone. I know you took it, now where is it?"

Elodie's eyes flashed. "I didn't take her stupid bloodstone.

183

Although if I *had*, it would've been totally justified after what she did to Chaston last night."

"She didn't do anything to Chaston, and you could have killed her!" I shouted.

"If she didn't attack Chaston, then who did?" Elodie asked, raising her voice. Little threads of light were racing under her skin, and her hair was starting to crackle. I could feel my own magic pulsing like a second heartbeat.

"Maybe that demon you were trying to summon," I fired back.

Elodie made a disgusted sound. "Like I said last night, if there were a demon, Mrs. Casnoff would know it. We *all* would."

"What's going on?"

We both whirled to see Anna standing in the doorway, her hair damp and a towel in her hand.

"Sophie thinks we took the vamp's stupid bloodstone," Elodie told her.

"What? That's ridiculous," Anna said, but her voice was tight.

I closed my eyes and tried to get control of my temper and my magic. Then, picturing Jenna's necklace in my mind, I murmured, "Bloodstone."

Elodie rolled her eyes, but there was a distinct squeaking sound as one of Anna's dresser drawers slid open. The bloodstone rose up from underneath a pile of clothes, its red center glinting.

It floated into my hand, and I closed my fist around it.

Surprise flickered across Elodie's face for a moment. Then it vanished. "You have what you came for, so get out."

Anna was looking at the floor. I wanted to say something withering, something that would make her feel ashamed for what she'd done, but in the end I decided it wasn't worth it.

When I got back to the room, Jenna's sobs had dwindled to sniffling. I opened the closet door a crack and handed her the bloodstone. Once it was back on her neck, she came out of the closet and sat on her bed, cradling her burned hand.

I sat next to her. "You should get this looked at." She nodded. Her eyes were still red and watery.

"Was it Elodie and Anna?" she asked.

"Yeah. Well, it was Anna. I don't think Elodie knew, but it's not like she would've disapproved."

Jenna released a shuddery breath. I reached up and brushed her pink stripe out of her eyes. "You need to tell Mrs. Casnoff what they did."

"No," she said. "No way."

"Jenna, they could have killed you," I insisted.

She stood up, pulling my comforter around her. "It'll

just make it worse," she said wearily. "Remind everyone that vamps are different from the rest of you. That I don't belong here."

"Jenna," I started.

"I said drop it, Sophie!" she snapped, her back still turned.

"But you're hurt—"

And then she whirled on me, her eyes bloodred, her face contorted with rage. Her fangs slid out, and she grabbed my shoulders with a hiss. There was nothing of my friend in her face.

Only a monster.

I made a shocked sound of hurt and fear, and she abruptly released me. My knees gave out, and I crumpled to the floor.

She was immediately beside me, Jenna again, her eyes pale blue and filled with apology. "Oh God, Soph, I'm so sorry! Are you okay? Sometimes when I get stressed . . ." Tears spilled down her cheeks. "I would never hurt you," she said, pleading.

I didn't trust myself to speak, so I just nodded.

"Girls? Is everything all right?"

Jenna looked over her shoulder. Mrs. Casnoff stood in our doorway, her face unreadable.

"We're fine," I said, standing up. "I just slipped, and Jenna was, uh, helping me up."

"I see," Mrs. Casnoff said. She looked back and forth between me and Jenna before saying, "Jenna, if you don't mind, I need to speak with you for a moment."

"Sure," Jenna replied, in a voice that was anything but certain.

I watched them leave the room, then sat down on Jenna's bed. My shoulders were sore, and Jenna's fingers had left a mark.

I sat there absentmindedly rubbing my arms, the smoky smell of Jenna's burned skin still stinging my nose.

And I wondered.

CHAPTER 18

A week later, things still weren't any better. No one had heard anything from Chaston, so Jenna was still the number-one suspect.

After dinner, I was in the cellar with Archer again. This was our fourth time down there, and we'd begun to work out a kind of routine. For the first twenty minutes or so we just worked on the shelves. Half the stuff we'd catalogued the last time had usually moved, so we'd spend time trying to sort that out. Once this was done we'd take a break and talk. Our conversations hadn't really graduated beyond small talk about our families and the occasional insult, which wasn't that surprising. Other than being only children, Archer and I had almost nothing in common. He'd grown up super wealthy in a big house on the coast of Maine. I'd lived with my mom in everything from the cottage in Vermont to a room in a Ramada Inn for six weeks. But I still found myself looking forward to our talks. In fact I'd started dreading the days when I didn't have cellar duty, which was almost too pathetic to contemplate.

Archer sat in his usual place on the steps while I hoisted myself onto a bare space on top of Shelf M.

He pointed at a pile of empty dust-covered jars in the corner. Two of them rose in the air and twisted and contorted until they were cans of soda. He flicked his hand in my direction, and one of them sailed straight toward me. I caught it, and was surprised by how icy cold it was.

"I'm impressed." I meant it, and he nodded his head in thanks.

"Yeah, turning jars into soda. Let the world tremble before my power."

"Well, at least it proves you still have powers."

He looked up at me quizzically. "What's that supposed to mean?"

Crap. "I—uh, I just . . . some people said that you left last year because you wanted to get your powers taken away."

I'd assumed he'd heard all those rumors, but he looked genuinely surprised. "So that's what everybody thinks. Huh."

"They know you didn't," I replied hastily. "Lots of people saw you drop Justin on the first day."

A smile played around the corners of his mouth. He looked up at me. "Bad dog."

I rolled my eyes, but I couldn't help smiling back. "Shut up. So where did you go?"

He shrugged and rested his elbows on his knees. "I just needed a break. It's not unheard of. The Council acts like it'll never let anybody out of Hecate, but they'll give you a leave of absence if you petition them. I guess they figured I needed it, especially after Holly."

"Right," I said, but the mention of Holly had me thinking about Chaston again. Her parents had come to get her the day after her attack. They'd been in Mrs. Casnoff's office for over two hours before Mrs. Casnoff had come to get Jenna.

When Jenna had come back to the room, she hadn't said a word, just gone to lie on her bed and stare at the ceiling.

The sudden shift in my mood must have showed on my face, because Archer asked, "Is Jenna okay? I noticed she wasn't at dinner tonight."

I sighed and leaned back. "It's not good," I told him. "She won't go to class or meals. She barely gets out of bed. I don't know what they said to her in that meeting, but the fact that they called her in there seems to prove her guilt to everybody."

He nodded. "Yeah, Elodie's pretty pissed."

"Wow, what a shame. I hope it doesn't give her wrinkles."

"Don't be like that."

"Look, I'm sorry your girlfriend is upset, but the only friend I have here is being accused of something she didn't do, and Elodie is leading the charge. I just can't feel sorry for her right now, okay?"

I waited for him to fire back, but apparently he decided to drop it. He got up off the steps and went back to his clipboard.

"Have you seen anything that looks like 'Demon-possessed Instrument: J. Mompesson'?"

"Possibly." I hopped off the shelf and went to the space where I'd found a drum the other day, but of course it had vanished. By the time we found it (it had hidden itself behind a pile of books that disintegrated when we moved them. "Really, really hope those weren't important" had been Archer's only comment), our hour was nearly up.

I heard the lock above us click open. The Vandy had stopped coming down to the cellar to get us; she just unlocked the door.

We tossed our clipboards down and headed for the stairs.

As we started up, I could've sworn I saw a flash of green out of the corner of my eye, but when I turned around to look, there was nothing. The hairs on the back of my neck stood on end, and I rubbed my hand absently over them.

"You okay?" Archer asked as he opened the door.

"Yeah," I said, but I was freaked out. "It's just . . . Can I ask you something really weird?"

"Those are my favorite kinds of questions."

"Do you think anyone around here could raise a demon?"

I thought he'd laugh or make a sarcastic comment, but instead he paused outside the cellar door and looked at me in that intense way he had. "Why would you ask that?"

"Something Jenna said the other night. She thinks Holly may have been killed because, uh, some people raised a demon."

Archer took that in before shaking his head and saying, "Nah, there's no way. Mrs. Casnoff would know if there was a demon on campus. They're pretty conspicuous."

"Why? Are they green and horny?" I willed a blush away and said, "I mean, as in having horns, not . . . the other."

"Not necessarily. They can look as human as you and me. Some of them even used to be human."

"Have you ever seen one?"

He looked at me incredulously. "Uh, no. Thank God. I like my face where it is and not eaten off."

"Yeah," I said as we reached the main staircase. "But you're a warlock. Couldn't you take a demon?"

"Not unless I had that," he said, pointing to the stained-glass angel above the stairs. "See that sword? Demonglass. Only thing that can kill demons."

"And so originally named," I commented, making him laugh.

"You mock," he said, "but that's some hardcore stuff. The only place you can find it is in hell, so it's kinda hard to come by."

"Wow," I said, looking at the window with new appreciation.

"Archer!" I heard Elodie trill from somewhere upstairs. I walked past him. "Well, thanks. See ya."

"Mercer."

I turned around.

He was standing at the bottom of the stairs, and in the soft lights of the chandelier he was so handsome that my chest hurt. It was easy to forget how irritating he was when he looked that good. "What?" I asked in the most bored voice I could manage.

"Arch!"

Elodie came bounding past me, and Archer's eyes went from me to her.

I turned and ran up the stairs before I had to see her in his arms.

CHAPTER 19

By the beginning of October, Chaston had sent written testimony into the Council, stating she couldn't remember anything about the attack, so Jenna was allowed to stay. I'd thought that news would do something to remove the shadows from under her eyes, but it didn't. She hardly talked to anyone besides me, and even then she barely smiled, and she never laughed.

As for me, I started to feel like I might actually be getting the hang of life at Hecate. My classes were going well. Elodie and Anna had been shaken up for about two weeks after Chaston and temporarily lost their sadistic urge to torture me. Instead they pretty much ignored me. But by the middle of October they were back to normal, which for them meant making nasty remarks and talking about clothes.

I avoided trouble with the Vandy even though she'd made Archer my permanent Defense partner, probably in the hopes that he'd inadvertently kill me. But even that wasn't going too badly, although being forced to spend more time in close proximity to him was its own type of torture. In fact, the more time we spent cataloguing in the cellar or blocking each other's blows in Defense, the more I began to suspect that my crush might be deepening into something else, something that I really didn't want to put a name to. It wasn't just that he was hot—although, believe me, that was definitely part of it—it was the way he ran his fingers through his hair. The way he looked at me like I was actually interesting to talk to. The way his eyes lit up when he laughed at my jokes. Hell, the fact that he laughed at my jokes.

And the more I got to know him, the more wrong his dating Elodie seemed. He'd sworn there was more to Elodie than met the eye, but in the two months I'd been at Hecate, practically the only things I'd heard her talk about were spells for making your hair shinier or freckles disappear. She'd looked at me when mentioning that one. Even her essay for Lord Byron's class was about the way physical beauty enhanced a witch's power, supposedly because it gave her easier access to humans. It was ridiculous. Now, sitting behind her in Ms. East's Magical Evolution class, I couldn't help but roll my eyes as she prattled on to Anna about the dress she was planning on conjuring for the school's annual All Hallow's Eve Ball in two weeks.

"Most people think redheads can't wear pink," she was saying, "but it totally depends on the shade of pink. Either really light pink or dark pink works best. And hot pink, of course, is just trashy."

This last bit was spoken in a louder voice for Jenna's benefit. She was sitting beside me, and even though she pretended to ignore them, I saw her fingers steal up to her pink streak a few minutes later.

I nudged her arm. "Don't listen to them. They're total bitches."

"Excuse me, Miss Mercer?"

I looked up to see Ms. East standing over my desk, one hand on her hip. Ms. East looked like she'd be one of the coolest teachers at Hecate. Jenna and I privately joked that her look was dominatrix-chic. She was rail thin and always wore her dark maroon hair pulled back in a tight bun. Factor in her all-black wardrobe and sky-high heels, and she looked like she could easily be walking the runways in Paris. But like all the teachers at Hecate, Ms. East seemed to have been born with her sense of humor gland completely absent.

Now I smiled weakly at her and said, "Um . . . there are witches? In this class?"

The class erupted into giggles except for Elodie and Anna, who had probably guessed what I actually said, and were glaring at me.

The corners of Ms. East's mouth turned down a fraction of an inch, which was about as close to a frown as she got. I think she was afraid of creasing her perfectly smooth face.

"What a thrilling observation, Miss Mercer. However, you know that I do not tolerate interruptions in my class—"

"I wasn't interrupting," I interrupted, and Ms. East's mouth tilted down ever farther, which meant I'd just crossed into the land of Royally Screwed.

"Since you have so much to say, perhaps you would like to write it in an essay on the different classes of witches? Two thousand words, let us say? Due tomorrow."

As usual my mouth opened before my brain had a chance to stop it, and I yelped, "What? That's totally unfair!"

"And now you may exit my class. When you come back, kindly have your essay and an apology in hand."

I bit off a retort and gathered my things under Jenna's sympathetic gaze and Elodie's and Anna's smirks. It took a lot of self-control, but I didn't slam the door as I left.

I checked my watch and saw that I had forty minutes to kill until my next class, so I ran upstairs and dropped my books off before heading outside for a little fresh air.

It was one of those insanely beautiful days that only October seems capable of producing. The sky was a deep clear blue, The trees were still mostly green, with a few orange and gold leaves poking out here and there. There was a pleasant sort of smoky-smelling breeze blowing, which felt just cool enough to make me glad I was wearing my blazer. So even though a part of me was still seething with the unfairness of getting kicked out of class, I was pretty happy about being given an unexpected free period, even though I should have been using it to write my stupid essay.

Just before I could do something super lame like spread my arms wide and burst into the chorus of "Colors of the Wind," I heard a voice say, "Why aren't you in class?"

I turned around to see the groundskeeper, Cal, standing behind me. As usual he was rocking his lumberjack look—all flannel and denim. And this time he even had a prop: a giant ax, which he held in his left hand, the lethal head gleaming dully against his boot.

I don't know what the expression on my face was as I stared at that ax, but I imagined I must have looked like Elmer Fudd when Bugs Bunny had dressed up as a girl—popping eyes, jaw dropped to the ground.

Apparently that wasn't too far off, because Cal seemed to stifle a laugh as he lifted the ax and rested it on his shoulder.

"Relax. I'm not a psycho."

"I know that," I snapped. "You're the healing janitor dude."

"Groundskeeper."

"Isn't that like a janitor?"

"No, it's like a groundskeeper."

From the two interactions I'd had with him, I'd assumed Cal was some sort of Neanderthal jock type. For one thing, he was super buff, and his hair was dark blond, making him look exactly like your average high school quarterback. Plus I'd barely ever heard him speak more than three words at a time. But maybe there was more than met the eye.

"So if you can heal with your touch, why are you working here as like, Hagrid, or whatever?"

He smiled, and I noticed his teeth were very white and very straight. What was with this place? Even the staff looked like Abercrombie & Fitch models.

"Shouldn't you be out there healing really important people instead of here, pulling weeds and patching up teenagers?"

He shrugged. "When I was released from Hecate last year, I offered my services up to the Council. They decided my talents were most useful here, protecting their most precious treasures. You."

There was something so . . . I don't know, intimate, about the way he said it that I felt like I might burst out in giggles and start blushing. Then I caught myself. I already had one stupid crush. I wasn't about to start lusting after the groundskeeper, for God's sake.

Maybe he realized the way he'd said it was weird too, because he quickly cleared his throat. "I mean, all of you. You know, their kids."

"Right."

"Anyway, now get back to Portraits of Faeries in Eighteenth Century France, or whatever other dumb-ass class you're skipping."

I crossed my arms, both because I was getting a little pissed and also because the breeze across the lake was turning chilly. "Actually, I got kicked out of Ms. East's class. Magical Evolution."

He snorted. "Man. Cellar duty for a semester, kicked out of class . . ."

"Tell me about it," I replied. "Apparently there's something about me that pisses off every teacher in this school."

To my surprise, Cal shook his head. "I don't think that's it."

Dimly in the distance, I heard the clanging bell

that signaled class changes. I knew I should hurry back for Byron's class, but I wanted to hear what Cal had to say.

"What do you mean?"

"Look at it from their point of view, Sophie. Your dad is head of the Council. Everybody at Hecate is bending over backward to not show favoritism to you. So maybe they're going a little overboard in the opposite direction, you know?"

I just nodded. Why wasn't I surprised to find out that yet another thing was my dad's fault?

"You okay?" Cal asked, his head tilted a little.

"Yeah," I answered way too brightly. I sounded like a cheerleader on a Kool-Aid high. "Yeah," I repeated, much more normally this time. "I gotta go. Don't wanna be late!"

I rushed past him, nearly colliding with one of his shoulders.

God, the guy's built like a freaking oak tree, I thought as I picked up my pace.

In the end, I was still late for Byron's class. Which meant that not only did I get yelled at—in iambic pentameter no less—but I also had to write a five-page essay on my "chronic and egregious tardiness."

"I think I need to find a homework spell," I whispered to Jenna as I slid into my seat.

She just gave a halfhearted shrug and went back to drawing faces in her notebook.

Faces, I couldn't help but notice, that looked a lot like Holly and Chaston.

CHAPTER 20

Later that night I worked on Ms. East's essay while Archer catalogued; I'd already written Byron's in my last class of the day, Classifications of Shapeshifters. Our teacher, Mr. Ferguson, was in love with the sound of his own voice, so he rarely paid attention to what we were doing at our desks. Jenna and I used to pass notes the whole time, but these days she usually spent the period doodling in her notebook and trying to shrink inside herself.

Archer and I had gotten to the point where we both barely catalogued more than ten things during our hour in the cellar. The Vandy hadn't said anything, which only confirmed my suspicion that the real point of cellar duty was being trapped down there for an hour three nights a week. After all, doing the work was pointless since everything we catalogued was in a different place the next time we arrived. We spent most of our time talking. Since Jenna had started swimming in the deep end of the pity pool, Archer was pretty much the only friend I had. Elodie and Anna had completely given up on my joining their coven, and from what I'd heard, they were looking for white witches now, a sure sign that I had fallen below contempt with them. I tried to tell myself that it didn't matter, but the truth was, life at Hecate had gotten pretty lonely.

"Do you think the teachers are hard on me because of my dad?" I asked Archer, looking up from the textbook spread across my lap.

"Probably." He hoisted himself onto an empty shelf. "Prodigium have pretty big egos. Not all of them are your dad's biggest fan, and Casnoff wouldn't want the other parents to think you're getting special treatment just because your dad is practically their king."

He raised an eyebrow. "Which makes you Crown Princess."

I rolled my eyes. "Oh yeah. Just let me polish my tiara and I'm set."

"Oh, come on, Mercer. I think you'd make a good queen. You've definitely got the snotty part down."

"I am not snotty!" I nearly yelped.

He leaned back on his elbows, a wicked smile on his face. "Please. The first day I met you, you practically had a layer of permafrost covering you."

"Only because you were a jerk," I retorted. "You told me I sucked at being a witch."

"You did suck," he said with a laugh.

And then, in what was becoming a running joke, we said in unison, "Bad dog!" and smiled at each other.

"You're just not used to meeting women who don't fall all over your ass like you're in a boy band or something," I said when our laughter had subsided a little.

I'd turned back to my essay, so I had to look up when I realized he hadn't answered me.

He was looking at me with a small smile, a strange glint in his eye. "So why didn't you?"

"Excuse me?"

"Well, according to you, women are always falling over me. So why didn't you? Not your type?"

I took a deep breath and hoped he didn't notice. Weird little moments like this one were getting too common with Archer and me. Maybe it was all the time we spent together alone in the cellar, or how familiar we'd gotten with each other's bodies while kicking the crap out of each other in Defense, but I was beginning to notice a subtle shift in our relationship. I wasn't delusional enough to believe that he actually liked me or anything, but flirting had definitely entered the picture. It left me feeling strange and totally unsure of myself in moments like these.

"Nope," I finally said, striving for a light tone. "I've always had a thing for the nerdy type. Arrogant pretty boys don't really ring my bell."

"So you think I'm pretty?"

"Shut up."

I needed to change the subject. "What about your family?" I asked.

He looked up, startled. "What?"

"Your family. Do they like my dad?"

He looked away quickly and gave a half shrug, but I could see something was wrong. "My family pretty much stays out of politics," he said. Then he held up his list. "Have you seen Vampire Fang: D. Frocelli?"

I shook my head.

As I turned back to my essay I wondered what the heck I'd said to freak Archer out so much. It occurred to me that in the past six weeks we'd been working together, Archer hadn't talked much about his family. It had never really bothered me before, but of course now that I knew he didn't want to talk about it, I was consumed by curiosity.

I wondered if Jenna would know anything about Archer's past, but then I quickly tossed the idea. Jenna was barely speaking to anyone and was clearly going through some major crap. The last thing she needed was me pestering her about my crush.

By the time the Vandy came for us, I'd already finished most of my essay, and I decided I would do the rest of it in the morning before class.

I walked back to my room, but as I did, I passed Elodie's open door and heard Anna's soft, lilting voice say, "Well, I'd be suspicious if it were my boyfriend."

I paused just outside the door and heard Elodie answer, "I would be if she weren't such a freak. Trust me, if Archer had to be stuck in the basement with any girl at this school, I'm positively thrilled it's Sophie Mercer. Archer wouldn't look at her twice."

It's funny. I knew that Archer wasn't interested in me, but actually hearing another person say it really, really sucked.

"She does have big boobs," Anna mused.

Elodie just snorted at that. "Please, Anna. Big boobs are not enough to compensate for being short and plain. And that hair!" Even though I couldn't see her, I imagined Elodie gave a shudder at that. I, meanwhile, was starting to feel vaguely nauseated. I knew I should walk away, but I couldn't stop listening. I wonder why it is that we always want to hear people talk about us, even if it's horrible stuff. And, you know, it's not like Elodie was saying anything I didn't know. I was short and plain and I did have crazy hair. I'd said these things about myself lots of times. So why were hot tears stinging my eyes?

"Yeah, but Archer is weird," Anna said. "Remember how mean he was to you first year? Like, didn't he call you a shallow bimbo, or something? Or dumb—"

"That's in the past now, Anna," Elodie said tightly, and I had to suppress a laugh. So Archer had apparently once been sensible. What had changed? Did Elodie actually have some depth to her, like he'd said? 'Cause I sure wasn't hearing anything deeper than a bedpan.

"Anyway, even if Archer was insane enough to have a thing for Sophie, after the All Hallow's Eve Ball, he won't even think about looking at another girl."

"Why?"

"I've decided to give myself to him."

Oh, gross. Who says stuff like that? Why didn't she just say "delicate flower" or "carnal treasure" or something equally stupid?

But Anna, of course, squealed. "Omigod, that is so romantic!"

Elodie giggled, which was a weird sound coming from her. Girls like Elodie should cackle. "I know, right?"

I'd definitely heard enough, so I tiptoed away and softly opened the door to my room.

Jenna was, as usual, curled up on her bed, one of her hot-pink throws pulled over her. She was doing this a lot now, pretending to be asleep so that I wouldn't talk to her. Normally I just gave her what she wanted and didn't attempt a conversation. But tonight I sat on the edge of her bed hard enough to bounce her a little. "Guess what I just overheard?" I singsonged.

She pulled down one corner of the blanket, and one eye blinked owlishly at me. "What?"

I repeated the conversation between Anna and Elodie, finishing up with, "Can you believe that? 'Give myself to him'? Ugh. What's wrong with just saying *sex*, you know?"

I was rewarded with a tiny smile. "That is pretty stupid," Jenna said.

"Totally stupid," I agreed.

"Did they say anything about Chaston?"

Surprised, I said, "Uh . . . no. Not that I heard, at least. But you heard what Mrs. Casnoff said at dinner a few nights ago. Chaston's fine and resting in the Riviera or some other glamorous place with her parents. She'll be back next year."

"I just can't believe they're gossiping about boys when one of their coven is dead, and another one nearly died just three weeks ago."

"Yeah, well, they're shallow jerks. Not exactly news, that."

"Yeah."

I stripped out of my clothes and pulled on a Hecate-issue blue tank top and a pair of pajama pants my mom had sent me last week. They were white cotton covered with tiny blue witches riding brooms. I think they were her way of saying she was sorry for the fight; I was sorry too, and had called her to tell her so. It felt nice to be on good terms with her again.

"Wow, I really bruised your shoulders," Jenna said, sitting up.

I glanced down. "Oh . . . right. No big deal. They don't even hurt."

They did still hurt a little.

Jenna's eyes were bright, and I think she was trying not to cry. "I'm still really sorry about that, Soph. I was just so freaked out and hurt, and . . . and sometimes I lose control."

Icy fear ran down my spine, but I tried to ignore it. Jenna was my friend. Yes, she'd vamped out on me, but she'd snapped out of it immediately.

But you're her friend. Chaston definitely wasn't. And who knows about Holly?

Nope. Not going there.

Instead I said with mock confusion, "Lose control of what? Your bladder? Because you might want to get that checked out. I'm *so* not loaning you any sheets."

"You're such a freak." She giggled.

"Takes one to know one!"

For the next couple of hours, we chatted and

attempted to study for Magical Evolution. By lights out, Jenna seemed almost like her old self again.

"Night, Jenna," I said when the lights finally blinked off.

"Night, Soph."

I stared at the slanting ceiling, my head full of thoughts: Archer, Elodie and Anna, Jenna, that conversation with Cal by the pond. I fell asleep wondering if Archer knew he was about to become the proud recipient of Elodie's virginity.

I didn't know what time it was when I awoke to find the girl in green standing at the foot of my bed. My heart in my mouth, I was sure I had to be dreaming, that there was no way this could be real.

Then she gave a exasperated sigh and, in a British accent, said, "Sophia Mercer. What trouble *you've* been."

CHAPTER 21

I sat up in bed, blinking.

It was the girl I'd been seeing since I'd started at Hecate, but she didn't look anything like a ghost; she looked very much flesh and blood.

"Well?" she asked, raising one perfect eyebrow. "Are you coming or not?"

I glanced over at Jenna. All I could make out was a dark lump. By the sound of her steady, even breathing, I knew she was still asleep.

The girl followed my gaze. "Oh, don't worry about her," she said with a dismissive wave. "She won't wake up and sound the alarm. No one will; I've taken care of that."

Before I could ask what she meant, she turned and swept out the door.

I sat frozen until she reappeared in the doorway

and said, "Oh, for Christ's sake, Sophia, let's *go!*"

Now, I knew that following a ghost was a Very Bad Idea. Everything in my body said that. My skin felt clammy and my stomach was in knots. But I found myself pushing off my covers, grabbing my Hecate blazer off the back of my chair, and catching up to her at the top of the stairs.

"Good," she said. "We have a lot of work to do and not much time."

"Who are you?" I whispered.

She flashed me that irritated look again. "I told you, you don't have to whisper. No one can hear us."

She stopped on the stairs and threw her head back, shouting, "Casnoff! Vandy! Sophia Mercer is out of bed and up to mischief with a ghooooooooooooost!"

I instinctively crouched down. "Shhhh!"

But just as she'd promised, there was no sign that anyone had heard her. The only sound was the muffled ticking of the grandfather clock in the main foyer and my own hard breathing.

"See?" she said, turning to me with a bright smile. "Taken care of. Now come along."

She ran down the last few steps, and before I knew it, we were outside on the front lawn. The night was cool and damp, and the grass squished unpleasantly under my feet. I looked down to make sure I was only standing on grass and noticed that my feet seemed a weird shade of green. Then I noticed I could see my shadow even though there was no moon.

I whirled around to look back at Hecate and gasped. The whole house was encased in a huge opalescent bubble that glimmered with dull green light. The bubble was in constant motion, undulating and shooting off pale green sparks. I had never seen anything like it; never even read about a spell like that.

"Impressive, isn't it?" the girl said smugly. "It's a basic sleeping spell that renders the victims totally insensible to the world for at least four hours. I just . . . enlarged it."

I didn't like the way she said "victims."

"Are they . . . are they okay?"

"Oh, perfectly safe," she answered. "Just sleeping. Like in a fairy tale."

"But . . . Mrs. Casnoff has spells all over the place. No one could just come in and do a spell that big."

"I can!" the girl said. Then she grabbed my hand. Hers was as solid and real as mine. I was sure Mrs. Casnoff had said ghosts couldn't touch us. But before I could ask, the girl started pulling me away from the house.

"Wait. I can't go anywhere with you until I know who you are and what you're doing here. Why have you been following me?"

She sighed. "Oh, Sophia, I had hoped you were

a little more perceptive. Isn't it obvious who I am?"

I studied her knee-length flowered dress and bright green cardigan. Her hair was shoulder length, curly, and held back from her face with bobby pins. Glancing down, I saw that she was wearing heinous brown shoes. I felt a little sorry for her: ghost or no, no one should have to go through eternity in ugly shoes.

But then I looked into her eyes. They were large and wide set, and even though the green light was reflected in them, I could tell that they were blue.

My eyes.

British, from the forties, and had my eyes.

"Alice?" I asked, my heart in my throat.

She smiled broadly. "Excellent! Now, just come with me and—"

"Wait, wait, wait," I said, holding a hand to my head. "You're telling me that you're the ghost of my great-grandmother?"

That irritated look again. "Yes."

"So what are you doing here? Why have you been following me?"

"I haven't been following you," she answered hotly. "I've been appearing to you. You weren't ready for me before, but now you are. I've worked very hard to get to you, Sophia. Now, can we please stop all this chattering and get down to business?"

I let her drag me away, mostly because I was afraid she might zap me if I didn't, but also because I was genuinely curious. How many people get pulled out of bed by their great-grandmother's ghost?

We walked away from Hecate and down the steep hill toward the greenhouse. I wondered if she was taking me there for training, but when we arrived, she veered off toward the left and pulled me into the woods.

I'd never been in the forest that surrounded Hecate, and for very good reason: it was spooky as hell. And of course it was doubly so at night. I stepped on a rock in my bare feet and winced. When something soft brushed against my cheek, I gave a little shriek.

I heard Alice murmur a few words, and suddenly a large orb of light appeared in front of us, bright enough that I had to shade my eyes. Alice muttered under her breath, and the orb jerked upward as if someone had it on a string. It floated away until it was about ten feet over our heads, casting light in all directions.

You would think that the light would make the woods less creepy, but actually it was worse. Now shadows moved across the ground, and I caught the occasional flash of animal eyes. We came across a dry creek bed, and to my surprise, Alice leaped nimbly into it. I followed, a lot less gracefully, tripping on loose soil and cursing.

If I'd thought the woods were spooky, they had

nothing on the dry creek. Rocks were sharp against my bare feet, and it seemed that everywhere I looked, there were dark hollows and exposed roots that looked like the entrails of some giant animal. In the end I just grabbed Alice's hand and kept my eyes shut until we came to an abrupt stop.

I opened my eyes and immediately wished I hadn't.

In front of me was a small wrought-iron fence flecked with rust. Behind the fence were six gravestones. Four were slightly crooked and covered in moss, but the other two stood straight and were as white as bone.

The gravestones were unsettling enough, but it was the other thing in this tiny graveyard that had my heart in my stomach, and the metallic taste of fear in my mouth.

The statue was about eight feet high, maybe a little taller. It was an angel carved in light gray stone, its wings spread wide. They were so finely carved you could make out every feather. Likewise, the angel's robes seemed to ripple and float in a nonexistent wind. In one hand it held a sword. The hilt was carved out of the same stone as the rest of the statue, but the blade was some sort of dark glass, which shone brightly in the light from the orb. The angel's other hand was held out in front of it, palm forward, as if it were warning others to stay back. The look on its face was one of such stern authority that it would have put Mrs. Casnoff to shame.

The angel was very familiar to me, and I realized with a start that it was the same one depicted in the stained-glass window at Hecate. The angel that cast out the Prodigium.

"What . . ." I broke off and cleared my throat. "What is this place?"

Alice was gazing up at the angel with a faint smile. "A secret," she answered.

I shivered and pulled my blazer tighter around me. I wanted to ask her what she meant by that, but there was a steely look on her face that told me I probably wouldn't get an answer. Hadn't the brochure said that one of Hecate's big rules was to never go into the woods? I'd just assumed the woods were dangerous or something.

But maybe it had been more than that.

The wind picked up, rattling the leaves and making my teeth chatter. Why hadn't I thought to grab shoes, I wondered as I rubbed one numb foot on top of the other.

"Here," Alice said, pointing to my feet. They tickled for a moment, and as I watched, my feet were suddenly encased first in wooly white socks and then in my favorite pair of fuzzy red slippers. Slippers that, as far as I knew, were still sitting in the bottom of my closet in Vermont.

"How did you do that?"

But Alice just smiled mysteriously.

And then without warning she whipped her hand through the air.

I felt a heavy blow right in my chest that knocked me off my feet. I hit the ground with a startled, "Oomph!"

Sitting up, I glared at her. "What was that?"

"That," she said sharply, "was a ridiculously simple attack spell that you should have been able to block."

I stared at her in shock. It was one thing to get laid out by Archer in Defense, but being attacked out of nowhere by my great-grandmother was just embarrassing.

"How could I have blocked it when I had no idea you were going to do that?" I fired back.

Alice walked over to me and offered her hand to pull me up. I didn't take it, mainly because I was pissed, but also because Alice looked like she weighed about ninety pounds, and I thought I'd probably end up pulling her down with me.

"You should have been able to sense that I was going to do that, Sophia. Someone with power as great as yours can always anticipate an attack."

"What is this?" I asked, dusting the dirt and pine needles of my now-sore butt. "A Star Wars thing? I was supposed to 'sense a disturbance in the Force'?"

Now it was Alice's turn to blink in confusion.

"Forget it," I mumbled. "Anyway, if you've been watching me at all over the past six weeks, you've probably picked up on the fact that I don't have any 'great power.' I'm like, the least powerful witch here. Clearly, the awesome family superpowers passed this gal by."

Alice shook her head. "No they didn't. I can feel it. Your powers are every bit as great as mine. You just don't know how to use them yet. That's why I'm here. To help you sharpen and mold them. To prepare you for the role you must play."

I looked up at her. "So you're like, my own personal Mr. Miyagi?"

"I have no idea what that means."

"Sorry, sorry. I'll try to stop with the pop culture references. What do you mean the *role* I must play?"

Alice looked at me like I was stupid. And in her defense, I felt pretty stupid.

"Head of the Council."

CHAPTER 22

"Okay, why would I want that?" I asked with small laugh. "I know nothing about Prodigium, and I'm a crappy witch."

The wind caught my hair, blowing it into my mouth and eyes. Through the strands covering my face, I saw Alice flick her hand toward me. My hair swept back from my face and gathered itself into a bun on top of my head. It was so tight my eyes watered.

"Sophia," Alice said in the tone used to placate a tantrum-throwing toddler, "you only think you're crappy."

The word "crappy" sounded ridiculously classy in Alice's cut-glass accent, and I had to smile a little. I guess she saw that as a good sign, because she took my hand. Her skin was soft and ice-cold to the touch.

"Sophia," she said in a softer voice, "you're incredibly

powerful. You're just at a disadvantage because you've been raised by a human. With the right training and guidance, you could put those other girls—what do you and your half-breed friend call them? 'The Witches of Noxema'?"

"Jenna's not a half-breed," I said quickly, but she ignored me. "You could be far, far more powerful than any of them. And I can show you how."

"But why?" I asked.

She smiled in that enigmatic way again and patted my arm. Even though I knew Alice had died at eighteen, which made her just two years older than me, there was something very grandmotherly in her touch. And after a lifetime of having just Mom as family, it felt nice.

"Because you're my blood," she answered. "Because you deserve to be better. To become what you are meant to be."

I didn't know what to say to that. Was head of the Council what I was meant to be? I thought of my one-time fantasy of owning one of those New Age bookshops, reading palms and wearing a big purple caftan. That seemed very far away now and, honestly, kind of stupid.

And then I thought of Elodie, Chaston, and Anna glowing and levitating in the library. They had looked like goddesses, and even though I'd been scared, I'd envied them. Was it really possible that I could become better than them?

Alice laughed. "Oh, you'll be much better than those girls."

Great, she could read my mind.

"Come, we haven't much time left."

We walked past the cemetery and into a clearing inside a ring of oak trees. "This is where we'll meet," Alice said. "This is where I'll train you to be the witch you should be."

"You do know that I have class, right? I can't stay up all night."

Alice reached down and slipped a necklace off her neck. Her hands glowed with a light brighter than the orb still floating above us. Then the light abruptly went out and she handed the necklace to me. It was almost too hot to touch. Just a simple silver chain with a square pendant about the size of a postage stamp. In the center was a teardrop-shaped black stone.

"There. Family heirloom," she said. "As long as you're wearing that, you'll never become too tired."

I looked at the necklace with appreciation. "Will I learn that spell?"

And for the first time, Alice smiled a real smile, a broad one that lit her whole face and made her slightly plain features beautiful.

She leaned in and took both my hands in hers, pulling me close until our faces were inches apart. "All that and more," she whispered. And when she broke out into giggles, I found myself laughing too.

Several hours later, I was not laughing. I wasn't even cracking a smile.

"Again!" Alice barked. How did a girl so tiny have a voice so loud? I sighed and rolled my shoulders. I focused as hard as I could on the empty space in front of me, willing with all my might for a pencil to appear. For the first hour, we'd just worked on blocking spells. I'd done pretty well blocking Alice's attack spells, even though I hadn't been able to sense them coming. But for the past hour we'd been working on making something appear out of nothing. We'd started small, hence the pencil, and Alice claimed it was just a matter of concentrating.

But I'd been concentrating so hard that I was afraid I'd now be seeing bright yellow Number 2 pencils every time I closed my eyes. I'd vibrated the grass a bunch, and after one particularly frustrating moment, I'd sent a rock flying toward Alice, but no pencils.

"Should we start even smaller?" Alice asked. "A paper clip, perhaps? An ant?"

I cut my eyes at her and took another deep breath.

Pencil, pencil, pencil, I thought. Bright yellow pencil, soft pink eraser, SAT, please, please . . .

And then I felt it. That feeling like water rushing up

from the soles of my feet and into my fingertips. But this wasn't just water. This was a river. Everything inside of me seemed to be vibrating. I felt a burning behind my eyes, but it was a good sort of heat, the way a sun-warmed car seat feels on your back on a cool day. My face ached, and I realized it was because I was smiling.

The pencil faded in slowly, looking like a ghost of itself at first, before finally becoming solid. I kept my hands out, the magic still pulsing through me, and turned to Alice to say something along the lines of "Neener neener!"

But then I saw that she wasn't looking at me. She was looking past me, where the pencil was. I turned back and gasped.

Now there wasn't just one pencil in front of me. There was a pile of maybe thirty spilling over each other, and more were popping up.

I dropped my hands and felt the magic stop instantly, like a connection had been severed.

"Holy crap!" I exclaimed softly.

"My, my," was Alice's only comment.

"I . . ." I stared at the pile. "I did that," I said finally, even as I mentally kicked myself for sounding so stupid.

"Indeed you did," Alice said, shaking her head a little. Then she smiled. "I told you so."

I laughed, but then a thought occurred to me.

"Wait. You said your sleeping spell lasts for only four hours." I glanced at my watch. "It's been almost four hours now, and it took us at least half an hour to get out here. How are we going to get back in time?"

Alice smiled, and with a snap of her fingers, two brooms suddenly materialized beside her.

"You're joking," I said.

The smile broadened, and she threw one leg over a broom and zoomed off into the sky. She came back down and hovered a few feet above my head, and her laugh echoed throughout the woods. "Come on, Sophia!" she called. "Be traditional for once!"

Heaving myself off the ground, I grabbed the slender neck of the broom. "Is this thing gonna hold me?" I called up to her. "We don't all shop at Baby Gap!"

This time she didn't bother to ask me what I was talking about. She just laughed and said, "I'd hurry if I were you! Fifteen minutes stand between you and year-long cellar duty!"

So I straddled the broom. I wasn't quite as ladylike as Alice, but when the broom suddenly lifted into the air, I didn't care how undignified I looked.

I grabbed the handle tighter and gave a startled yelp as the night air rushed over me. And then I was in the sky.

I'd assumed the broom would rush off and that I'd be hanging on for dear life, but instead it sort of glided, and

I caught my breath, not out of fear but out of a feeling of sheer exhilaration. The air was cold but soft around me, and as I followed Alice back to the school, I gathered the courage to look down at the trees below me. Alice had extinguished the orb, so all I could really make out were dark blobs, but I didn't care. I was flying—actually honest-to-God *flying*.

The stars overhead felt close enough to touch, and my heart felt like it was floating free in my chest. In the distance I could see the green glow of the bubble around Hecate, and I hoped we would never get there, that I could just go on feeling this light, this free, forever.

Too soon, we touched down just in front of the porch. My cheeks felt chapped and my hands were numb, but I was smiling like a lunatic.

"That," I pronounced, "was the most awesome thing ever. Why don't all witches do that?"

Alice laughed as she dismounted. "I suppose it's thought of as a cliché."

"Well, screw that noise," I said. "When I'm head of the Council, that's going to be the only way to travel."

Alice laughed again. "Glad to hear it."

As we watched, the bubble around Hecate began to dim.

"Guess that means I should go in," I said. "So, same time, same place tomorrow?"

Alice nodded and then reached into the pocket of her dress and pulled out a small pouch. "Take this with you."

The bag was soft in my hand, and I could feel its contents shifting. "What is this?"

"Dirt from my grave. Should you ever need extra power for a spell, just pour a little on your hands and that should do it."

"Okay. Um, thanks." It would be nice to have a little extra magic mojo, but inside, all I could think was, Grave dirt? Gross.

"And, Sophia," Alice added as I turned to go.

"Yeah?"

She walked up to me and took my shoulders, pulling my head down to her mouth. For a second I thought she was going to kiss me on the cheek or something, but then she whispered, "Be careful. The Eye sees you, even here."

I jerked back, my heart pounding and my mouth dry, but before I could reply, Alice gave a sad smile and faded away.

CHAPTER 23

"So," I breathlessly asked Archer a week later, "have you picked out the perfect shade of pink for your tux yet?"

We were in Defense, and I was only winded because I'd just delivered a blow that had sent Archer to the mat for the fifth time that day. My lack of oxygen had nothing to do with how good he looked in his tight T-shirt. I couldn't believe I'd knocked him down so many times. Either he was getting worse, or I was getting a lot better. I mean, I was never going to be on *American Gladiators*, but I wasn't half bad. *And* I'd been out all night.

My necklace bumped against my chest as I leaned down to offer Archer a hand. Alice's charm had worked like a . . . well, you get it. I'd only gotten about two hours of sleep for the first three nights, and yet I'd woken up feeling fine. The first morning I'd lived in fear that Mrs.

Casnoff was going to pull me into her office and ask if I knew anything about a sleeping spell someone had put on the school, but when that hadn't happened, I'd started to relax a little. Now I didn't even bother to sleep. I'd just lie there in the dark, feeling as antsy as a kid on Christmas Eve until I saw the soft green glow spill through my windows. Then I'd rush outside, jump onto my broom, and soar through the night sky until I got to the cemetery.

I knew what I was doing was dangerous and maybe a little stupid. But when I rode through the sky or did spells so powerful I'd never dreamed they existed, it was hard to remember that.

Archer grinned as I helped him to his feet.

"No, seriously," I said. "Elodie was saying earlier that you two were going to match. So what shade is it? 'Tickled Pink'? 'Rambling Rose,' maybe? Ooh, ooh, I know! 'Virgin's Blush'!"

The All Hallow's Eve Ball was just a week away, and it seemed like that was all anyone was talking about. Even in Byron's class our assignment had been to compose a sonnet about the outfit we were going to wear. I still had no idea what I was wearing. Ms. East was in charge of teaching us the transformation spell that would create our dresses and tuxes. Just yesterday she'd given us each a dummy dressed in something that looked like a pillow-case with armholes. I didn't know why we couldn't just transform clothes we already owned, but I figured it was just another one of Hecate's dumb rules.

The shapeshifters and faeries had to get their own clothes, which meant that boxes had been arriving nonstop for the past few days.

And then there was Jenna. I'd offered to make her a dress, but she'd looked at me like I was completely stupid and said there was no way she was going to that "idiotic dance."

We'd been working on the spell every day in Ms. East's class, but so far everything I'd attempted had come out a little too poufy. Ms. East said that was just because I was too excited, but I didn't really buy that. There was nothing all that exciting about the ball for me. I wasn't "giving myself" to anyone.

"Shut up," Archer said good-naturedly, lifting his arms over his head to stretch. "For your information, only my bow tie will be pink, and I plan on *rocking* it, thank you very much."

I tried to smile back, but I was trying not to stare at the ribbon of skin that was showing beneath his T-shirt as he bent over.

As usual, my mouth went a little dry and my breathing sped up, and that weird, almost sad feeling settled in my stomach.

I never thought I'd be glad to hear the Vandy's braying

voice, but when she shouted, "All right! That's it for today!" I could have kissed her.

Well, on second thought, no. Maybe a firm handshake.

"Holy hell weasel," I muttered an hour later.

I was staring at my latest attempt at a ball gown. At least this one had avoided a serious case of the poufies, but it was also a noxious shade of yellow-green usually found in baby's diapers or around nuclear disasters.

"Well, Miss Mercer. That's . . . an improvement, I suppose," Ms. East said. Her lips were pursed so tightly, it was a wonder any words had come out at all.

"Right," Jenna said. She was sitting on a desk next to me. She spent most of the class reading those mangas she liked so much. "You're getting better," she said encouragingly, but she frowned as she took in my latest creation.

"Yeah, at least this one didn't knock over three desks," Elodie sneered from beside me.

Her dress, of course, was gorgeous.

I'd assumed the ball was like the monster version of prom, and that the dresses would be similar to anything you'd see in a regular high school. Yeah, not so much. The dresses most of the girls were working on looked like something out of a fairy tale.

But Elodie's dress was easily the prettiest in the class. High-waisted with delicate cap sleeves and frothy skirts, it looked like something you'd wear if you were in a Jane Austen book. I'd teased Archer about it being pink, but even I had to admit that the shade of pink was really lovely. Nowhere near "Electric Raspberry," it was more the pale pink that you sometimes find inside shells. It seemed to glow like a pearl, and Elodie was going to be devastatingly beautiful in it.

Damn it.

Frustrated, I turned back to my own dress. I put my hands on either side of the dummy's waist and thought, *Beautiful dress, beautiful dress, something blue,* as hard as I could. It was so annoying to know that I could now make something as big as a chair appear out of thin air, but I couldn't seem to make a dress that wasn't completely heinous. Okay, so the chair I'd conjured up last night was toddler-size, but still.

I felt the material shift and slip under my hands. *Please,* I thought, my eyes squeezed shut.

Then I heard Elodie and Anna burst out laughing.

Crap.

I opened my eyes to stare at a bright blue tulle monstrosity with a skirt that would hit me at mid thigh. I'd look like the really slutty bride of Cookie Monster.

I muttered a really bad word under my breath, which earned me an evil look from Ms. East, but surprisingly, no punishment. I guess she couldn't really blame me after she looked at the dress.

"Wow, Sophie, that's really something." Elodie sauntered over to me, one hand on her hip. "I think you have a real future in fashion design."

"Ha-ha," I muttered, which, as far as comebacks go, is about as cool as saying, "So there."

"I can't believe I actually invited you to join my coven," she said, turning those bright green eyes on me.

I groaned inwardly. Elodie's eyes were only that bright when she was about to deliver a huge smackdown. The last time I'd seen her like this was the night she'd called Jenna a bloodsucking freak after they'd found Chaston.

"Here you are, the head of the Council's daughter, and you can't even make a *dress*. Pathetic."

"Look, Elodie, I don't want to fight. So just . . . just leave me alone and let me work on my dress, okay?"

But she wasn't remotely finished with me.

"Why do you even care about making a dress for the ball? Who have you got to look pretty for? Archer?"

I fought very hard to keep cool, even as my hands tightened around the material in front of me.

Elodie leaned in closer, so I doubted anyone else heard it when she whispered, "You think I don't see the way you look at him?"

Keeping my eyes on the dummy, I said in the

lowest, calmest voice possible, "Stop it, Elodie."

"I mean, your crush on him is just so sweet. And by sweet, of course I mean *tragic*," she continued. From the corner of my eye, I could see that almost everyone had stopped working and was watching us. Ms. East was pretending to ignore us, so I knew I was being thrown to the wolves on this one.

I took a deep breath and turned around to face Elodie, who was smirking at me in triumph.

"Oh, Elodie," I said in a voice that was so sweet it practically dripped syrup, "don't worry about me and Archer. After all, I'm not the one planning on having sex with him at the ball."

The class erupted into giggles, and Elodie did something I'd never seen her do: she turned bright red and actually sputtered in her attempt to come up with a serious put-down.

Ms. East chose that moment to shout, "Miss Mercer! Miss Parris! Back to work!"

Smiling, I turned back to my dress. But the feeling of triumph was immediately deflated by the bright blue disaster in front of me.

"Does your magic feel off or anything?" Jenna asked softly.

"No, it feels the same as always. Water rushing up from my feet and all that."

"What?" Anna sneered, propping a hand on her hip. "*How* does your magic feel?"

"Uh . . . like something coming up from underneath me," I said, rushing to get the words out.

"That's not what magic feels like," Anna said.

I glanced around and saw that there were a few other witches staring at me in confusion.

"Magic comes from above," Anna continued. "It feels like something falling over you, like . . ."

"Snow," Elodie finished.

My face was hot when I turned back to my dummy. "I guess mine is just different, then."

I heard some whispers, but I ignored them.

"You'll get it," Jenna said, shooting Anna a dirty look.

"Oh, I know I'm gonna get better," I told her, running a hand over the tulle bustle in the back of the dress. (A *bustle*? Screw you, magical powers.) "This is the dress I'm making for you."

"Oh, really?" she asked, her smile widening.

"Yeah, we'll probably have to hem it, though. Don't want it dragging on the floor."

She playfully smacked my arm with the back of her hand, and before I knew it, we were laughing.

I spent the rest of the class attempting to make the ugliest dresses possible, which was only funny to me and Jenna. I lost count of how many times Ms. East threatened to throw us out of class, and Elodie rolled her eyes so much that Jenna finally asked if she was having a seizure. This made us laugh so hard that Ms. East finally did kick us out, and gave us both a seven-page essay to write on the history of clothing spells.

I didn't care. To have Jenna laughing again, I would have written a hundred pages.

"I don't know what changed," I told Alice later that night as we moved through the forest, picking mint for some spell that could slow time. "One minute she was the same sulky Jenna she's been for the past month, the next we were friends again."

Alice didn't say anything, so I said, "Isn't that great?"

"I suppose."

"You suppose?" I said, mocking her accent.

She straightened and glared at me. "It's just that I don't approve of your having a vampire for a bosom companion. It's beneath you."

I laughed. "Oh my God, *beneath* me? Come on."

Alice sighed as she shoved another bunch of leaves into the small leather sack she'd conjured. "Your friends are your concern, Sophia. I'll try to respect that. Now tell me about this party you have coming up."

I bent down to pick another bunch of mint. "It's a ball, actually. For Halloween. It should be awesome. Especially since I can't manage to make a dress that doesn't completely suck. Oh, and—bonus—I get to suffer through watching a girl I despise be totally beautiful and seduce a guy I like. Should be good times."

"Elodie?"

I nodded.

Alice scowled. "I don't care for that girl. She's been quite hateful toward you. Undoubtedly because your powers are so superior to her own. There are few things more abhorrent to me than a weak witch."

"Wow, tell me what you *really* think."

Alice blinked at me. "I just did."

"Forget it. It's just so unfair that she's such a heinous person, but her dress spell has turned out so beautifully. She's going to look amazing."

And have sex with Archer, I added silently.

I'd forgotten Alice could read my mind. "Oh. Is Archer that boy you fancy?"

There was no use in denying that I "fancied" him. I nodded.

"Humph," Alice replied. "Why not just use a love charm on him? They're frightfully simple."

I shoved some more mint into my bag. "Because I . . . Look, this sounds stupid, but I really like him, and I don't want him to like me back if it's just, like, some spell."

I thought Alice might argue with me, but she just

238

shrugged and said, "Attraction has its own magic, I suppose."

"Yeah, well, there's probably no chance of him ever being attracted to me. I thought maybe at the ball . . . but I can't even make a decent dress."

I turned to Alice. "Why is it that when I'm out here with you, I can do completely kick-ass spells, but when I'm in the school, everything I do blows up in my face?"

"Confidence?" she suggested. "You feel unsure of yourself in that school, and it's reflected in your magic."

"Maybe."

We continued picking plants for a while until Alice said, "You say this girl's dress is beautiful?"

I sighed. "It's perfect."

Alice smiled, and in the light from the orb, I could swear her teeth actually gleamed.

"Would you like to change that?"

CHAPTER 24

Classes were canceled the day of the ball, and since it was another one of those beautiful, clear October days, nearly everybody spent it outside. Everybody but me. Well, me and Jenna. Even with her bloodstone, she wasn't the biggest fan of the outdoors. She was curled up in her usual spot, on her bed, covered with her throw, and a manga in her hand.

I sat on my bed staring at my stupid dress dummy, which was still wearing the pillowcase. I'd spent most of the morning trying to turn it into something at least halfway presentable, and had had absolutely no luck. I couldn't figure it out; I knew I wasn't the world's best witch, but a transformation spell just should not have been this hard. True, I'd never attempted anything as elaborate before, but I should have at least been able to make a little black dress. But even that had turned out shapeless, with a crooked hem to boot.

I sighed, and Jenna exclaimed, "Damn, Sophie, I'm supposed to be the moper. What is your problem?"

"This freaking dress." I pointed at the offending object. "Nothing I do works."

Jenna shrugged. "So don't go."

I glared at her. Jenna wasn't going to the ball, so she didn't understand why I so badly wanted to go. I didn't really understand why I wanted to go either, although it probably had a lot to do with Archer in a tux.

I didn't want to tell Jenna that, though. "It's not the ball; it's the principle of the thing. I should be able to do this spell. It's just not that hard."

"Maybe somebody cursed your dummy," she joked, turning back to her manga.

My hand sneaked into my pocket and closed around the small object that seemed to be burning a hole there.

When Alice suggested doing a spell on Elodie's dress, I had initially said no way. "I could get kicked out for doing magic on another student," I'd told her.

"But it wouldn't be you," Alice argued. "It would be me. You would just be the carrier, as it were."

That had made sense, and I have to admit I'd felt a little giddy when Alice had reached into her pocket and pulled out a tiny bone, probably from a bird. Alice having bones in her pocket probably should've freaked me out, but by that point I was used to Alice's weirdness. Like the necklace that first night, the bone glowed softly in her hands. She'd smiled as she gave it to me. "Just slip this into the hem of her dress."

"Do I need to say any special words or anything?"

"No. The bone will know what to do."

I remembered those words now as I fingered the small, smooth bone. I'd had it for a week, and I still hadn't used it. Alice had promised that the bone would only turn Elodie's dress some horrible color when Elodie put it on, and that didn't sound too bad. Still, I was worried. Every spell I'd ever tried to do on another person had gone badly, and even though I didn't like Elodie, I didn't want to accidentally hurt her. So the bone had stayed in my pocket.

But if I wasn't going to use it, why hadn't I thrown it out?

With another sigh, I got off my bed and went to the dummy. Even though it didn't have a head, its very posture seemed to be mocking me. "What up, loser?" I imagined it saying. "I'd rather wear this pillowcase than any of your ugly designs."

"Shut up," I murmured as I put my hands on it and, yet again, concentrated as hard as I could. "Blue, pretty, please . . ." I muttered.

The fabric rippled and promptly became a sequined, bright blue hot pants outfit that looked like a majorette's uniform.

"Crap, crap, crap!" I cried, hitting the dummy so that it spun on its stand.

Jenna looked up from her book. "Now that's fetching."

"Not helpful," I growled. God, what was *wrong* with me? I'd done spells way harder than this, and they'd never, ever come out this badly.

"I'm telling you," Jenna said, "you got a bum dummy. Nobody else seems to be having this hard a time with theirs."

"I know," I said, leaning my head on the dummy. "Even Sarah Williams, who is, like, the worst witch ever, made this really pretty red dress. It's not as fancy as Elodie's but—"

I stopped, a sinking feeling in my stomach.

It didn't make sense for me to be having so much trouble making a dress. Maybe Jenna was right: maybe my dummy was cursed.

I pressed my hands to the pillowcase again, but this time I didn't think of a dress. I just said, "'Fess up."

For a moment nothing happened. I wasn't sure whether I should feel relieved or disappointed.

Then, very slowly, two glowing handprints the faint

burgundy color of watered-down wine appeared on the front of the dress.

Relief surged through me, but that was quickly swallowed up by a white-hot wave of anger.

"How did you do that?" Jenna asked from behind me. She was on her knees staring at the handprints.

"It's a revelation spell," I said through clenched teeth. "Lets you know if an object has been messed with magically."

"Well, at least you know that you're not a crap witch."

I nodded, but I was nearly shaking with fury. Here I'd been thinking I was just useless, and it had been Elodie all along. It had to be her. Who else would want to make sure I couldn't go to the ball? God, the whole thing was almost too fairy tale to handle.

And the thing that really bothered me was that I hadn't used my curse on her dress. I'd felt *bad* about using it.

Well, screw that.

"Where's Elodie right now?" I asked Jenna.

Her eyes were wide, so I knew I must have looked pretty scary.

"Um, I heard Anna say they were going down to the beach with a bunch of people."

"Perfect."

I headed for the door, ignoring Jenna as she called out, "What are you going to do?"

I hurried toward Elodie's room. There was no one in the hall to see me as I slipped in.

My heart pounding, both out of fear and anger, I walked over to the window, where Anna's and Elodie's dress dummies stood. Anna's dress was black with purple trim and a short train. She'd look amazing in it, but it was nothing compared to Elodie's dress.

I hesitated for a moment.

Then I thought of Elodie laughing at me in class as I'd tried so hard to make just one damn dress, and my nerve came back.

I dropped to my knees and fished around in the filmy layers of skirts until I found a small gap in the hem. I slid the tiny bone inside and gave it a light pat. It glowed brightly inside the dress, shining dull red through all the layers of pink. I held my breath until the glow went out, then I ran for the door.

The hall was empty, so I was able to sneak back to my room unseen.

Jenna was still sitting on her bed when I came in.

"What did you do?"

I walked over to my bed and pulled out the small pouch of dirt I'd hidden there. "Let's just say turnabout is fair play."

Jenna opened her mouth, but then closed it again as she watched me pour some of the dirt on my hands. She probably thought I'd totally cracked up as I marched over to my dummy with dirt-covered hands, grasped it around the waist, and closed my eyes.

This time I didn't even think anything specific. "Dress," was all I said.

As usual, I could feel the dress slip and slide under my hands, but it was different this time. My hands felt hot, and it was like there was an electric current running through me.

I heard Jenna gasp, and when I stepped back and opened my eyes, I gasped too.

The dress wasn't just beautiful, it was stunning.

It was peacock blue satin, and green lights seemed to dance inside the fabric. The top looked like a corset, strapless and boned in the front, and as I spun the dummy to the back, I saw that it laced up with a bright green ribbon.

The skirt belled out from the cinched-in waist, and, most impressive of all, there was a panel of actual peacock feathers running down the front, starting at a point just under the corset top and widening as it reached the bottom, like an upside-down triangle.

"Whoa," Jenna breathed. "Now that is a dress. Sophie, you're going to be gorgeous."

She was right, I thought, feeling dazed. I would look gorgeous.

"What was that stuff you put on it?"

I wasn't ready to tell Jenna about Alice, and I had a feeling she wouldn't take the words *grave dust* well, so I just shrugged. "Magic powder."

Jenna looked skeptical, but before she could ask any more questions, I gave her a bright smile and said, "Let me make you one."

She gave a startled laugh. "You really wanna make me a dress?"

I nodded. "Why not? It'll be fun, and then you can come with me to the ball."

"I don't think so, Soph," she protested weakly, but I was already pulling one of her nightgowns out of her dresser. I pressed my still-dirty hands on it and just thought, *Jenna*.

All of Jenna's protests died on her lips when she saw the dress: hot pink, with thin straps and a sparkling belt at the waist that I thought might be made out of real diamonds. The dress was perfect for her, and before long she was holding it up and spinning around.

"I don't know what your 'magic powder' is, and I don't care," she said with a laugh. "This is the most beautiful dress I've ever seen!"

We spent the rest of the afternoon transforming our shoes until we each had the perfect pair. By the time evening fell, we were both dressed, and if I do say so myself, looking pretty hot. Jenna had piled her white-blond hair on top of her head, with her pink streak falling over one eye. My own hair was actually behaving for once, and I'd let Jenna arrange it into a low bun at the base of my neck, a few tendrils escaping around my face.

We walked downstairs arm in arm, giggling. There was a crush of people in the narrow hallway leading to the ballroom. I craned my neck, looking for Archer and Elodie, hoping to discover what gross color Elodie's dress had become, but I couldn't see them.

I'd been pretty impressed with Jenna's and my dresses in our room, but now I saw that we were hardly the most spectacular people there. A tall blond faerie bumped into me, and her dress, a concoction of ice-green sparkles, chimed softly, like bells. I also saw a shapeshifter in what looked to be a gown made entirely of white fur.

The boys were a little more sedate. Most of them were just in tuxes, although a few had been more daring and were wearing long coats and breeches.

We were just about to enter the ballroom when I felt something warm press up against my back. I thought it was just some random person crowding me, until a voice whispered in my ear, soft and low, "I knew it was you."

CHAPTER 25

I tried to whirl around, but it's hard to do when you're squashed between a bunch of people and wearing a big dress. I ended up accidently elbowing Jenna, who gave a startled squawk, before I could finally turn to face Archer.

Both of us widened our eyes and said, "Whoa."

Then I immediately blushed. Oh my God, had I just looked at Archer and said, "Whoa"?

But . . . wait a minute. Had Archer just looked at *me* and said, "Whoa"?

We just kind of stared at each other. Archer more than deserved his "whoa." This was a boy who could make a school uniform look good. What he did to formal wear was damn near criminal. He had lied about his bow tie being pink. He wasn't even wearing a bow tie, just a regular tie, and it was black, like everything else he was wearing.

But the best part wasn't the way he looked. It was the way he was looking at me.

"That dress," he said at last, his eyes still skimming over me. "It's . . . something."

I fought the urge to self-consciously tug at the low neckline and just smiled. "Thanks. I just, uh, whipped it up."

He nodded, but he still looked a little shell-shocked, and it was all I could do to keep a big goofy grin off my face.

Then I remembered what he'd said. "What do you mean, you knew it was me?"

He shook his head a little, like he was trying to clear it. "Oh, right. Elodie."

My heart seemed to stutter in my chest, and I could actually feel my face paling.

"I just saw you from the back and said that had to be you. Elodie said there was no way it could be."

"Oh." I glanced over and saw Elodie coming up behind him. She glared at me, and I was surprised to see that her dress looked perfect.

The bone will know what to do, my ass, I thought, but I was kind of relieved. My anger had faded once I'd been able to make a killer dress. I figured that was a way better revenge than messing up her dress anyway.

"How on earth did you pull that together?" Elodie

asked. She tried to keep her tone sweet, but her eyes were cold and angry.

I just smiled back and shrugged. "It was the weirdest thing. Apparently I got a cursed dummy."

Her eyes widened a little before she broke my gaze. "Weird," she mumbled.

"Yeah, it was. Luckily, I was able to lift the curse, and then—tada!" I held my skirt out with a bright smile, and was rewarded with Elodie's scowl.

"Don't you think it's a little . . . loud?" she asked.

Before I could answer with something cutting, Archer turned to her. "Oh, come on, El. She looks great and you know it."

That did it. The goofy grin could no longer be held back. Archer smiled and winked as he and Elodie slid past us and into the ballroom.

I turned to Jenna, who laughed and rolled her eyes. "Oh, girl, you got it *bad*."

She was still giggling, and I was still smiling like a lunatic when we entered the ballroom. I don't know what I had been expecting, but the ballroom blew me away. There were no paper streamers and balloons here. Instead, the room glowed with soft faerie lights, smaller and softer versions of the orb Alice always made for us. Each light rested on what looked like a dark purple flower. They floated high in the air, bobbing softly like they were caught in a gentle breeze. The chandeliers weren't lit, but their crystals had been turned violet for the occasion, and the fairy lights made them sparkle like amethyst. The mirrors were uncovered too. I thought that might bug Jenna, but when we looked in them and saw only me, she just pointed and said, "Look. In Mirrorland, you're still a dateless wonder," which made us both laugh.

The floors were no longer the shiny light wood they usually were, but a deep and glossy black. I shook my head in wonder. "This is . . . wow."

"I know," Jenna said. She took my hand and squeezed it. "I'm so glad you made me come."

We hovered on the edge of things for a while, watching everybody dance. I remembered the prom I'd gone to with Ryan, where everybody had danced like they were auditioning for a rap video. This could not have been more different. The witches and shapeshifters were all waltzing, which freaked me out a little. No one had told me ballroom dancing lessons were a prerequisite for going to Hecate. The faeries were off to one end of the ballroom by themselves, doing some elaborate dance that looked like something out of Elizabethan England.

I spotted Archer and Elodie dancing, and my breath caught at how beautiful they both were: Archer, tall and dark, and Elodie, her hair glowing in the lights, her dress floating around her. But then I looked at their faces and saw that they were clearly arguing. Archer was frowning and looking at a spot somewhere over her head, and Elodie seemed to be talking a mile a minute.

Then suddenly Elodie pulled her hands from Archer's and clutched her side.

A slow feeling of dread rose up in me as I watched Archer lead her off the dance floor. She was trying to smile, but it was more like a grimace. I saw her wave him off and mouth the words "I'm fine." But then she gasped and clutched her side again. I saw Anna push her way through the crowd, Mrs. Casnoff in tow. By now Elodie was nearly bent double.

"I wonder what's going on," Jenna said.

"Maybe she got a stitch in her side."

"Yeah. Maybe."

I looked over and saw that Jenna was looking at me with a troubled expression.

"What?"

"What did you do to Elodie's dress this afternoon?"

"Nothing!" I insisted, but I'm a terrible liar and I knew it was showing all over my face.

Jenna just shook her head and turned back to watch Elodie, who was now being led from the room by Mrs. Casnoff and Anna. Archer went to follow, but Elodie turned back and said something to him. We couldn't hear, obviously, but it was clear from her expression that she was pissed. Whatever she said, Archer backed up a couple of steps and raised his hands in front of him. Elodie turned back to Mrs. Casnoff, and the two of them left the ballroom, Anna and Archer trailing behind.

Archer came back about twenty minutes later, looking flustered and angry.

I could feel Jenna's eyes on my back as I crossed the room to him.

"What was all that about?" I asked him.

He was still looking at the door they'd led Elodie out through. "I don't know. She was fine, then she started saying her dress felt too tight, like it was shrinking or something. It just kept tightening she said, and she was having trouble breathing. Mrs. Casnoff thinks the dress was cursed."

I was glad he was still looking away from me so that he didn't see me flinch.

The bone will know what to do.

Had Alice known this would happen, or had I screwed it up somehow? Maybe I was supposed to use it right away, and the magic on it had, I don't know, soured or something in the week I'd held on to it.

Or she'd known, a voice kept whispering. She never meant for the dress just to change colors. She'd meant for it to hurt Elodie.

But why would Alice want to do that? I knew she

didn't like Elodie, but this seemed really harsh. No, I must have screwed it up somehow, like the love spell on Kevin.

"Hey," Archer said.

"Yeah," I said weakly. Then I smiled and tried to sound more enthusiastic. "Yeah, I'm fine. That's just . . . you know, weird about Elodie."

"Yeah," he agreed, looking back toward the door.

"Is she mad at you or something?" I ventured.

Running a hand though his hair, he sighed and said, "I guess. She told me I should be glad because now I could spend the ball with the person I really wanted."

He looked down at me. "I guess she meant you."

There were people all around us, but suddenly I felt like we were totally alone. And in that moment I swore I could feel something shift between us. Some spark flared that hadn't been there before, at least not on his part.

He looked away again, back toward the door, and then smiled at me. "Well, it seems a shame not to show off that dress. Wanna dance?"

"Sure," I said, going for the most casual tone possible, but my heart was beating so hard I was afraid he'd actually be able to see it. A lot of my chest was on display, after all.

He pulled me onto the dance floor, one hand warm on my waist, the other holding my hand high at shoulder level. I was scared to death that I would trip on my dress or step on his feet, but thanks to Archer, we glided across the ballroom.

"You can dance?" I asked.

He looked down at me with a smile. "A few years ago, Casnoff decided to teach a formal dancing class. Attendance was mandatory."

"I could've used that."

"Nah, you're doing fine. Just hold on to me."

I'd never been given better instructions. There was no band or sound system that I could see, just dreamy music that seemed to float in from everywhere and nowhere. My fingers rested lightly on Archer's shoulder as we spun around the room. We danced near the spot where I'd left Jenna. I looked for her, but I couldn't see her. I wondered if she had gone back up to the room, and felt a little guilty. But then Archer's hand tightened on my waist, and Jenna slid completely from my mind.

I looked up to see him studying me intensely with an expression I'd never seen before. Well, one he'd never directed at me before.

"She was right," he murmured.

"About what?" I said, and my voice didn't even sound like mine. It was low and breathy.

"I did want to spend the ball with you."

I felt like a thousand sparklers had just gone off inside me. The smile that began to spread across my face actually made my face hurt, and for the first time I didn't care if he saw it.

I knew I didn't have a crush on Archer anymore.

I was in love with him.

His face lowered, and my heart stopped. "Sophie—"

But before he could finish, a scream pierced the air.

The music stopped abruptly. Nearly everyone turned to see Elodie rushing back into the ballroom, a green silk robe flapping around her pale legs, and a look of horror on her face.

"It's Anna!" she was screaming. "It's happened again! I . . . Oh God, I think she's dead."

CHAPTER 26

Anna wasn't dead, thank God. They'd found her sprawled in the hallway just in front of her room. Elodie said Anna had gone to get her some tea from the kitchen. When she hadn't come back, Elodie had been worried and went to look for her.

That's when she'd discovered her, facedown in the hall, a puddle of tea and her own blood soaking into the thick cream-colored rug. Just like Holly, just like Chaston, she had two small holes in her neck, but her wrists weren't cut.

Cal had gotten to her in time, and by the time Mrs. Casnoff came running up the stairs, Anna was sitting up, her head lolling against Cal's shoulder.

Just like Chaston, she couldn't say who had attacked her.

Jenna had been back in our room, and seemed totally unaware of what had happened to Anna.

But she'd been right down the hall.

Sometime around midnight, Mrs. Casnoff had come to get her. They hadn't come back.

I lay awake in my bed, still in my dress, long into the night. Luckily, Alice and I had decided not to meet tonight, so I didn't have to worry about her sleeping spell suddenly taking hold.

Around three, I finally fell asleep, but I spent the rest of the night tossing and turning from nightmares. I saw Jenna, her mouth stained with blood, and Anna at her feet. I saw Archer and Elodie dancing, only Elodie was pale, her lips blue and her eyes staring as her dress clutched around her like a snake. And strangest of all, I saw Alice in the cemetery, clutching the iron fence while three men in black descended upon her, silver knives raised high.

I woke up as the first rays of sunlight swept across the floor.

I felt disoriented. My mouth was dry and sticky, like I'd spent the night eating lint. There was also a low, hollow ringing sound. At first I thought it was just in my ears. Then I realized it was the bell on top of the house, the bell that usually called us to classes. Why was it ringing this early in the morning?

Then last night came back to me in a rush. I looked over to Jenna's bed, but it was still empty.

I pushed myself out of bed and stuck my head out the door. Several girls were already dressed and headed down the stairs. I saw Nausicaa and called out to her, "Hey! What's going on?"

"Assembly," she answered. "You'd better get dressed."

I shut the door and shimmied out of my gown. It became a pillowcase again as soon as it hit the floor. I set some sort of land-speed record for getting dressed, and decided to just leave my hair up in the chignon I'd worn last night. It was a lot messier now, and half of it was falling around my face, but I figured no one would care.

We all met in the ballroom, which had been transformed back into the room we all knew, complete with mismatched tables. As I sat at a table near the back, I looked up and noticed a lone fairy light high on the ceiling. It bumped gently against a corner, like it was trying to find a way out.

All the teachers had gathered on the dais up front, except for Byron. Mrs. Casnoff looked tired and older than I'd ever seen her. I noticed with a shock that her hair wasn't in its usual complicated bun, but was caught in a sloppy knot at the back of her neck.

Archer and Elodie were sitting up front and to the left of me. Elodie looked pale, and there were still tears streaking down her face. Archer had his arm around her, his lips moving in the hair at her temple. Then, like he knew I was watching them, he turned and looked at me. I dropped my eyes, my hands fisted in my skirt.

After Anna and Jenna, I'd nearly forgotten about me and Archer, but now our encounter from last night came flying back at me, slamming into my heart.

Thankfully, Mrs. Casnoff stood up and raised her hands for silence, so I could turn my eyes to her and not Archer.

"Students," she began, "as I'm sure you know, there was another attack last night. Miss Gilroy is going to be all right, but as this is the third attack in less than a year, we obviously have had to take some drastic measures. As I'm sure you've all noticed, Lord Byron is not here. Nor is Miss Talbot. Until the Council can get to the bottom of these attacks, vampires are no longer welcome at Hecate."

My heart sank as everyone around me burst into applause. I thought of Jenna, how happy she'd been last night in her pink dress, and felt tears prick my eyes. Where had they taken her?

Mrs. Casnoff said a few more things, mostly about being careful and aware of our surroundings, and that we couldn't drop our guard until we knew for sure what had happened, but I barely heard her. It was true that Jenna had been back up in our room when Anna was attacked, but I'd seen Jenna after she came back from a feeding at the infirmary. She was always worn out and almost drugged. Last night, when Casnoff came to get her, she'd just looked scared.

I didn't realize that the assembly was over until a shapeshifter boy stepped on my toes, getting out of his seat.

Numb, I stood, only to hear Mrs. Casnoff say, "Sophie, Elodie, please wait a moment."

I turned back. Elodie looked as confused as I felt.

"If the two of you would kindly go to my office."

Archer gave Elodie's arm a quick squeeze before leaving. His eyes met mine as he passed me. He gave me a smile, and I tried to smile back. Whatever had happened between me and Archer last night had been a freak incident, one I knew would just be easier to pretend had never happened. He was clearly with Elodie, and I couldn't blame him. Not only was she gorgeous, but now all her friends were gone. What kind of jerk would break up with a girl the day after her best friend had had nearly all her blood drained?

Not that it was a situation that came up often, I guess.

Elodie and I walked to Mrs. Casnoff's office, our shoulders brushing in the narrow hallways.

"I'm really sorry," I started, but Elodie cut me off with a glacial stare. "What, that your best buddy nearly killed another one of my friends, or that you tried to kill me with my own dress?"

I was too tired to even give my crappy lying skills a shot. "The spell wasn't supposed to hurt you. It was just going to turn your dress a different color when you put it on."

Elodie was silent, and when I glanced over at her, I saw that she was watching me with an appraising look. "That was some pretty powerful magic," she said. "And while I don't appreciate nearly being strangled by clothes, it might be a cool spell to learn."

"I'll teach it to you if you'll teach me the curse you put on my dummy," I offered.

Before she could reply, Mrs. Casnoff ushered us into her cramped office. "Come along, ladies."

Once Elodie and I were seated in the tiny chairs, Mrs. Casnoff moved behind her desk. "I'm sure you both know why I wanted to speak with you."

She sighed as she sat down. If it had been anyone else, I would've said she flopped into the chair, but Mrs. Casnoff was way too formal to flop. It was more like a graceful collapse.

"I'm sure it's occurred to you that all these attacks have been exclusively on members of your coven, girls."

Confused, I said, "Oh, I'm not a member of their coven."

Now Mrs. Casnoff looked puzzled. She glanced over

at Elodie, who I now noticed was looking anywhere but at either of us.

"You joined Sophia to your coven without her knowledge?" Mrs. Casnoff asked.

"What?" I yelped. "How is that even possible?"

Elodie blew out a long breath that ruffled her bangs. "Look, we didn't have a choice," she said, still looking down at her lap. It was weird to see Elodie so subdued. Normally she would have rolled her eyes a bunch of times and said something dripping with contempt.

But now she looked downright guilty.

"We needed her," Elodie said to Mrs. Casnoff, her tone pleading. "She wouldn't join with us willingly, so we did the joining ritual without her."

Mrs. Casnoff was glaring at Elodie. "And what did you use in place of her blood?"

"I snuck into her room and took some hair from her brush," Elodie muttered. "But we didn't think it had even worked. There was just this big black puff of smoke when we threw her hair in the fire. That's not supposed to happen."

"Oh my God!" I exploded. "You can't just *do* something like that! I can't believe I felt bad about putting that stupid bone in your dress."

Mrs. Casnoff's glare swung back to me. "You did what?" she asked in a voice so frosty, I was sure I was about to be flash-frozen like a wooly mammoth.

Elodie saw her chance. "That's right! She's the one who nearly killed me last night by putting a charmed bone in my dress!"

"Only because you put a curse on my dress," I fired back.

"Only because you're trying to steal my boyfriend!"

That was apparently the last straw for Mrs. Casnoff.

"Girls!" she yelled, standing up and slamming both of her hands on the desk. "The time for bickering about dresses and boys is over. Two of your sisters were severely injured, and another is *dead*."

"But . . . you've fixed it," Elodie said softly. "You kicked out the vampires."

Mrs. Casnoff sat down in her chair and rubbed a hand over her eyes. "We can't be sure that Jenna or Byron was responsible. Both claim their innocence, and last night neither showed signs of having recently fed."

I thought of the picture in the book about L'Occhio di Dio, the one with the witch drained of blood, and Alice saying that The Eye saw me, even here.

"Mrs. Casnoff," I ventured, "do you think . . . Do you think it's possible that L'Occhio di Dio has gotten into the school?"

"Why would you even think that?" Elodie asked, but Mrs. Casnoff held up her hand.

"It's just that I saw this picture of a witch they had killed, and she had two holes in her neck and hardly any blood, just like Holly and Chaston and Anna. I mean, maybe it's possible—"

Mrs. Casnoff interrupted. "I've also seen that illustration, Sophia, but there is no way L'Occhio di Dio could infiltrate Hecate. There are simply too many protection spells. And even if they could somehow get past those, what would they do? Hide out on this tiny island for months waiting until they could sneak into the school?" She shook her head. "It doesn't make sense."

"Unless they were already in the school," I said.

Mrs. Casnoff raised her eyebrows. "What, as a teacher? Or a student? Impossible."

"But—"

Mrs. Casnoff's voice was gentle, and her eyes were sad as she said, "Sophia, I know you don't want to believe that Jenna is responsible for this. None of us do. But I'm afraid that at this time, it's the most plausible explanation. Jenna is being transported to Council headquarters now, and she'll have a chance to plead her case. But you have to accept that she may be guilty."

My chest tightened at the thought of Jenna, scared and alone, on her way to London, where she'd probably be staked. Maybe even by my own dad.

Reaching across the desk to pat my hand, Mrs. Casnoff

said, "I am sorry." She looked over at Elodie. "I'm sorry for both of you. But perhaps this will give you an opportunity to put aside your differences for now. After all, you're the only members of your coven left here." She looked back at me and gave a wry smile. "Whether you like it or not. Now, I'm excusing the two of you from classes today. Until we get the results of the Council's inquiry, I want you to keep a close eye on each other. Understood?"

We both mumbled yes and then shuffled out of Mrs. Casnoff's office.

I spent the rest of my day in my room. Without Jenna, it felt big and lonely, and it was all I could do not to cry when I looked at her stuffed lion, whom we'd named Bram as a joke, and all her books. They hadn't let her take anything with her.

I stayed in bed through dinner. Sometime after night had fallen, I heard a soft knock on my door, and Archer saying, "Sophie? You in there?" But I didn't answer, and after a while, I heard him walk away.

I lay awake until midnight, when the soft green glow of Alice's spell crept through my windows.

Throwing off my covers, I jumped to my feet, eager to get out of this house and into the sky, and wanting to tell Alice everything that had happened.

I didn't even bother being quiet on the stairs as I

walked to the front door. My hand had just turned the knob when I heard a voice hiss, "Busted!"

My heart in my mouth, I turned around and saw Elodie standing at the foot of the stairs, her arms crossed, and a smirk on her face.

CHAPTER 27

"I knew it," she said, louder now. "I knew you were up to something. When Mrs. Casnoff finds out you've been doing a spell on the whole school, you're going to join your little leech friend in London."

I was still frozen at the door, the knob half turned in my hand. Of all the people to catch me sneaking out, why did it have to be the one person who hated me the most? I stood there thinking of something to say that would keep her from running to Mrs. Casnoff right then and there.

Then I remembered the look on her face when she'd asked me about the bone spell, and an idea occurred to me. I just hoped Alice would go with it.

"Okay, you caught me." I tried smiling sheepishly, but probably just looked deranged, because Elodie moved back a step as I came closer.

"Since my magic was going so badly—no thanks to you—I've been taking, um, private lessons from one of the ghosts here."

Elodie rolled her eyes. "Oh, please," she said. "A magic tutor? Who happens to be a ghost? You must think I'm completely brain dead."

Her eyes narrowed. "Who are you really meeting out there? A guy? Because if it's Archer—"

"There is nothing going on between me and Archer," I said, which wasn't technically a lie. I mean, I was pretty sure I was in love with the guy, and I think he might've kissed me at the ball if Elodie hadn't rushed in, but it's not like we were meeting for secret trysts in the woods. No matter how much I wished that might have been true.

Now I smiled at Elodie and held out my hand. "You wanna learn some awesome magic? Come with me."

Just as I'd hoped, the thought of learning new magic was too seductive for Elodie to pass up.

"Fine," she said. "But if this is some trick that ends up getting me killed, I'm so haunting your ass."

Alice must've known Elodie was coming, because there were two brooms waiting outside.

Elodie's eyes widened like a kid's on Christmas morning. "You ride brooms?"

I just smiled and hopped on. "Come on," I told her, repeating Alice's words to me. "Be traditional for once."

Then we were riding through the night, the cold, clear air burning our lungs. Overhead, the stars sparkled in the inky sky. I could hear Elodie laughing next to me, and I looked over at her, our eyes meeting in the first smile we'd ever shared.

After we landed in the cemetery, I introduced Elodie to Alice, leaving out the part where Alice was my great-grandmother, and introducing Elodie as a "member of my coven."

Alice gave me a sideways glance at that, but she didn't say anything.

"So. What sorts of magic do you two do out here in Creepyville?" Elodie asked.

"A number of things," Alice replied. In the moonlight, her skin looked like porcelain and her cheeks were rosy. Even her eyes seemed brighter. I wondered if she had some sort of beauty spell. If so, I really hoped we'd learn that one next.

"Sophie has mastered summoning objects," Alice continued, "and she is currently working on a transportation spell."

Elodie turned to me, surprised. "You can make things appear out of nothing?"

"Yeah," I said, like it was no big deal even though I still couldn't summon anything bigger than a lamp, and that made me sweat buckets. Concentrating on something

271

small that wouldn't leave me gasping for breath, I waved my hand and an emerald brooch appeared in the air right in front of Elodie. Her mouth fell open, and I smiled at Alice.

Elodie reached out and took the brooch, turning it over and over in her hands. "Teach me."

She was a quick learner, faster than I had been, and within an hour she had made a pen and a tiny yellow butterfly appear. I was a little jealous; I'd never conjured anything that wasn't inanimate. On the bright side, Alice didn't seem very impressed with Elodie, and she didn't praise her nearly as much as she had me.

While they worked on that, I worked on transporting myself from one spot to another, a spell I still couldn't master. Alice said the best witches could cross oceans with that spell, but so far I couldn't even move one inch to the left.

Finally, Elodie and I were both exhausted and pretty tipsy with magic, so we sat on the grass, our backs against the cemetery fence while Alice leaned against a tree, staring off into space.

"I hope it's okay that I'm here," Elodie said to her.

"Why did you come with Sophia tonight?" Alice asked. She didn't sound angry, just curious, so I answered, "Elodie caught me sneaking out, so I invited her to come along. I thought she might like to learn some new magic, too."

"Mrs. Casnoff said to keep an eye on you," Elodie said to me, but she was smiling. I wasn't sure if it was from the magic or if she was just genuinely happy to be here.

"Why?" Alice asked, and both Elodie and I turned more serious. Briefly, I told Alice what had happened to Anna, and how Jenna and Byron were gone.

"Are they sure it was a vampire?"

"No. They don't know who else it could be, though," Elodie said.

"The Eye," Alice said, and I felt Elodie stiffen next to me.

"I asked them about that," I said. "But Mrs. Casnoff said there was no way they could get to us. There are too many protection spells."

Alice gave a low laugh that sent chills up my spine. "Yes, that's what they said to me too. It was nothing for my sleeping spell to blast through their pathetic defenses. Do you really think The Eye couldn't do the same?"

"They don't have magic, though," I argued, but I sounded unsure. Elodie scooted a little closer to me.

"Don't they?" Alice asked. She walked toward us and crouched down in front of me. I saw her long white fingers go to the buttons of her green cardigan, and when she'd discarded that, she unbuttoned her dress.

I sat, frozen in horror, as she pulled her arm out of the left side of her dress and pushed down her slip.

There, just where her heart would have been, was a large gaping wound.

"This is what The Eye did to me, Sophia. They tracked me down, they chased me until I could run no farther, and they cut out my heart. Here. At Hecate."

All I could do was stare at that hole and shake my head. I could feel Elodie trembling beside me.

"Yes, Sophia," Alice said quietly. I looked up at her face and saw that she was watching me with pity, like she was sorry she had to tell me all this.

"It was the head of the Council himself who set them on me, who tricked me into feeling safe here, and then offered me up like a lamb to sacrifice."

"But why?" I asked, my voice no more than a strained whisper.

"Because they were afraid of my power. Because it was greater than theirs."

My head was spinning and I felt like I might throw up. Somehow all the horrors we'd been shown that first night at Hecate were nothing compared to this one wound, this one story.

"Your father believed you'd be safe here because he didn't know the real story of how I died. But, Sophia, you have to believe me. You are in very real danger here."

She looked over at Elodie. "Both of you are. Someone is targeting powerful witches, and you two are the only ones left."

Now it was Elodie who was shaking her head. "No, no, there's no way. It was Jenna. It was a vamp. It . . . it has to be."

Alice's face went very still, like a mask had come down, and her eyes seemed to be looking through us. "Perhaps it was. For both of your sakes, I hope it was."

She reached out and took one of my hands in hers, and one of Elodie's in the other. "But in case it wasn't . . ." Suddenly my hand was hot in hers. Too hot, and I winced, trying to pull back. I could feel Elodie trying to do the same, but Alice held on until we were both making little whimpering sounds. Finally the heat faded, and she let us go. I studied the hand that now lay in my lap, thinking it would at least look red, if not blistered, but it looked normal.

"What was that?" Elodie asked in shaky voice.

"A protection spell. It will help you know your enemies, should the time ever come."

Elodie and I were quiet as the three of us flew back to the school. This time there was no delighted laughter, no weightless feeling of freedom.

When we landed, Alice reached around her neck and pulled off the necklace she was wearing. It was just like the one she'd given me. Elodie didn't put it on right away. She just looked at it, frowning, before closing her hand around it.

"Thanks for the lesson," she told Alice. Then she looked at me, her face still troubled, and said, "See you tomorrow, Sophie."

"Do you really think The Eye is here at Hecate?" I asked Alice once Elodie had gone inside.

Alice glanced past me at Hecate. The huge shadowed mansion looked like a many-eyed monster slumbering in the dark.

"Something is here," she said at last. "But what, I don't know. Not yet."

I looked back at the house and knew Alice was right. A shadow had fallen over the school and seemed to be creeping closer and closer to me. Overhead, clouds snaked across the crescent moon, and the night became even darker. I dreaded the thought of walking into the dark hallways by myself and up to an empty room.

"Do you—" I started to ask Alice, but when I turned, she was gone, leaving me shivering and alone in the night.

CHAPTER 28

I'd figured that Elodie wouldn't want to go back with me to see Alice again after the "my gaping chest wound, let me show you it" thing, but she surprised me by meeting me on the stairs the next night.

"So when did you meet Alice?" she asked on our way down.

"Middle of October?" I answered. Elodie nodded, like that was the answer she'd expected. "So after Chaston, then."

"Yeah," I said. "What does that have to do with it?"

But she didn't answer.

Elodie came with me for the next two weeks. Alice didn't seem to mind her tagging along, and I was kind of shocked to discover that I didn't find her presence completely abhorrent either. In fact, I started to suspect that I might actually like Elodie.

It's not as if her whole personality changed or any-thing, but she was definitely becoming a kinder, gentler Elodie. Maybe she was just using me for Alice. I mean, after just a couple of nights of training, Elodie could already make a small couch appear out of nothing, and she'd moved on to the transportation spell. Not that either of us could do it yet.

But I didn't think it was just about the magic; I think she was lonely. Anna and Chaston were both gone, and I'd never really thought about how they were the only people Elodie ever talked to, besides Archer. And even they seemed to be spending less time together. Elodie said she was too busy with "other stuff" for a boyfriend, while Archer said he was giving her some space.

Archer and I were weird too. After the ball, some-thing had changed between us, and the easy camaraderie we'd shared during cellar duty had evaporated. Now we usually spent the full hour actually cataloguing instead of teasing and joking, and sometimes when he didn't know I was looking, I'd see this really faraway look cross his face. I didn't know if he was thinking about Elodie, or if, like me, he was disappointed by the uncomfortable distance that had sprung up between us.

November at Hecate was gray and rainy, which seemed to suit my mood. Even though I was glad Elodie and I were becoming sort-of friends, she wasn't Jenna, and

I missed my real friend. About a week after Anna had been attacked, Mrs. Casnoff announced at dinner that the Council had cleared Byron of any suspicion. Apparently, he had a solid alibi; he'd been telepathically talking to someone at the Council at that time. But no matter how many times I asked, Mrs. Casnoff would never give me an answer about where Jenna was or what was going on, and I worried about her pretty much all the time.

Mom, being a mom, could sense something was up whenever I called her, but I told her that I was swamped with classes. I hadn't mentioned anything about Chaston or Anna or Jenna; it would have freaked her out, and I knew she worried about me enough as it was.

I hated being alone in the room at night, so I started spending my cellar duty–free evenings in the library, reading up on Prodigium lore in the hopes that I could find something that might clear Jenna. So far, the only creatures I knew of who took blood from their victims were vampires, demons, and, if that one book was to be believed, L'Occhio di Dio. Since Mrs. Casnoff had already shot down my L'Occhio di Dio theory, I tried finding books about demons. But it seemed that every book about demons in the whole library was written in Latin. I tried pressing my hand to the pages and saying "Speak," but the books seemed charm proof. The only parts I could make out were facts I already knew, like how they had to be killed with that demonglass. I sincerely hoped there wasn't a demon at Hecate, because I suspected you couldn't just run down to Williams-Sonoma to pick some up.

One drizzly evening in late November, just after dinner and before I was supposed to report for cellar duty, I took a few of the books to Mrs. Casnoff. She was in her office, writing in a big black ledger. Lamplight cast a warm glow over the room, and classical music was playing softly. Like on the night of the ball, the music wasn't coming from anywhere that I could see.

She looked up when I came in. "Yes?"

I held the books out. "I had some questions about these."

She frowned a little, but closed her ledger and gestured for me to sit down.

"Is there a reason you're researching demons, Sophia?"

"Well, I read that they sometimes drink the blood of their victims, and I thought, you know, maybe that's what happened to Chaston and Anna."

For a long moment Mrs. Casnoff studied me. I realized the music wasn't playing anymore.

"Sophie," she said. It was the first time she'd ever called me that. Her voice was tired. "I know how much you want to exonerate Jenna."

I knew what she was going to say: the same thing

she'd said about The Eye. I rushed on. "I can't read any of these books because they're all in Latin, but there are pictures in them that show demons who pose as humans."

"That's true. But it's also true that we would know if such a thing was on school grounds."

I stood up, slapping one of the books on her desk. "You said yourself that magic isn't always the answer! Maybe your magic is broken. Maybe something has a power stronger than yours and got in."

Mrs. Casnoff rose from her desk, her shoulders drawn back. There was a sudden charge in the air, and I was suddenly—painfully—aware that Mrs. Casnoff was much more than just a principal. She was an extremely powerful witch. "Do not raise your voice with me, young lady. While it's true that magic is not always infallible, what you are suggesting is *not possible*. I'm very sorry for you, but you have to face the fact that in the three weeks Jenna has been gone, neither you nor Elodie nor any other student at this school has been attacked. You made a poor choice for a friend, but it cannot be helped."

I stared at her, my breath coming in and out in a harsh rasp, like I'd just run a race.

Mrs. Casnoff ran a hand over her hair, and I saw that her hand was trembling. "I apologize if I seem blunt, but you have to understand that vampires are not like us; they are monsters, and I was foolish to forget that."

Her expression softened. "This hurts me as well, Sophie. I backed your father's decision to let vampires attend this school. Now I have a dead student, two more who may never return, and a lot of very powerful people very angry at me. I would love to believe that Jenna had nothing to do with any of this, but the evidence strongly suggests otherwise."

She took a deep breath and pressed the books into my numb hands. "You're a loyal friend for trying to find a way to clear her, but in this case, I'm afraid your efforts are wasted. I don't want you doing anymore research on demons, is that understood?"

I didn't nod, but she acted as if I had. "Now, I believe you're late for your cellar duty, so I suggest you hurry on to that before Ms. Vanderlyden comes looking for you."

Through a film of tears, I watched her sit back down at her desk and open her ledger. I was angry with her for refusing to admit there could be something at Hecate she didn't know about. I also felt a bone-deep sadness. It didn't matter what I found, or what theories I tried to work on; the easiest explanation was that Jenna had killed Holly and tried to kill the other two, so that was all anyone was ever going to believe. Anything else might mean admitting they were wrong or, worse than that, not omnipotent.

The tears were gone when I reached the cellar.

They'd been replaced by a dull steady ache just behind my eyes. The Vandy was waiting for me at the door. I expected her to bite my head off—maybe even literally— but she must've seen something in my face, because all she did was grunt, "You're late," and give me a light push toward the stairs.

As she locked the door behind me, Archer looked up from behind one of the shelves. "There you are. Did the Vandy send out the hellhounds after you?"

"No." I picked up the clipboard and headed to the farthest corner of the cellar.

"What, no witty retort? No standard-issue Sophie Mercer comeback?"

"I'm not feeling very witty right this second, Cross," I said as my eyes scanned the shelves without seeing.

"Huh," he said softly. "What's up with you?"

"Let's see, shall we? The only real friend I have here is gone and will probably never come back. Everyone is determined to think she's a monster, and no one will listen to any other ideas."

"What other ideas?" he asked. "Sophie, she's a vampire. It's what they do."

"So you believe that too?"

He tossed his papers down. "Yeah, I do. I know she was your friend, and that it sucks, but she wasn't the only friend you have here."

I was so angry, I felt like I was vibrating. I crossed the room to stand in front of him. "Are you saying you're my friend, Cross? Because I could swear you've barely talked to me since the night of the ball."

He looked away, and I could see the muscles working in his jaw.

"You've been completely weird ever since that night."

"Me?" He swung his gaze back to me. "You're the one who hasn't been able to look at me. And excuse me if I think it's a little suspicious that as soon as Elodie started spending time with you, she suddenly breaks it off with me."

I shook my head, confused, until what he was saying dawned on me. "What, you think I told Elodie what you said about wanting to spend the ball with me so that she'd dump you and I could have you all to myself?"

When he didn't say anything, I gave him a light shove. "Get over yourself," I nearly snarled. I tried to walk past him, but he caught my arm, pulling me up short so that I nearly collided with him.

For a few charged seconds we froze, glaring at each other, breathing hard. I saw his eyes darken just a little, like Jenna's had the day she'd seen my blood. But this was a different kind of hunger; one I felt too.

I didn't let myself think. I just leaned forward and pressed my lips to his.

He took a split second to respond, but then he made a sound almost like a growl from low in his throat, and his arms were suddenly around me, holding me so tightly I could hardly breathe. Not like I cared. All I cared about was Archer, his mouth on mine, and his body pressed against me.

I'd been kissed a few times before, but nothing like this. I felt electrified from the top of my head to my toes, and somewhere in the back of my mind I heard Alice saying that love had a power all its own. She was right: this was magic.

We broke apart to catch our breath. I wondered if I looked as dazed as he did, but then he was kissing me again and we were stumbling against the shelves. I heard something fall and shatter against the floor, heard the soft crunch of glass underfoot as Archer pushed me against the wall.

There was a sensible part of me somewhere that clutched its pearls and hissed that I better not give up my V-card in a *cellar*, but when Archer's hands slid under my shirt and onto the skin of my back, I started thinking that a cellar was as good a place as any.

As if they didn't even belong to me, my hands reached up between us and unbuttoned the first few buttons of his shirt. I wanted to touch his skin the way he was touching mine. He must've felt the same way, because he backed up a little to give me better access. His lips trailed from mine to my throat, and I closed my eyes and let my head tip back against the wall as I slid my hands inside his shirt.

His mouth on my neck felt so good that it took me a while to realize that my left hand was burning.

My head felt heavy as I lifted it to look at my hand on his chest, just over his heart.

And then the haze of desire clouding my brain gave way to a numbing wave of shock as I watched a tattoo—a black eye with a golden iris—appear under my fingers.

CHAPTER 29

At first I refused to believe what I was seeing. Then Archer, noticing how I'd frozen up, pulled back and looked down.

When he lifted his face back to mine, he was pale, and there was a panicked look in his eyes. That's when I knew that what I was seeing through my fingers was real: it was the mark of L'Occhio di Dio. Archer was an Eye. I said the words in my mind, but it was like they wouldn't compute. I knew I should scream or run or something, but I couldn't move.

Archer spoke. "Sophie."

It was as if my name was the code word to break my paralysis—I pressed both of my hands hard against his chest and shoved. I caught him by surprise or I never would've been able to knock him down. But he fell back, crashing into a shelf, sending its contents to the floor. A viscous, yellow liquid spilled from one of the broken jars. I slid in it as I turned to run.

But Archer was already steadying himself, and he grabbed my arm. I thought he said my name again, but I wasn't sure. I whirled around, and my momentum knocked him off balance again. As he slipped in the yellow ooze, I shoved my elbow as hard as I could into his chest. He bent over as the air rushed out of his lungs, and I took that as my chance to slam the heel of my hand into his jaw.

Skill Number Three, I thought.

Just like in Defense.

Archer clutched his mouth as bright red blood seeped through his fingers. I felt the crazy urge to laugh bubble up inside of me. I had just kissed that mouth, and now it was bleeding because of me.

He reached for me, but he was moving slowly, and I was able to spin away from him.

How many times had we fought each other in Defense? Had we just been preparing for this moment? Had Archer watched me struggle to deflect his blows, and laughed at how easy it would be to kill me?

I dodged his last grasp and ran for the stairs. My mind felt like it was going down one of those spiral slides. All I could think was that Archer had kissed me, Archer had killed Holly, Archer had hurt Chaston, Archer had attacked Anna. I didn't look behind me, but I thought I felt his fingers brush my ankle. I ran for the door, only to remember that it was locked . . . Oh my God, it was locked.

I fell against the wood, screaming, "Vandy! Mrs. Casnoff! Somebody!"

Banging as hard as I could on the door with my fists, I finally looked behind me in time to see Archer pulling up his pant leg. It took me a minute to figure out that he was reaching for something strapped to his leg.

A knife. A silver knife, like the one that had cut out Alice's heart.

My scream turned breathy and weak with fear, like something out of a nightmare.

But Archer didn't come near me. He ran for the low window in the back of the room, sliding the knife along the ancient lock.

I could hear people on the other side of the door— footsteps and, I thought, the jangle of keys.

The lock on the door and the lock on the window gave way at the same time.

Archer looked at me one last time as I sagged against the door. I couldn't read the expression on his face, but I was shocked to see that there were tears in his eyes. Then he turned and shimmied out the window just as the door opened behind me, and I fell, shaking, into the Vandy's arms.

I sat on the couch in Mrs. Casnoff's office, a cup of hot tea in my hands. From the smell of it, there was more than just tea in the cup, but I hadn't taken a sip yet. I couldn't get my teeth to stop chattering long enough to drink, even though Mrs. Casnoff had wrapped a heavy afghan around me. I wasn't sure I was ever going to stop shaking.

Mrs. Casnoff sat next to me, stroking my hair. It was a weirdly motherly gesture from her, and it was more unsettling than comforting. The Vandy was leaning against the door, rubbing the back of her neck. It had been a long time since anyone had spoken.

Then Mrs. Casnoff said, "You're sure it was the mark of The Eye."

It was the third time she'd asked me, but I just nodded and tried to bring my shaking teacup to my lips.

She gave a sigh that made her sound a hundred years old. "But how?" she asked for the third time. "How could one of ours be L'Occhio di Dio?"

I closed my eyes and finally drank. I was right: the tea was fortified with some kind of alcohol. It hit my stomach in a warm wave, but it did nothing to stop the shivering.

How? I thought. *How?*

I tried to answer the question for myself, wondering if he'd sought them out last year when he'd left Hecate for a while. But that was a logical question, and my brain felt totally incapable of dealing with logic right now.

Archer was an Eye. Archer had tried to kill me.

I kept repeating it in my head. Almost from a distance, I wondered if Archer had only befriended me, pretended to like me, so that he'd have a chance to get close to me. Was that the reason he'd started dating Elodie?

I rubbed my hand over my chest, just above my heart. Mrs. Casnoff watched with a look of concern. "Did he hurt you?"

"No," I told her. "He didn't."

Nowhere you could see, at least.

"Looks like you got a few good blows in, though," the Vandy piped up, nodding toward my right hand, which was turning purplish and swelling up from its run-in with Archer's jaw.

I raised my eyes to her. "Yeah," I said flatly. "Thanks for your high-quality defense lessons. Much appreciated."

"I just don't understand," Mrs. Casnoff said, dazed. "We should have known. We should have been able to sense it. Or someone should have seen his mark."

I shook my head. "It was hidden. It only appeared because . . ." Because of Alice's protection spell, I thought, but I didn't want to tell them about Alice. "I did a protection spell on myself," I lied. As usual I sucked at lying, but they were too shaken up to notice. "When I touched the mark, it appeared."

Mrs. Casnoff looked at me. "You touched it?"

I felt my face flame with embarrassment. Like it wasn't bad enough that the boy I loved had turned out to be an assassin, now I was going to get busted for making out in the cellar.

Luckily, Mr. Ferguson, the shapeshifter teacher, came in, shaking rain off his heavy leather coat. There was an enormous Irish wolfhound at his side, as well as a golden mountain lion. As I watched, the wolfhound stood and became Gregory Davidson, one of the older kids on campus. The mountain lion was Taylor. For the first time since Beth had told her who my father was, Taylor wasn't glaring at me. In fact, I was pretty sure I saw pity in her eyes.

"No sign of him, Mrs. C.," Mr. Ferguson said. "We searched the whole island."

Mrs. Casnoff sighed. "None of my tracking spells have turned up anything either. It's as though he vanished into thin air."

She massaged her temples and said, "The much more pressing issue now is informing the Council that we were infiltrated. Your father will definitely want to hear of this, and then of course, our security spells will have to be strengthened, and the other students will have to be told what happened."

Her voice wavered on the last word, and to my horror, she dropped her face into her hand with what sounded like a sob.

I shrugged off the afghan and draped it over her shoulders.

"It'll be okay."

She looked up at me, her eyes bright with unshed tears. "I'm so very sorry, Sophie. I should have listened to you."

Just a few hours ago, those words from Mrs. Casnoff would have had me dancing in the streets. Now I just smiled sadly and said, "Don't worry about it." I was glad that this meant Jenna might be able to come back, but that one piece of happy was buried under a compost pile of hurt, sadness, and anger. I'd wanted to be proven right, but not like this.

I left Mrs. Casnoff, Ferguson, and the Vandy planning an assembly for the next morning, and headed for my room. Though I missed Jenna, tonight I was actually looking forward to being alone.

Cal met me at the foot of the stairs.

"I'm okay," I said, holding up my hand. "It'll heal on its own."

"It's not that. Mrs. Casnoff doesn't want you going

anywhere on your own for now. Not until we find Archer."

I sighed. "So . . . what? You're going to follow me to my room?"

He nodded.

"Fine." I laid a hand on the smooth wood of the banister and attempted to drag my weary self up the stairs. Now I finally understood the term *heartsick*. That's exactly how I felt. Like I had the flu, but in my soul instead of my body. I was so tired, and everything seemed to hurt. Just as I was thinking I might reconsider my pledge to never get into one of those spooky bathtubs, I heard Elodie say, "Sophie?"

I turned around to see her standing in the foyer. Her face was pale, and it was the first time I'd ever seen her look anything less than beautiful.

"What's going on?" she asked. "All these people are saying that Archer, like, attacked you in the cellar, or something, and I can't find him anywhere."

Just when I thought the pain in my chest couldn't get any worse, it seemed to bloom like a thorny plant.

"Wait here," I said to Cal.

I took Elodie's hand and led her into the nearest sitting room. Sitting next to her on the sofa, I explained what had happened, leaving out the whole me and Archer kissing part and mainly telling her about the fight and the mark over his heart.

Halfway through, she started shaking her head. Tears pooled in her eyes. I just kept talking and watched those tears spill down her cheeks and onto her lap, leaving dark spots on her blue skirt.

"That's impossible," she said when I was through. "Archer . . . couldn't hurt anyone. He . . ."

By then she was crying too hard to talk, and I reached out to hug her, only to have her slap my hands away. "Wait," she said, and a sliver of the old Elodie began to reemerge. "How did you see his mark?"

"I told you," I said, but I couldn't look her in the eyes. I looked at the lamp behind her instead, keeping my eyes on the blank face of the shepherdess at its base. "That protection spell Alice put on us."

"I know that," Elodie said, scooting back from me. "But why were you touching his chest?"

I lifted my eyes to hers and tried to think up a plausible lie. But I was tired and sad, and nothing would come. Guiltily, I looked down at my lap.

I waited for Elodie to yell or cry some more, or hit me, but she didn't do any of that. She just wiped her face with the back of her hands, stood up, and walked out.

CHAPTER 30

I thought the news about Archer would really upset people, but the opposite ended up being true. Instead of freaking out that L'Occhio di Dio had been inside our school, everybody seemed relieved that the mystery behind the attacks had been solved and that life could finally go back to normal. Well, normal for a school like Hecate, which meant the shifters could go outside at night again, and the faeries were allowed to roam the woods at sunrise and sunset.

A few days later, Mrs. Casnoff pulled me aside and told me that Jenna would be coming back, and my dad would be arriving a week or so after that.

I should probably have been excited to finally meet him, but all I felt was nervous. Was he coming to Hecate in his official capacity, or was it because I was his daughter and I'd nearly been attacked? What would we talk about?

I called Mom one night to talk to her about it. I hadn't told her about Archer. It would've only scared her. I just said there'd been some trouble, and Dad was coming to check it out.

"You'll like him," Mom said. "He's very charming and very smart. I know he'll be thrilled to see you."

"Then why hasn't he tried to see me before? I mean, I get when I was little you didn't want us hanging out. But what about after I came into my powers? You'd think he could've spared a visit somewhere in there."

Mom got quiet before finally saying, "Sophie, your dad had his reasons, but they're his to tell, not mine. But he loves you." After another pause she asked, "Is there something else going on?"

"I'm just really swamped with school," I lied.

I tried to be happy about seeing Dad, but it was hard to be enthusiastic about anything. I felt like I was moving underwater, and anything people said to me seemed muffled and distant.

On the other hand, I found myself suddenly popular. I guess nearly getting murdered in the cellar by an undercover demon hunter is all it takes to make people want to be your friend. Who knew?

I made that joke to Taylor one evening at dinner. Ever since that night in Casnoff's study, she'd been a lot friendlier to me, now that she finally realized I wasn't a spy for my dad. She laughed. "I didn't know you were so funny!"

Yeah, I was a regular laugh riot. Maybe because making jokes meant that I didn't burst into tears.

I watched people gather around Elodie and cluck over her sympathetically, murmuring how heartbroken she must be. She wasn't talking to me, and I missed her. It sounds weird, but I really wanted to talk to her about Archer. She was the only person who was feeling the same thing I was.

I'd stopped meeting Alice in the woods. Mrs. Casnoff had been true to her word and put about a dozen new protection spells over the house, so even Alice's super-powerful sleeping spell didn't work anymore. I could've just snuck out, but I had a feeling that was what Elodie was doing, so I left her to it. I mean, I'd stolen her boyfriend, even if it had been only temporarily. She could have my great-grandmother. Not exactly a fair trade, but as far as amends went, it was the best I could do.

Besides, I wasn't sure if I trusted myself with Alice anymore.

Looking back on it, a tiny part of me had been thrilled when that spell on Elodie's dress had started working. I hadn't wanted to hurt her—at least I don't think that I had—but there'd been a definite rush knowing I was capable of a spell like that.

Where would that thrill end?

My attraction to the dark side wasn't the only thing occupying my thoughts. I thought about that night in the cellar constantly. I kept coming back to Archer pulling out that knife. He'd had plenty of time to stab me and run. So why hadn't he? I kept turning that question over and over in my head, but I couldn't come up with a scenario that gave me the answer I really wanted; that Archer wasn't an Eye, that it had all been a horrible mistake.

A week after Archer left, I was perched on my window seat, flipping through my *Magical Literature* textbook. Even though he'd been cleared, Lord Byron wasn't coming back to Hecate. I got the impression he'd said something really rude to Mrs. Casnoff when she'd asked him back, because she pursed her lips a lot when she said we'd have a new teacher. It ended up being the Vandy. I'd thought she might be a little nicer to me after she'd rescued me from a killer, but other than canceling my cellar duty for the rest of the semester (all three weeks of it—really big of her), she showed no signs of softening. We already had three essays due by Friday, which was why I was attempting to find something in the stupid textbook that half interested me.

I'd just started to read a paragraph about Christina Rossetti's "Goblin Market" when movement out on the lawn caught my eye. It was Elodie walking purposefully toward the woods. I guess she and Alice had decided the brooms were a little too attention-grabbing.

I told myself that I wasn't jealous, and that it was fine Alice hadn't made any attempt to contact me in the past few weeks. Elodie was a better student anyway. I glanced over to the closet, where I'd stashed Jenna's lion, Bram. I'd had to hide it a few days after she'd left because it hurt too much to look at it. Last week I'd hung the necklace Alice had given me around Bram's neck for a similar reason. Not like I needed it to keep me awake anymore anyway.

I was still looking at the closet when my door opened.

"Miss me?" Jenna asked with a grin. I don't know which one of us was more shocked when I burst into tears.

She was across the room in an instant, wrapping her arms around me and leading me to my bed. She hugged me while I cried.

Jenna reached behind her and pulled a box of Kleenex off my desk. "Here," she said, handing it to me.

"Thanks." I sniffled into my tissue. Then I let out a deep shuddering breath. "Whew. I feel better."

"Rough couple of weeks, huh?"

I glanced at her. She looked the best I'd ever seen her. Her skin was still pretty pale, but there was a light rose flush on her cheeks. Even her pink stripe looked brighter.

"Did they fill you in?"

Jenna nodded. "Yeah, but I can't believe it. Archer really didn't strike me as the secret demon hunter type."

I snorted and wiped my nose again. "You or anybody else. You were with the Council. Are they freaked?"

"Big time. From what I heard, Archer and his whole family disappeared off the face of the earth. No one knows what happened, but it seems pretty clear they were all in on it." Jenna ran a hand through her hair. "It's crazy to think he was hiding that all this time."

"Yeah," I said, looking down at my hands. "It just sucks because . . ." I sighed.

"You hate him for what he did, but you miss him," Jenna finished.

I looked up at her, surprised. "Exactly."

She reached up and swept her hair to one side, revealing a pair of light blue puncture wounds just below her ear. "I know a little something about falling for the enemy."

With a sad smile, she let her hair fall back.

I shifted on the bed to make more room for her, and we both leaned back against my pillows.

"So tell me about London."

Jenna rolled her eyes and kicked off her shoes. "I never even got to London. The Council has a house in Savannah they use when they have stuff to do at Hecate. I just hung out there while they asked me a bunch of questions, like what vampire made me, and how often did I feed. I'm not gonna lie: it was pretty scary at times. I was sure they were bringing in Buffy at any moment to give me the ol' stake and shake."

I choked on a laugh. "The what?"

Blushing, Jenna looked away and rubbed one foot on top of the other. "It's just this thing this girl there said."

"A pretty girl?" I asked, bumping shoulders with her.

"Maybe," she said, but she was grinning from ear to ear. All I could get out of her was that the girl's name was Victoria, she worked for the Council, and she was a vampire too.

"They have vampires that work for the Council?"

"Yeah," Jenna said, more animated than I'd ever seen her. "They work all sorts of cool jobs, mentoring younger vamps and acting as security for VIPs in the Council."

"Speaking of which, you didn't run into my dad by any chance, did you?"

Jenna shook her head. "Nope, sorry. But I overheard Vix say he would be out here in a few days."

"Vix?" I asked, doing my startled eyebrow thing.

Jenna blushed all over again, and I laughed. "Wow, does Bram know he might have to share you soon?"

"Shut up," she said, but she was still smiling. "Hey, where is Bram?"

"Saved him for you," I said, hopping off the bed and

going to the closet. I fished Bram out from underneath some laundry and tossed him to Jenna. She caught him with a smile. "Ah, Bram, how I've miss—"

Her expression changed, and I watched that pretty flush seep from her cheeks as she stared at the stuffed lion.

Or, more accurately, at the necklace around his neck.

"Where did you get this?"

"The necklace? It was a present."

"From who?" She raised her eyes to mine, and I saw real fear in them. An uncomfortable prickling sweat broke out on the back of my neck.

"Why? What is it?"

Jenna shuddered and pushed Bram away from her. "It's a bloodstone."

I crossed the room and picked up Bram, pulling the necklace over his head.

The large flat stone looked nothing like a bloodstone. It wasn't even red.

"It's black," I said to Jenna, holding it out to her, but she scooted back against the headboard.

"That's because it's demon blood."

Everything within me went completely still. "What?"

Jenna reached into her blouse and pulled out her bloodstone. The liquid inside was pitching and rolling, like there was a storm inside the tiny capsule. "See?" she said. "There's white magic in my stone. It only reacts like that if black magic is near. And that's some seriously dark stuff, Sophie."

Her fingers were clutching her necklace so hard her knuckles were white. "It did this the day of the ball too," she said, her eyes still on the pendant in my hands. "When you got that dirt out. I should have said something then, but you seemed so happy with the dress, and I thought black magic couldn't make something so pretty."

I was barely listening to her. I was remembering that Mrs. Casnoff said no one knew how Alice had become a witch. How she had only spoken to me after Chaston was attacked, how much more alive she'd seemed after Anna.

And Elodie's face when Alice had given her her necklace.

Elodie was with her right now.

I dropped the necklace, and the stone cracked against the corner of my desk. A drop of black liquid seeped from the crack and sizzled on the floor, leaving a small burn mark.

I was amazed at how stupid I'd been. How naive.

"Jenna, get Mrs. Casnoff and Cal. Tell them to go to the woods, to Alice's and Lucy's graves. She'll know where that is."

"Where are you going?" she asked, but I didn't answer. I just ran—the way I had the night I'd found Chaston.

I plunged into the woods, branches scratching at my face and arms, rocks cutting my feet. I was only wearing pajama pants and a T-shirt, but I barely felt the cold. I just ran.

Because now I understood how Alice had been corporeal, how she had all that power even though she was supposed to be dead. That black magic ritual Alice had gotten caught in hadn't turned her into a witch: it had made her a demon.

You too, my mind whispered. *If that's what she is, that's what you are.*

CHAPTER 31

Iwas certain I'd find Elodie lying bleeding or maybe even dead when I got to the cemetery. So I was shocked when I saw her standing next to Alice, smiling as she faded away—only to reappear seconds later about a yard away.

She'd finally mastered the transportation spell.

Alice saw me first and lifted her hand in greeting. I stared at her and wondered how I'd ever believed she was just another ghost. None of the ghosts at Hecate had ever looked so real, so whole. Life radiated from her. I felt stupid for not seeing it before.

I neared them, fear racing through me. Elodie had stopped smiling the instant she saw me and was now looking somewhere over my head.

"Elodie," I said in what I'd meant to be a calm voice, but I know I sounded as strained and scared as I felt. "I think we should go back to the school. Mrs. Casnoff is looking for you."

"No she's not," Elodie answered. She reached down into her blouse and pulled out her necklace. "It glows whenever someone's looking for me, and tells me who it is. See?" The pendent was glowing, and I could make out my own name etched across it in dull gold.

"Family heirloom, huh?" I asked Alice.

She smiled, but I saw something flicker in her eyes. "Now, Sophia, don't be jealous."

"I'm not jealous," I said too quickly. "I just think Elodie and I should head back to the school now."

Mentally, I was calculating how long it would take Mrs. Casnoff and, I hoped, Cal to get out here. If Jenna had found them right after I'd left, surely they were only a few minutes behind me.

Alice frowned and lifted her head, sniffing the air—there was nothing even remotely human in the gesture. I felt myself start to shake.

"You're frightened, Sophia," she said. "Why on earth would you be afraid of me?"

"I'm not," I replied, but again my voice gave me away.

The wind blew through the trees, making them creak against each other and sending strange shadows skittering across the ground. Alice turned her head and took a deep breath. This time her expression hardened. "You've brought intruders on us. Why would you do such a thing, Sophia?"

She flicked her hands toward the woods, and I could hear a loud groaning, like the trees were uprooting themselves and moving. She was slowing Mrs. Casnoff and Cal down, I realized with horror.

"You led Casnoff here?" Elodie asked, but my eyes were locked on Alice.

"I know what you are," I said, my voice little more than a whisper. I'd expected Alice to look surprised or at least angry, but she just smiled again. Somehow, that was much scarier.

"Do you indeed?" she asked.

"A demon."

She laughed, a low throaty sound, and her eyes flashed a reddish-purple.

I turned to Elodie. She looked guilty, but she didn't flinch from my gaze.

"You did summon a demon," I said, and she nodded, like I'd just accused her of dyeing her hair, or something equally innocuous.

"We had no choice," she insisted. "You heard what Mrs. Casnoff said: our enemies are getting stronger all the time. I mean, my God, Sophie, they turned one of ours and used him against us. We had to be prepared."

She said all of this in the patient tone of a kindergarten teacher.

"So what?" I asked, my voice shaking. "You let her kill Holly?"

Now her eyes dropped, and she said, "A blood sacrifice is the only way to bind a demon to you."

I wanted to run at her, hit her, scream, but I was frozen in place.

Elodie looked at me with wide, begging eyes.

"We didn't mean to kill Holly. We knew we needed four to hold the demon and make it do our bidding. But we had to have blood. So I did a sleeping spell on her and Chaston pierced her neck with a dagger. We thought we could stop the bleeding before it was too late, but she just bled so *much*."

I could taste bile at the back of my throat. "You could have taken blood from anywhere," I said. "You took it from her throat so you could blame Jenna for it. Kill two birds with one stone, huh?"

I went on. "You knew that you killed Holly, but you let everyone think it was Jenna. You made me wonder if it had been her."

"I thought it *was* her who attacked Chaston and Anna," Elodie said, a tear trickling down her cheek. "We just thought the ritual had backfired. I never saw Alice before that night with you, I swear."

Now I looked at Alice. "Why didn't you appear to them?

Alice shrugged. "They weren't worth my time. They pulled me out of hell, but I felt no need to serve three schoolgirls."

She lifted one hand, and Elodie jerked.

"I wondered why it took you so long to figure it out," Alice said, still looking at me. "You're supposed to be such a bright girl, Sophie, and yet you couldn't tell the difference between a ghost and a demon? Or was it more?"

She turned her hand a little to the left, and Elodie screamed as she flew to the side, landing in a heap against the graveyard fence. She lay still after that, but I didn't know if she'd been knocked out or if Alice was using magic to keep her from moving.

"Do you know what I think, Sophia? I think you knew what I was but you didn't want to face it. Because if I'm a demon, then what does that make you?"

My whole body was trembling now. I wanted to cover my ears to block out what she was saying. Because she was right. I'd known there was something off about her, but I hadn't wanted to question it because I'd liked her. I'd liked the power she'd given me.

"I've waited for you for so long, Sophia," Alice said, and now she looked like she always did—just a girl my age. "When those pathetic excuses for dark witches did their summoning spell, I clawed my way over a horde of demons to be the one brought forth. In the hopes that I could find you."

Blood was rushing in my ears, pounding at my temples.

"But why?" I whispered through chattering teeth.

Her smile was beautiful and terrible. Her eyes glowed as bright as a furnace. "Because we're family."

Then I was flung backward, my back slamming painfully against a tree, the bark scraping me through my shirt. I tried to move, but my limbs were heavy and useless.

"I apologize for that," she said, moving toward Elodie, "but I can't have you in the way just now."

She knelt beside Elodie while I sat helpless and paralyzed. As gently as a mother with a baby, Alice lifted Elodie's head into her lap. Her eyes unfocused and half shut, Elodie rolled her head to one side as Alice stroked her temple. Then Alice lifted her hand to Elodie's neck. Two thin claws shot from her fingertips, illuminated by the light from the orb.

Elodie barely flinched as the claws punctured her neck, but I screamed. When Alice lowered her mouth to drink, I shut my eyes.

I didn't know how much time had passed before I could suddenly move again—but when I finally stood, Alice was standing in front of me, and Elodie lay, very pale and very still, against the cemetery gates.

I ran to her, and Alice didn't try to stop me.

Kneeling at Elodie's side, I felt the damp earth beneath us. Elodie's face was cool under mine, but her eyes were still half open, and I could hear her shallow breathing.

The wounds at her neck were red and raw, the rest of her very white. Our eyes met and her lips moved, like she was trying to say something.

"I'm sorry," I whispered. "I'm so sorry, for everything."

She blinked once, and her lips moved again. *Hand.*

Thinking she wanted me to hold her hand, I reached down and took her left hand in mine.

She gave a deep sigh, and I felt a low vibration, like a low voltage current.

I felt her magic settle over me, just like she'd described. It felt soft and cold, like snow. Then her hand slipped from mine, and she went very still.

I heard Alice laugh. I turned to see her twirling in a circle, her skirt held out to her sides. "I must say, of all the gifts you could have given me, that one was the best."

Slowly, I rose to my feet. "Gift?"

Alice stopped twirling, but she was still giggling. "That night you brought her with you, I was sure you had figured out what I really was. It was kind of you to bring her to me and save me the risk of getting caught in that horrid school."

The magic Elodie had passed on to me still thrummed

in my veins, but I had no idea what to do with it. I knew I was no match for Alice, even if we did share the same type of power. She'd had a lot longer to use it, plus I guessed her stint in hell had taught her a few tricks. So the only thing I had going for me were the few paragraphs I could remember from the demon books I'd read, and pure, clean rage.

Alice was laughing again, magic drunk on Elodie's blood. "Now that I've regained my full strength, we'll be unstoppable, Sophia. Nothing will be out of our reach."

But I wasn't listening to her. I was looking at the statue of the angel and the black sword in its hands. Black rock.

Demonglass.

In Defense, the Vandy was always going on about how everyone had a weakness, and I knew what Alice's was.

Me.

"Break," I murmured, and with a loud crack, the sword split in half. The jagged stone landed in the grass just in front of me. I picked it up even as it burned hot and its edges sliced my hand. It was heavier than I'd thought it would be, and I hoped I'd be able to lift it high enough to do what I had to.

Alice turned around and saw me holding the shard, but she didn't look scared, just confused. "What are you doing, Sophia?"

She was standing about ten feet from me. I knew that if I ran at her, she'd flick me into a tree like a bug. But she was so giddy and didn't think I'd hurt her. After all, we were family.

I closed my eyes and concentrated, calling on my own power and the magic Elodie had given me. A fierce wind whipped around me, a wind so cold that it took my breath. My blood slowed in my veins even as my heart raced. I opened my eyes to find myself directly in front of Alice.

Her eyes widened, but not with fear or surprise. With delight.

"You did it!" she said excitedly, like we were at my ballet recital.

"Yeah. I did."

And then I hefted the shard of demonglass and sliced her neck.

CHAPTER 32

"So it turns out I'm a demon," I told Jenna the next afternoon.

We were sitting in our room, or, more accurately, she was sitting. I was still in bed, where I'd been pretty much ever since Cal and Mrs. Casnoff had dragged me back to Hecate. Cal had been able to repair most of the damage done to my feet by my crazy bare-footed run through the woods, but my hand was another story.

I looked down. My left hand was fine, but the right had three long gashes across my fingers, palm, and the heel of my hand. They were puckered and angry looking, the edges of each slash a vivid purplish-red. Cal had done the best he could to heal them, but the demonglass had done too much damage. I'd probably always have scars.

Or maybe Cal just hadn't had much magic left after

trying to revive Elodie. He and Mrs. Casnoff had come crashing into the clearing only moments after I'd cut off Alice's head and watched her body dissolve into the dirt. Cal had run to Elodie right away, but we'd all known it was already too late. Anna had told me Cal couldn't raise the dead, but he had tried that night. Only when it was obvious that Elodie was gone did he turn to me and take the blade out of my hand.

On the way back to the school, I'd been pretty out of it, but I remember Mrs. Casnoff telling me that Alice's body had been buried in the cemetery, along with a few other demons. That's why the angel had held the blade of demonglass—just in case any of them ever managed to get out.

"You people are more prepared than the Girl Scouts," I'd muttered. Then I'd fainted.

"I always thought you were pretty evil. I just never wanted to say anything," Jenna said now. Her voice was light, but her eyes were sad when she looked down at my hand.

I'd gotten most of the story from Mrs. Casnoff that night. She hadn't lied when she'd told me that Alice had been changed through a black magic ritual. She'd just neglected to tell me that Alice's ritual had been a summoning incantation, designed to bring forth a demon and make it do your bidding.

I had no idea what anyone would ever need a demon for. Errands? General evil tasks that needed doing around the house?

But demons are tricky, and so instead of becoming Alice's do-boy, it had stolen her soul and made her a monster. Since she was pregnant at the time, her baby had been a demon too. Lucy had married a human, so Dad was half demon, making me only a quarter demon.

"But," Mrs. Casnoff had told me as Cal had tried to heal my hand, "even a diluted amount of demon blood can result in enormous power."

"Great," I'd replied, my hand on fire as Cal's white magic raced over it.

Mrs. Casnoff had known what I really was all along, of course. That's why she hadn't been able to sense Alice. She thought she was just picking up on my demon vibes.

"So what happens now?" Jenna asked, getting off of her bed to sit gingerly on the edge of mine. "What about Archer and your dad?"

I shifted, wincing as my hand bumped against my leg. "I haven't heard anything about Archer other than what you told me about how he and his family have dropped off the face of the earth. Apparently there's a big group of warlocks out hunting for him."

And what they would do when they caught him. . . ?
I didn't want to think about it.

"Cal thinks he and his family probably ran to Italy," I continued, trying to ignore the pain in my heart. "Since that's where The Eye is based, it seems like a safe bet."

To my surprise, Jenna shook her head. "I don't know. Something I overheard in Savannah. A few witches were talking about the L'Occhio di Dio contingent in London. There've been a few sightings of a new guy with them. Dark-haired, young. Could be him."

My chest constricted.

"Why would he go there? He'd be right under the Council's noses."

She shrugged. "Hiding in plain sight? I just hope they catch him. I hope they catch *all* of them." Her eyes were cold as she said it, and a little shudder ran through me.

"As for my dad, I don't really know. The Council always knew he was half demon, but I guess since he'd never attempted to eat anybody's face and was super powerful to boot, they decided it was okay to make him Head, so long as no other Prodigium found out what he really was."

"And Mrs. Casnoff knew too?"

"All the teachers did. They work for the Council."

Jenna reached up and started twirling her pink streak. "So you're not a witch," she said. It wasn't a question.

Now my wince had nothing to do with my hand. I wasn't a witch. I never had been. Mrs. Casnoff had explained that the powers of demons are so similar to those of dark witches that it's easy for a demon to "pass" as a witch, so long as she doesn't do anything crazy, like . . . well, like drinking the blood of a bunch of witches to make herself stronger.

I'd liked thinking of myself as a witch. It was a lot nicer than demon. Demon meant monster to me.

Jenna suddenly reached over and started scratching the top of my head. "What are you doing?"

"I was seeing if you have horns under all that hair," she said, giggling.

I swatted her hand away, but I couldn't help smiling back. "I'm so glad my monsterness amuses you, Jenna."

She stopped playing with my hair and wrapped an arm around my shoulder. "Hey, speaking as one monster to another, I can tell you it's not so bad. At least we can be freaks together."

I turned and dropped my head on her shoulder. "Thanks," I said softly, and she gave me a squeeze in return.

There was a soft rapping at the door, and we both looked up. "It's probably Casnoff," I said. "She's checked on me like five times already today."

What I didn't tell Jenna was that the last time we had talked, I'd asked Mrs. Casnoff what all this meant for me.

"It means that you will always be incredibly powerful, Sophia," she'd answered. "It means that, like your father, you will be expected to use this power in service to the Council."

"So I have a destiny," I said. "Crap."

Mrs. Casnoff smiled and patted my hand. "It's a glorious destiny, Sophia. Most witches would kill to have your power. Some have."

I'd just nodded because I couldn't tell her how I really felt: I didn't want to be Sophia, the Great and Terrible. That sort of thing should belong to girls like Elodie, girls who were beautiful and ambitious. I was just me: funny, sure, and smart, but not a leader.

Sitting there that night with Mrs. Casnoff, Cal still holding my hand even though all of the magic was out of him, I'd asked the one question that had been buzzing in my brain.

"Am I dangerous? Like Alice?"

Mrs. Casnoff had met my eyes and said, "Yes, Sophia, you are. You always will be. Some demon hybrids, like your father, are able to go years without any incident, although he is accompanied by a member of the Council at all times just to be cautious. Others, like your grandmother Lucy, are not so lucky."

"What happened?"

She looked away and said, very quietly, "L'Occhio di Dio did kill your grandmother, Sophie, but with good reason. Despite living thirty years without ever harming a living soul, something . . . something happened to her one night, and she reverted to her true nature."

She took a deep breath and said, "She killed your grandfather."

There was no sound for a long time until I asked, "So that could happen to me? I could just snap one day and demon-out on whoever is with me?"

And when I said that, all I'd been able to see was my mom lying bloody and broken at my feet. My stomach rolled and I'd tasted bile.

"It's a possibility," Mrs. Casnoff answered.

And then I asked Mrs. Casnoff if there was a way I could ever stop being a demon—if I could ever return to normal.

She had studied me for a long time, before saying, "There's the Removal. But it would almost assuredly kill you."

Her answer was still sitting like a stone in my chest. The Removal might kill me.

It probably *would* kill me.

But if I lived the rest of my life as part demon, I might kill someone. Someone I loved.

The door opened, but it wasn't Mrs. Casnoff standing there. It was my mom.

"Mom!" I cried, leaping out of my bed and throwing

my arms around her. I could feel her tears as she buried her face in my hair, so I hugged her even tighter and breathed in her familiar perfume.

When we broke apart, Mom tried to smile at me, and reached down to take my hands. I couldn't hold back a soft cry of pain, and she looked down.

I thought Mom would cry again when she saw my hand, but she just raised it to her lips and kissed the palm, like I was three and had a skinned knee.

"Sophie," Mom said, smoothing my hair away from my face, "I've come to take you home, okay, sweetie?"

I looked back over my shoulder at Jenna, who was trying really hard to ignore us, but I saw the hurt look flash across her face. If I left, Jenna would have no one. So much for being freaks together.

I took a deep breath and turned back to my mom. I didn't know if I would be strong enough to look in her eyes and tell her what I had to say, what I'd known I had to do as soon as Mrs. Casnoff had given me her answer.

Then, before I could say anything, I saw Elodie walk by my doorway.

Rushing out, my heart in my throat, I wondered if Cal had saved her after all. Maybe she'd been recovering in the school this whole time, and they just hadn't told me.

The hall was empty except for her, and she had her

back to me. "Elodie!" I cried, running up to her. But she didn't look at me, and I realized I was looking through her.

She walked on, pausing in doorways like she was looking for someone—just another Hecate ghost stuck here forever. I knew she deserved it, in a way. She and her friends had summoned a demon and paid the price.

I watched her for a long time, until she finally faded into the late afternoon sunlight. We'd never really been friends, but she had given me the last little magic she'd had inside her so that I could defeat Alice, and I would never forget that.

And in the end, it was seeing Elodie that gave me the strength to turn to my mom and say, "I'm not going home. I'm going to London, and I'm going through the Removal."

Acknowledgments

Writing a book has been compared to crossing the Atlantic in a bathtub, so I'm very grateful to have had the following people on my "crew"!

First and foremost, a HUGE thank you to my agent, the incomparable Holly Root, the first person not related to me to fall in love with Sophie & Co. Your enthusiasm and killer sense of humor make you the definition of a dream agent! Also, to Jennifer Besser, Emily Schultz, and everyone at Disney-Hyperion Books, all of whom are freaking geniuses and made this book so much better than I thought it could be.

Big neuroses-laden hugs to all my writer friends in The Tenners, namely Kay Cassidy, Becca Fitzpatrick, and Lindsey Leavitt. Writing can be a lonely business, and you always gave me a shoulder to cry on (or an inbox to fill).

Thanks, too, to Sally Kalkofen and Tiffany Wenzler,

who were my first readers, and whose questions, comments, and encouragement helped shape *Hex Hall* into something actually resembling a book. And to Felicia LaFrance, whose cupcakes helped me write the last hundred pages. You rock, friend!

Few people are lucky enough to have had the same best friend for more than twenty years, so I am very grateful for Katie Rudder Mattli, who's been reading my stories since 1987, and is probably even now plotting to sell them on eBay. Thank you for your unwavering faith, and for always "validating" me!

Because I always promised I'd do this if I got published: Hi, Dallas!

Thanks to Crys Hodgens, Alison Madison, Debbie McMickin, and Amber Williams. Y'all are phenomenal teachers, and even better friends.

I was lucky enough to have some pretty phenomenal teachers of my own. Alicia Carroll, Alexander Dunlop, James Hammersmith, Louis Garrett, Jim Ryan, Judy Troy, and Jake York were all mentors and friends, and their guidance is much appreciated.

A special thanks to Nancy Wingo, who made me enter writing contests, and compete in English tournaments, and go to Southern Literature conferences. . . . You're the best, and this book truly would not exist without you.

So much of *Hex Hall* is about the power of women, and I know few women more powerful than the formidable WOS—Tammi Holman, Kara Johnson, Nancy Wingo, and my mom, Kathie Moore. You ladies are an inspiration in more ways than one!

For my parents, William and Kathie Moore. I would have to write a whole other book just to express a fraction of how thankful I am to you. You have supported me even when my path took some crazy turns, and I love you more than I can say.

John and Will, you are the brightest part of every day. Without the two of you, none of this would've been possible. I love you both "infinity"!

And last but not least, thank you to every student who sat in my classroom from 2004–2007. You guys were the reason I came to work every day, and I'm so thankful that I got to be a part of your lives. This book is for all of you.